"I'm truly moved to see such blindness in a piece of literatu[r]... the most wonderful, three-din[...] countryside on my mind's eye[...] tale that is at times chilling and at others cosily poignant in its sublime evocations of youth and summertimes past."

Maud Rowell, author of *Blind Spot: Exploring and Educating on Blindness*

"Susanna Clarke meets Robert Aikman in this heady, melancholic, nuanced coming of age story. I was utterly entranced by *Never the Wind*."

Paul Tremblay, author of *A Head Full of Ghosts* and *The Cabin at the End of the World*

"This book is so good that I am speechless. Staggeringly good! An extraordinarily powerful work. Dimitri casts his net into the sea of myth, and brings up a remarkable catch. Family, friendship, horror, humor, wit and deception—I have seldom read a book so powerful."

Ellen Kushner, author of *Swordspoint*

"It's a ghost story and a love story, full of life and passion, and knowledge. It's a wonderful book."

Aliya Whiteley, award-winning author of *The Beauty, The Loosening Skin* and *Skyward Inn*

"A sensory treat! *Never the Wind* is richly realised, and Francesco Dimitri is a marvel."

Oliver K. Langmead, author of *Birds of Paradise* and *Glitterati*

"A tender and magical take on all the potential – and horrors – of adolescence. Dimitri's writing is full of wonder at the natural world, beautifully mediated through Luca's heart-rending personal circumstances, and a narrative voice full of pathos and wisdom. An utterly fresh take on the coming-of-age tale."

Ally Wilkes, author of *All the White Spaces*

"Francesco Dimitri has set himself what would be a daunting challenge for any writer, and he has risen to that challenge with aplomb. The result is beautiful and life-affirming and profound, and I am more than a little in awe. Dimitri is a phenomenon. Read this book. Read it now!"

A. J. Elwood, author of *The Cottingley Cuckoo*

"Damn, this is good. This is the kind of fantasy that I wish I could write, and I am awestruck."

James Brogden, author of *Hekla's Children*

"Francesco Dimitri is a true visionary in contemporary fantasy fiction. His masterful storytelling has echoes of Alan Garner in its invocation of the landscape … and the ancient magic that throbs just beneath the surface. Fiercely intelligent, achingly heart-felt, *Never the Wind* will live on in your dreams long after the last page has been read."

Mark Chadbourn, author of *Age of Misrule*

"Truly spooky...plenty here to fascinate fans of cerebral horror."

Publishers Weekly

NEVER THE WIND

NEVER
THE
WIND

FRANCESCO DIMITRI

TITAN BOOKS

Never the Wind
Print edition ISBN: 9781789099812
Electronic edition ISBN: 9781789099829

Published by Titan Books
A division of Titan Publishing Group Ltd
144 Southwark Street, London SE1 0UP
www.titanbooks.com

First edition: June 2022
2 4 6 8 10 9 7 5 3 1

A CIP catalogue record for this title is available from the British Library.

Printed and bound in the United States.

For all those who accept reality
just enough to change it.

We can ask and ask but we can't have again
what once seemed ours for ever.
J. L. Carr

What was previously thought to be nonsense
is, in fact, almost certainly the case.
Jeffrey J. Kripal

I became friends with Ada Guadalupi in the June of '96, at the start of a summer that would shape my existence the way the wind shapes the land. Mum and I had recently moved South, and I was not adapting well. My troubles began straight away, on our first night in the farmhouse that had been Grandpa Ferdinando's and now was ours, when I woke up needing to pee, terrified that I wouldn't make it to the loo.

Yes, I do appreciate the funny side of this – now. At thirteen, I didn't. I had been fully blind for a grand total of eight months, too short a time to master my new life; once or twice I had lost my way to the bathroom and peed myself like a baby, and even though I'd learnt the route since, the humiliation stayed with me. Half-asleep, I reached out for my cane, stood up and headed out, or so I believed, until I ran into a wall where I was expecting a door. *I must have overshot*, I thought, and shifted left. The wall was still there.

My brain finished rebooting. I had instinctively followed my Turin routine, but there was a silence around me which did not belong in a city: no hum of cars, no high-pitched sirens, only a faint chirping of crickets. I was not in Turin. I was not home. I was in the village of Portodimare, a thousand miles south of everything I knew, in a room which – up until this year – I had occupied for no more than one week every summer. I'd gone to sleep without first practising the itinerary from bed to loo – a rookie mistake.

The sighted master any place the moment they are in it, whereas I need practice. To the sighted, space is a container of things, such as trees and houses and people; to me, space is movement, a dance of things reaching to me with their sound while I reach out to them with my limbs and my cane. As I move, space moves with me, and I need to get the rhythm right, for if I fall out of time and pick the wrong landmark to turn past, I find myself down the wrong alley, and by the time I notice it I am utterly lost. I am a drummer, playing beats with feet, cane and hands. I practise a new place in the same way as a musician practises a new song; if I lose the rhythm, I lose the way, because the rhythm *is* the way, and I need to practise until I get it right, and then keep practising until I cannot get it wrong, until my body takes over.

I hadn't rehearsed that room, that house, at all. I was not a deft blind person yet – there is only so much you can learn in eight months.

My anxiety racked up a notch. I *badly* needed to pee. I turned my back to the wall and stepped towards the bed, from where I hoped I'd manage to make my way to the door, using what visual memories I had. Tricky, but doable.

The bed was not where I thought it was.

Because I had followed my Turin regime, I must have veered right after leaving the bed; I had to correct to the left on my way back. Pee bubbled in my bladder like soup in a cauldron, sending steam up to my brain. It took me precious moments I didn't have to realise that I had to correct to the *right*, because I was going the opposite direction, *towards* the bed rather than

14

away from it. I veered right, too much, for my cane still didn't encounter the bed. It found another wall. There were walls everywhere, encroaching on me from all sides. Where was this one? Left of the bed, or right, or…?

I was lost.

I was lost in my own room and I was going to wet myself.

Fuck. The indignity of it made me furious. I spun round, sweeping my cane in a semicircle, a Hail Mary for something, anything, that would help me locate myself.

My cane bumped into something hard.

I edged closer, tested the darkness with my hands, and felt sweaty cotton and a soft surface giving under pressure – a mattress. *The bed.* I swept my hand over it, searching for the pillow, to locate the bed's head, and thus its orientation. *I can make it.* Or not: the soup in my bladder would slosh over any moment.

I knew that I had to go through the bedroom door – which was on the wall parallel to the bed's feet – and turn right under a small archway, which gave on to a hall with four doors, and the second from the right was the loo. I walked quicker than I normally would, quicker than it was wise for a blind boy. I managed not to trip, found the door and marched out in triumph.

My cane bumped into something once again. I hadn't a clue what it could be, so I squatted to touch it, letting my hand sink into a collection of broken objects, hard and cold. I almost cut myself on the edge of one of them. *A brick in a pile of rubble.* Like the one Mum had mentioned that afternoon. My parents were renovating the property; builders were at work during the day, knocking down walls, raising new ones, changing the layout of the house.

I waved the cane to the left, where I remembered there being a wall.

There was no wall.

I reached out further. My arm was extended to full length, the cane too, and I was trembling by then, as I still couldn't find any wall. The references I remembered from my sighted days were gone; I was lost again.

It's not fair. My eyes welled up. *It's not fair, it's not fair, it's not fair.* When I'd found my way, the way had changed; I couldn't win a game stacked against me. I had no option left other than to pee here, on dirt and broken stones, and tomorrow everybody would pretend not to notice, but I would know they did. I hated myself for that, and I hated myself for these baby tears. I sniffled and took a hand to my eyes to wipe them.

I felt on the back of my palm, not exactly a breeze, but a cold spot, like the ones said to manifest when a ghost is close. A ghost, or a draughty window. *There's one in the corridor.* The tears stopped as quickly as they'd come. There was still a chance.

I trailed the cold, slow steps this time, squeezing my dick between my thighs (I wore only pants; it was too hot for pyjama bottoms), willing the window to be in its place. When I touched the glass, it was like unwrapping the best Christmas present ever. I groped for the handle. I found it and turned it right, too quickly for the old wood. It got stuck. I took a breath, turned the handle again, slower, and pushed the window open.

I pulled down my pants and fire exploded out of my bladder, along my dick, and out of the window, a blazing waterfall splattering on the pavement two floors below. It felt amazing. I peed and peed and got high on the unadulterated joy of it.

I whipped my dick to shake off the last drops and pulled up my pants. I was pleased with myself, like when I'd managed to complete *Wario Land* on the Game Boy just before the Game Boy had smouldered out.

I stood there, facing a landscape I couldn't see, quaffing the last traces of urine in the cool night air, the sweet scent of victory. I listened to distant waves coming ashore, the ever-present crickets and a lunar barking of dogs. Packs of strays roamed the countryside, where they found no shortage of things to bark at – foxes, hedgehogs, cats, the moon.

A change in sound occurred.

I noticed when I tried to switch back from the barking to the waves, finding their sound was gone. The sea had stopped making any noise. And now that I was paying attention, the crickets had stopped. Only the barking remained, fading away. Soon that was gone too; and the night was perfectly silent.

I could still hear my own breath, my beating heart, the brushing of my palms on the windowsill, but no sound, no sound at all, reached me from the outside. It was the silence our world would make if our world were dead, if it had stopped moving and breathing. I swallowed. I had no way of discerning what crawled under the cover of that silence, sneaking closer.

The air was thick with the anticipation that comes before something momentous is said. I expected to hear a voice, a call – human, or otherwise. I heard something else: a breeze barely blowing, like the breath of a child fast asleep. Before I could fully appreciate the uncanniness of it all, it was over. The night sounded like itself once again, with waves and crickets joining the wind. Not the dogs: those didn't return.

I shut the window and forgot about it, as we do with things we would rather not confront, when we are pleased with ourselves.

The near-miss tragedy with the loo made it plain that I had to get a grasp of my new home. I told Mum that I was going to explore the farmhouse and the fields, to which she said, 'I'll go with you.'

'You can't! That's the point. I don't want to rely on you for ever.'

'Just to get you started. I helped you in Turin.'

'And how many times did I manage to go out alone in Turin?'

The answer was *none*, so she said instead, 'You didn't have enough time to learn.'

'Mum, I'm begging you. It's difficult enough as it is.'

That shut her up. She and Dad didn't like to hear me say that blindness was hard, and not some great, madcap boy's adventure.

The Masseria del Vento – the Grange of the Wind, to use its full name – had been built in the seventeenth century, one of the countless fortified masserias dotting the countryside. Puglia, the region in the heel of Italy, used to be invaded every other day by anyone who had ever built a boat, so the locals, that is, the descendants of older waves of invaders, came up with these self-sufficient structures, halfway between a modest castle and a glorified farm, in which to take refuge when a new wave came. Small communities would live in the vicinities of a fortified masseria, and when the invaders *du jour* arrived, they would retreat within the walls, where they would keep producing their own food and wait for the invaders to get bored.

Our place was never one of the most formidable, and it hadn't aged well; today budding invaders could simply wander in from one of the many points where the walls had crumbled. But the property comprised a decent-sized vineyard, century-old olive trees and an area of Mediterranean scrub scattered with more trees – carob, almond, walnut, peach, apricot, plums and a copse of eucalyptus. Wild prickly pears stood here and there, with fruits whose mad colours were wasted on me now.

Back in my sighted days I'd liked all of that. Now I found it daunting. Walking down a city road is a cinch, once you get the hang of it; cars are frightening, but after you get used to their roar, you appreciate the easy rationality of the road layout. The countryside is another matter. Mediterranean scrub will get you lost in a heartbeat. There are no straight lines, no neat corners or markers, and what sparse landmarks you might come across – rocks, shrubs – are almost indistinguishable from one another to the unskilled touch of a newbie blind person. Also, it can shift: a passing herd of sheep might upturn rocks, change the shape of shrubs, and the next time you go there you better get the hang of the change at once, or you will be hard-pressed to find your way back without help. Nothing is certain in a living world; nothing is defined.

This was 1996, before mobiles were cheap enough to become ubiquitous. If I got lost, I would have to wait for Mum to come and find me. I wasn't planning on straying far. *No big deal*, I thought. I had never ventured out on my own in Turin, a city full of strangers and fast-moving things, where walking was easier but also riskier. Here, I thought the only danger was humiliation. I was wrong about that, as I was wrong about a great many things that summer.

My young brain was a blank page easily written on. I learnt in no time the way from bed to loo, from bedroom to staircase to kitchen, from kitchen to garden door, from garden door to porch table. Seven steps, turn right, three steps, turn right, twenty steps, turn left. Those were simple beats. The challenging ones came in the wilds beyond the porch.

I started with the least ambitious routes: from the porch to the walnut tree, from the walnut tree to the wide-leaved carob tree that had been a favourite reading spot, from there to the vineyard. My right arm aches when I think of it. Sweeping the white cane on bare earth was hard, more of a continuous tapping than a smooth arc. I was using my marshmallow cane tip, one whose lightness and bulbous shape was meant for paved roads. It was only the following spring, if I remember, that I would discover the bell-sized flex tip for rough terrain, which I still use today.

In two or three days I was confident handling those routes and decided to venture into the vineyard. The vines were neatly planted in parallel lines, so I could enter a corridor between two rows, then get to the end of it and back without fear of getting lost. I planned to use the vineyard as a platform for further exploration: each line would take me to a slightly different point in the next field, so all I had to do was count rows and I'd know where I would end up. From there, I could push myself further, knowing that, as long as I made my way back to the vineyard, I could make my way back home. It seemed easy enough.

I first entered the vineyard late one morning. Not being able to see the other side, I couldn't estimate how long it would take me to get there. The vines were only slightly shorter than me, and their coarse leaves brushed my face whenever I veered too much one way or the other.

There was a strong aroma – one I would come to cherish in later years – of not quite wine, but what comes before, like the yeasty scent of dough that will become bread. I touched a bunch of young grapes, each one little and firm like a milk tooth. I picked one and put it in my mouth. I spat it out immediately; it was tart, bitter. I wished I had water with me. I never carried water with me in Turin, where it was rarely that hot, and where I could just *buy* water at every corner.

I remember the air being motionless. The noise of the building works, until now an ever-present hubbub at the edge of my consciousness, didn't make it here. I was lost; a dread came over me and choked my throat like a thief in the night. It was a terror completely out of proportion to the objective circumstances. I think what I felt was a sense of foreboding – of the encounter I was about to have, of the extraordinary events I was to go through before summer's end. I think I was afraid because of things yet to come.

Don't be absurd, I told myself. I put one hand on the vine next to me and reached out with the other to a vine on the opposite side, and I remained with my arms spread for a while, like a statue of Christ abandoned in the sticks. There we go. I was still in the same place, I wasn't lost, I couldn't be lost. *Nothing to fear*. And yet I wanted to go back to the farmhouse, to human sounds and voices.

I forced myself to push forward, until my cane told me the vines had come to an end. I moved another step and felt a breeze on my face. I was out. I was far from home, a grizzled adventurer who had just landed on the other side of the world. It gave me an intoxicating sense of freedom. It also made me uneasy. *That's enough for one day.*

Or was it?

The vineyard had been a piece of cake, as I'd expected. To break free I had to push myself. On this side was an expanse of scrub, a terrain I had to explore sooner or later. *Only a few steps.* I'd walk in a straight line, until I reached a rock, a tree, anything I could make into a landmark; and then I would move on from there.

I gave myself forty steps. If I didn't find a landmark in forty steps, I would turn around, re-trace my path. *It's safe*, I told myself. *Safe*, I repeated.

I walked on, conscious of the flip-flops I was wearing. Trainers would have been better on that rocky, spiky soil, but I didn't want to go back and change, and have to answer Mum's questions. Eight, nine, ten steps. I barely avoided kicking a half-buried rock, and kept walking. Eighteen, nineteen, twenty. My feet were rough with grit. I was thirsty: the grape's tartness had taken root in my mouth. The sun was beating hard. I passed a hand through my hair, wishing I'd put my baseball cap on. I'd gone for a walk with no water, no shoes and no hat; I knew the Southern ways as little as I knew the ways of the blind. Twenty-nine, thirty. A stab of pain. I panicked for a second, before realising that something had slipped between a flip-flop and my foot. Leaning on my cane for balance, I lifted the foot, and took out of my sole a tiny hard object with spikes on all sides. Some drops of a substance more viscous than sweat poured onto my fingers. I smelt it, and it was metallic – blood. Only a few drops. I flipped the thorny thing away. I wiped a layer of sweat from my forehead, and took off my soaked t-shirt, leaving me in just flip-flops and shorts. *What are the signs of heatstroke?*

Forty steps; no landmark.

A part of me was grateful, because if I had found one I would have had no excuse to head back. Rationally I *knew* I was close to the farmhouse and civilisation, but it didn't feel like it. I felt like an astronaut whose cable had snapped; I was floating in space, unmoored. A memory came back to me of the impossible silence I'd heard on my first night in the Masseria del Vento, of the certainty that something crawled beneath it. But there was no silence here. There was a soundscape of crickets, rustling leaves, an intense chirping of birds. Something else too; a different kind of rustling, coming from below rather than above, from the soil rather than the foliage. Coming closer. And behind the rustling, I picked up an undefinable gait, a *tap, tap*, which sounded like nothing in nature. They sounded like steps of sorts; an animal's, perhaps? *Tap, tap*.

'Who's there?' I called.

The wind took the gait away, but the rustling got stronger, and whatever was coming started running towards me. I heard heavy breaths, beastly pantings. I turned and hurried back towards the vineyard, too late, for now the pantings were accompanied by guttural growls, and when the barking started I knew it was stray dogs. The breeze brought the rotting scent from their throats.

The barking got louder, and it got closer.

Every cell in my body begged me to break into a run. I managed not to listen, and just keep walking. I only had to make it to the vineyard, and then…

… then what?

The vineyard was not a magic circle, and the dogs were not foul-smelling demons; leaves and grapes offered no protection. If the dogs wanted to get me they would, and there was not one thing I could do about it.

'Bastards!'

I was thirteen, in equal parts stubborn and naive. My mind was crammed with stories of heroes fighting against all odds to come up on top, strong men who could handle themselves in a fight and tell a Martini's quality at first sip. So I did something notable by its idiocy: I turned towards the barking noises, flailing my cane, as if that could ever look like a weapon. I must have cut a pathetic image, but it was imposing in my head. Perhaps it still is.

'Go away!' I shouted. In my head it had been a threat, but I suppose it came out more like a plea. I threw my t-shirt at the dogs.

The dogs barked closer, barked furiously, barked so loud they covered all other sounds, and I started making myself ready for pain, ready to go down, yes, but with a swing, when a powerful voice broke from the depths of the Earth shouting, 'Hey!'

The dogs stopped barking for a fraction of a second, then started again.

The voice said, 'What do you think you're doing?' And there was a sense of the person moving, the voice coming from a lower point now.

The barking subsided to a growl. One of the dogs made another attempt, to which the voice commanded, 'Don't!'

The growling stopped. There was a rustling once again, paws moving, this time away from me.

'Are you okay?' the voice said.

When my tale becomes too dark, just bear in mind that I survived to tell it: I survived the summer of '96, the savage season in which Ada Guadalupi and I trespassed into another world. It was a miracle – I use the word in its most literal sense – that I made it all the way to September. I was lucky. Others weren't. In later years I came to consider this as a fact of life: we are lucky until we aren't. Every summer must end, and another will come.

Before I lost my sight, my family's summer had been long, fat. We were in good health; we lived in a spacious three-bedroom flat in Turin; we went on holiday every August, one week at Grandpa Ferdinando's in Puglia, two weeks somewhere else. Our summer lasted for years, decades; it lasted for so long that Mum and Dad convinced themselves that through brains and hard work they had made summer eternal. As people do while their luck holds, they flat-out refused to admit luck had any hand to play. 'We reap what we sow,' Dad used to say.

Mum nodded and sagely added, 'Nothing more and nothing less.'

Then the black spot came. It started, as far as I can tell, on an early evening in October 1994, at the end of an epic battle with homework. Mum was frying artichokes in the kitchen; the smell infiltrating my room was killing me. I was tired and hungry. I put away the maths book. I yawned, rubbed my eyes, and the black spot remained, in the bottom right edge of my vision, too tiny to be seen, almost. I thought it was a hole in the desk's old, battered wood, but when I moved my head the hole moved too. It was on my wardrobe now.

I rubbed my eyes again. The hole remained. It was completely black, darker than the dark behind my eyes when I shut them to go to sleep. I was too young for health scares, and I shrugged it off. The hole would go when it would go.

It didn't go the next morning, or the morning after that. It was a harmless puncture in reality and I didn't have much use for the bottom right edge of my vision anyway. In a matter of days, the puncture became a part of my world and I stopped noticing it altogether; the same as a tall person sees the world from above, and a short person from below, I saw the world with a puncture in it. It was just the way it was. My parents never believed me on this, but I swear to this day that the only reason I didn't mention it immediately was that it didn't occur to me that it might be worth mentioning.

I forgot about the hole, and so I didn't notice that it was growing. I noticed, sometime in December, that it *had* grown; it was still small, but not as small as it had been. I was with Dad in a comic book shop, flipping through a Fantastic Four book, and the hole was large enough to hide Galactus the Devourer of Worlds. I shrugged it off again, and moved my head to look at Galactus's awesome purple and blue suit. Everything was forever changing – a month ago I had grown out of my best jumper, a week ago I had decided that *The Hobbit* had beaten *The Neverending Story* in the ranking of my favourite books – and this was just one more new development to add to the pile.

Three days later, Grandpa Ferdinando died.

My last visual memory of the Masseria del Vento is from the night of the wake. I went back there once while I was technically sighted, but by then I was in steep decline, and frightened of what was coming, so the visit didn't leave much of an impression. In that last memory, the main building of the grange stands as it will always stand for me: white and decrepit, longer than it was tall, with a squat tower almost entirely ruined on one end, and a smaller one, intact, more or less, on the other.

I remember stepping outside with Ferdi, my big brother, to catch some fresh air. Inside, Grandpa's body, dressed in a brown moleskin suit, lay in an open coffin in a living room full of friends and family. Food had been set on a table. Uncle Mario sat his enormous frame on a wicker armchair, crying loudly, surrounded by his famously beautiful children, Maddalena and Ferdinando, who, like my brother, was named after Grandpa. There were flowers on every table and in every corner, obscene in their colour. It was a warm night for winter, following a warm day, and it took many flowers to hide the acrid smell of Grandpa's meat rotting.

Under the arches of the porch, Ferdi lit a roll-up. He said, 'Thank you for coming. I needed to get out of there.'

I inhaled his smoke. I was training myself to like cigarettes, so that in five years, when I'd be Ferdi's age, I could start smoking as well. 'I couldn't stand them anymore either.'

Behind us, the masseria was almost entirely dark. Grandpa had been using a handful of rooms, and light only came from those windows. The bulk of the building was left to spiders, bats and other wild things. Ferdi walked beyond the reach of the light, into the winter mist hovering over the countryside. The mist made the world soft; moonlight took its time to trickle down to us, like syrup falling in a pool of water.

'It didn't look like Grandpa,' I said.

'What did it look like?'

'A mannequin.'

Ferdi took a drag of his cigarette. 'People look different after they die.'

'Why?'

'They're not people anymore.'

I marvelled at my brother's wisdom. 'Do you think they're still alive? In Heaven.'

'Sure,' Ferdi said.

'You don't sound convinced.'

'Grandpa was.'

'Praise God, never the wind. He always said that.'

'Yeah, praising God is good for you. He did believe that stuff.'

'I hope he was right,' I said.

Out of the mist appeared the tall walnut tree that stood on the edge of the vineyard. Not a single leaf was left on its branches. In summer Ferdi and I would gorge on fresh nuts, still not entirely ripe, which made our fingers black when we peeled off the skin. I touched its bark and said, 'I've never seen this tree bare before.'

'Give it four months.'

'Summer won't be the same, without Grandpa.'

'No, it won't.'

I had been crying a lot, and I felt I could have another go. Grandpa's death had not been unexpected to the adults in my family, but I had been positive that he, like pretty much everybody I knew, was immortal. This idea that death was a real thing that could reach everybody, even us, was new to me. My other grandparents had all died before I was born.

'Hey,' Ferdi said. 'Hey, Scrawny.' That was what my brother used to call me, and it was, back then, a fair description of my appearance. 'Are you crying?'

I sniffled. 'No.'

'There's no shame, you know. Dad's been crying too.'

'You've not.'

'Yeah, when you weren't watching. Don't tell anyone though.'

That was reassuring. I gave the lump in my throat time to subside before saying, 'If tomorrow is clear, can we climb on the roof and watch the stars?' It was another of my summer treats: Ferdi and I would lie on the masseria's rough roof terrace, to look at the stars and make up our own constellations. I'd discovered Elvis Presley, a cluster of stars which looked uncannily like Elvis's head and hairdo.

'We can go now if you want.'

'Not with this mist.'

Ferdi chuckled. 'Come on, let's go.'

'Where?'

He froze mid-movement. 'On the roof.'

'But, the mist!'

He said, 'Scrawny, what mist?'

The wild dogs were gone. I was alone in the field with this stranger who had saved my life. I was shaking like a willow in a gale, to the point that the muscles in my throat didn't allow me to form words. I had to sit. I settled down carefully, after checking the soft earth with the side of my foot for rocks or thorny bushes. 'You… you still there?' I managed to ask.

'Yes.' The voice was female, a little husky, with the unhurried vowels of the local accent. 'Water?'

'Please!'

There was silence. 'Are you handing me a bottle?' I asked.

'Yes,' she said. 'Sorry.'

I felt her coming closer. She put a lukewarm bottle in my

hand. 'Thank you,' I barely said, before bringing the bottle to my mouth. I drank and drank until not a drop of water was left. 'I emptied it. Sorry.'

'No worries.'

It occurred to me that it was a ridiculous scene, me sitting there in the middle of a field, exchanging apologies with this stranger looming over me. With some effort, I stood up. My legs were still shaking. I leaned on my cane for balance and extended the bottle roughly in the direction of the voice. The stranger shifted, took the bottle.

'Do I know you?' I asked.

'Don't think so. Ada?'

'Ada Guadalupi?'

'That one.'

Ada was a girl my age, from Casalfranco, the closest town to Portodimare. Her family had a holiday home right next to the masseria, where they spent the summer. I was aware that she existed, but we weren't friends. We had crossed paths in the village or on the beach sometimes, and our families had been polite with each other, that was all.

'You must be Luca Saracino.'

'You heard of the blind boy.'

'I knew of a boy my age living next door. I'm sorry for Ferdinando.'

'Did you know Grandpa?'

'A little.'

Another silence.

'What are you doing?' I said. I felt frustrated; my condition made simple tasks – like talking to girls – harder than I ever thought they could be.

'Oh fuck, sorry!' She took my hand in hers, which was small and sweaty. 'I was offering you my hand to shake. Kind of a welcome.'

Now that I had touched the sweat, I could smell it on her: not unpleasant, it was the gentle smell of sweat on clean skin in the sunshine. I said, 'You're not supposed to be here, are you?'

'Sure I am.'

'This is my family's land.'

There was a silence; Ada blinked out of existence.

'You still there?' I asked.

'Yeah.' She blinked in. 'Did I just save your arse, or did I imagine that?'

'I didn't mean it in a bad way.'

'In which way did you mean it, then?'

I felt a surge of resentment. Ada could go wherever she wanted and do whatever she pleased, and took for granted she had a right to that. 'This *is* our land though.'

'And this is the girl who chased away those big bad dogs.'

'Don't patronise me.'

'You know what, I don't have to do this.'

'No, you don't.'

'Goodbye and fuck you, then.'

Same here, I thought, and said, 'Bye.'

I made to go, and realised I didn't know which way. I tried to remember the fields, the way they looked, which didn't help. Then I did what doctors had suggested and focused on the four senses I had rather than on the one I missed. The sun beat on my face, and was its warmth on my back earlier, or on my front? I didn't know. I didn't know how long ago 'earlier' was. I heard the birds and the crickets and, as a bass line beneath it all, the huff of the girl's breath moving away from me. I'd got lost in my bedroom; I could easily get lost here in the open. With no water, under a scorching sun. My foot may still be bleeding from where the thorny thing had punctured the skin. What if the dogs caught a scent? Like sharks. They could do that, couldn't they?

What if the dogs come back?

I called, 'Wait.'

'What?'

I couldn't quite bring myself to say it.

'What's the matter?' she asked.

'Could you help me out?'

'Doing what?'

'Getting back to the farmhouse.'

She didn't answer. I zoned in on her breath to make sure she was still there.

She said, 'But I'm a trespasser.'

'I didn't say that.'

'Not in so many words.'

'Could you take me just to the vineyard? I can take it from there.'

'Fine.'

'And by the way – do you see a t-shirt?'

I heard her come closer with a thumping noise.

'What are you doing?'

'Kicking your t-shirt. I won't touch it. It's gross. Here, right in front of you.'

I squatted and found it, caked in sweat and dirt. I stood up while Ada was saying, 'I wouldn't put it back on.'

'Me neither.'

'Why's it in the dirt?'

'I threw it at the dogs.'

'You were holding back a pack of dogs with a filthy t-shirt.'

'Seemed a good idea at the time.'

She chuckled. 'A biological weapon, I see.'

'Which way is the vineyard?'

I suddenly felt a hand on my arm, and jumped. Ada said, 'Trust me.' She hooked her arm under mine.

We walked in silence. Some people, and I am talking about well-intentioned people, forget that when I rely on them to walk I have to rely on them completely. Even Mum and Dad had made me trip, even Ferdi. Not Ada: she was a natural. She understood that, no matter how small, a rock would send me sprawling, and that if she were to speed up her pace I wouldn't follow. She adopted a slow, steady gait, and almost convinced me that it was her usual one.

'They're not dangerous, you know,' she said. Ada couldn't do silence for long, which suited me. Silence is a lifeless void.

'Who?'

'The dogs. They're only scared.'

'*They're* scared?'

'Dogs don't like having no master.'

'I don't like being chased.'

'They wouldn't have touched you. I think. Next time just pretend you're picking up a stone.'

'What?'

'A stone. Bend down and pretend to pick up a stone. They're used to having stones thrown at them. Pretend you're picking one up and show no fear and they'll go.'

'Is this what you did?'

'Indeed.' She stopped. 'The vineyard,' she announced.

Yes, the vineyard; its scent merged with Ada's. 'Thank you.'

'Do you mind if I come to yours for a glass of water?'

'Sure.'

We went into the vineyard together, with me still hanging by her arm, and now that I had company the space between the vines felt smaller, more domestic. I was grateful she was with me. I am almost certain that she found an excuse to take me all the way back home, a thought that didn't cross my mind until many years later.

Ada said, 'Might be too much of a hassle, to give water to a trespasser.'

'Yeah, about that. Sorry. I overreacted.'

'Don't say.'

'It wasn't about you. I was upset. Because of the dogs.'

'I get it. We're good.'

'But seriously, what were you doing out there in this heat? Just asking.'

'A walk,' she said. 'My parents were driving me crazy. It's too hot to walk all the way to the beach, so I was having a stroll here.'

'You don't have a bike?'

'The front tyre went bust during the winter.'

'I used to like going to the beach.'

'Why the past tense?'

'Can't go on my own.'

'Your old people won't let you?'

I tapped my wraparound sunglasses. 'I've been this way since October. Still learning, and the beach is a bit much. My mum would take me, but I don't want to go with her.'

'We could go together.'

'Some time,' I said, without enthusiasm.

'Dad's getting the bike fixed. I'll come tomorrow and get you.'

'Can't do tomorrow,' I lied.

'Another time, then.'

'Another time.'

She took me all the way back, to the racket of building works. Mum wasn't home, which was good. I could take cover in the shower and never tell her what happened. Ada drank a glass of iced tea in one long swallow, said, 'See ya,' and left me alone with the drilling and the hammering.

Dad dismissed Ferdi's worries with another, 'It's nothing.'

Ferdi and my parents were arguing again, on the night of Grandpa Ferdinando's wake of all times, and for once it wasn't because of Ferdi, but because of me. They were doing a bad job of keeping their voices down. I could hear everything, tucked in bed under a double duvet. The room had a mustard tiled floor and a tuff, vaulted ceiling, blackened by time. The black spot was in its usual place, at the bottom right edge of my vision. The mist had followed me inside.

'He kept saying he's seeing *mist*!'

'Have you smoked?' Mum asked. 'Because I can smell it on you.'

'*Everybody* was smoking in that fucking room. You stink like a gambler.'

Dad said, 'Language, Ferdi.'

'I'm telling you, there's something wrong with Luca.'

'His grandfather – *your* grandfather – just died. That's what's wrong with him.'

Mum said, in her let's-be-reasonable voice, 'Luca's been crying his heart out. He's tired.'

Ferdi said, 'There's more than that.'

'He was *Mum's father*,' Dad said. 'I know you won't give a damn when our time comes, but I was hoping you'd give up the spotlight just this once.'

I heard Ferdi's heavy footsteps, a door slamming; then my mum's and dad's voices, too low for me to make out the words. I shut my eyes to try and catch some sleep. Ferdi thought there was something wrong with me, and Ferdi was always right. That night I felt the first pang of a fear which would be my faithful companion for years to come, and maybe never left – the fear that I might be flawed, and beyond repair.

The thing is, I did want to go to the beach – badly – but not as someone's charity case. I distinctly remember how sulky I was for the rest of the day. I'd have talked to Ferdi, if long-distance calls weren't so expensive and strictly policed; tomorrow afternoon we'd call Turin to wish Ferdi good luck on the eve of his end of school exams. Tomorrow, not before. 'Until we're up and running,' Dad had explained, 'we're going to be a little careful with money. That's how business works.' Maybe, but meanwhile I missed my brother.

It wasn't one of my highest moments, out there with the dogs; I couldn't go for a walk *in my own fields*. I found myself stumbling that day, as if I was newly blind again, like an acrobat who looks down and suddenly forgets how to walk the tightrope, and falls.

I did fall, too, in the shower, bumping my head against the wall. I stopped the fall with a hand; I was lucky my wrist didn't snap. I sat with water pouring over me, my arms hugging my legs and my chin on my knees, too weary to stand up again. There was no hurry. Mum hadn't come back. I could stay in the shower for as long as I wanted without her knocking on the door and asking, 'What's the problem?' What could be the problem? That I was trapped in a cage the size of my body and I had no way out, but the teeth and claws of the world had plenty of ways in. I imagined the dogs as these immense wolf-like beasts, eyes red, mouths foaming, razor-sharp fangs.

They're not dangerous.

Easy for Ada to say, but everything is dangerous when you don't see it coming. *Just pretend you're picking up a stone.* It wouldn't work for me; the pack would smell my helplessness. A girl had come to my rescue. That was beyond embarrassing. I was the man, I should do the rescuing, and instead here I was, sitting on my arse in the shower. I didn't want to be that kind of man. Grandpa hadn't been that kind of man. Ferdi wasn't that kind of man.

I hauled myself up.

I had forgotten all about the undefinable gait, the *tap, tap* I'd heard just before the dogs attacked, for other thoughts were louder. I wondered how Ada Guadalupi looked. I had last seen her briefly three, four years earlier, and I vaguely remembered curly hair, but I could be wrong. I was sure she had to be cute. Ferdi said that cute girls think they can do whatever they want, and that they might even be right. What Ada wanted was, obviously, to turn me into her special project. I wouldn't allow that. I turned off the tap, fumbled for my towel. I'd never talk to her again. That, I decided, was set in stone.

She came by the next day.

I woke up on the morning of Grandpa's funeral, the day after the wake, to find Ferdi in the courtyard, kicking a leather football on his own. I made a point of putting up a front and saying, 'Gorgeous day!'

'Mist is gone?'

'Totally.'

It wasn't true, but I hoped that by ignoring the mist I'd convince it to leave me alone. Besides, Mum and Dad had enough on their plate. Me too. I'd loved Grandpa Ferdinando almost as much as I loved Ferdi.

The day rolled among clouds. The hearse drove Grandpa's coffin over clouds, and we walked on clouds behind it; the clouds came with us inside the small church by the sea where the function was held, and from the clouds the priest grandiosely praised Grandpa's life. When we left the church, there were clouds all around the stone building, and on the square, and on the sea behind it. I was looking at the misty sea, while my parents received condolences, when Ferdi came to me and said, 'It's still there, isn't it?'

I hesitated, then said, 'Yes.'

It took another argument, in which words difficult to forgive were exchanged, but at last Mum and Dad agreed to take me to the doctor as soon as we were back in Turin. I have a perfect recollection of that visit. I could re-enact it step by step: the ophthalmologist's fingertips on my eyelids, the pressure of cool gas on my pupil, the eyedrops. When it was over, the doctor wanted to have a word in private with one of my parents. Dad took me to a café around the corner and bought me hot chocolate; Mum emerged from the mist a half hour later, her eyes red.

The news wasn't great, but it wasn't terrible either. I was going through something called *retinitis pigmentosa*: hidden parts of my eyes were coming undone. Dad asked, 'Okay, what do we do next?'

'The doctor says we cannot do much,' she answered. 'So we find another doctor.' We had sound judgement and we worked hard, so good things came to us: that was my parents' credo.

The Christmas holidays came and went, as doctors did. There were many of them, all with similar faces and similar voices. After a string of visits, after hearing the same words over and over again, and after I was stuffed with Vitamin A to no avail, we had to accept that it was likely that I would end up losing my sight, all of it. *Blind people who cannot see anything at all, no shapes, no light, are very rare*, a junior doctor said, as if joining their ranks would be a praiseworthy achievement of mine. There were explanations, very good medical explanations, which I could chant as a litany right now, but they were explanations, not *reasons*; I was told in great detail how I was going blind, never *why*. Of course, I know now there was no why. Some things happen because they do, and whatever meaning we want to find in them, we have to make it ourselves.

'We could have saved him!' I heard Ferdi bellow one night. 'If only you fuckin' listened to me *for once!*'

Ferdi was wrong; the season had turned for our family, and when bad weather is coming all you can do is brace yourself, and prepare.

A sound like a whir of mechanical wings got closer, then stopped suddenly, and whatever had existed disappeared.

I was sitting on the porch, brushing the dots of a Braille edition of an old translation of *Moby-Dick* (my choices for reading being somewhat limited). It weighed almost as much as the real whale, which made reading it harder. I was improving with Braille, not quickly. The rumble of building works had a numbing effect – perhaps I should have walked somewhere quieter, but after meeting the dogs, I didn't feel like leaving the safety of the house for now.

'Hello hello?' her voice came. 'It's me, Ada.'

'Hi.'

She left something on the ground with a light *clang*. '*Moby-Dick*,' she read aloud, which is less impressive than it sounds, because most Braille books bear their title in print letters as well. 'How is it?'

'Great, if you like whales.'

'Do you?'

I waved my hand in a *so-so* gesture. I was proud of my so-so wave. I was making an effort to hold on to the use of gestures in conversation, and the so-so one was, I reckoned, one of my best.

She said, 'The bike's as good as new. Coming to the beach?'

So that was what produced the whir – a bike. I stored the information for future reference. 'As I said, no.'

'Why? What are you up to?'

'Reading *Moby-Dick*.'

'He's a whale. He'll want to come too.'

We could have spent the whole day arguing if Mum hadn't come out saying, 'Who's here?' and after a pause, 'Hello.'

'I'm Ada Guadalupi,' Ada introduced herself, with her impeccable manners. In my mind's eye she curtsied. 'Your neighbour's daughter.'

'Yes, Ada, I remember you. I didn't know you and Luca were friends.'

Ada would tell Mum about the fields and the dogs. I was rushing to stop her somehow (I didn't know how), but her mouth was quicker than mine. 'We're not, yet. I heard you guys moved in and came to say hi.'

'That's very kind, thank you. Luca needs to make friends.'

'Yeah, he was just saying he'd love to come to the beach with me. Isn't that right, Luca?'

She'd already got me painted: saying no at that point would be too awkward for me to bear. 'Yes,' I said.

'That's wonderful!' Mum said. 'Be careful, okay?'

I put on my trunks and fetched a baseball hat and a backpack, into which I tossed a towel, a bottle of water, and *Moby-Dick*. No sunscreen; sunscreen was for wusses. We promised Mum that we would walk the mile to the beach rather than ride, and we respected the promise for the whole length of the drive leading to the rusty old thing which my family insisted on calling a *gate*, even though it had been jammed open for ever. When we turned right on the road – still unpaved, full of pebbles and holes, not the strip of smooth tarmac it is today – Ada said, 'Jump on.' She took my hand and placed it on the pillion to show me where it was. I wasn't sure I could climb on it. Losing my sight had made my balance wonky too. I would fall and make her fall and we would hurt ourselves.

'Luca?' she called. 'Any problems?'

'No.' I folded my cane and put it in the backpack. I mounted, put my hands on Ada's waist, and lo!, we were moving.

In April '95 I signed up to a Karate dojo. The hole in my eye had split in two, and then four then eight, each one roughly the dimensions of the first one; the mist seemed to get heavier by the day; lights projected rainbow halos and explosions flashed suddenly with no noise. I was slipping into a parallel universe of strange colours and fuzzy edges, and I was slipping fast. The doctors said I would lose what was left of my vision in one year or less. It was time to talk about what happened next, and I decided that was martial arts. I was a comic book nerd (I suspect I still would be, if I'd had the chance) so my model of a sightless man was Matt Murdock, aka Daredevil, a blind Ninja lawyer whose other senses were so developed that it was as if he wasn't blind at all. Even his blindness was sort of a superpower: you cannot fool a blind man, not in comic books.

Matt Murdock had a gaunt, severe sensei; mine was good-hearted, pot-bellied, with a handlebar moustache and receding hairline. He only agreed to take me on after I promised – without really meaning it – that I would tone down my expectations. I lasted six weeks. Even at the slowest speed, when I saw a blow come, it was too late to parry. I was punched and kicked repeatedly, and I kept tripping on my own feet. I felt no sharpening of my awareness. I felt, if anything, more disabled than ever. I'd make better use of my time studying Braille. So I quit, with the lingering suspicion that, had I been stronger, faster, better, I would have turned into a Ninja after all.

Shortly after that, Dad dropped the bomb. He said one evening at the dinner table, 'We need to discuss Grandpa Ferdinando's masseria.'

I remember I was polishing off a plate of polenta and sausage, eager to finish and go play with my new Game Boy (a perk of looming blindness was that Mum and Dad would let me satisfy whims they never let me satisfy before, in much the same spirit in which prison directors set up last meals for death row inmates). 'When are we going?' I asked. I always looked forward to Portodimare.

'Are you sure you want to go this year?'

'Yes,' I said. 'Why?'

'Because…' Dad couldn't bear himself to as much as *name* what was happening to me. 'It might be easier for you to stay home.'

'I want to see the beach one last time.'

'Luca…'

'And the trees and the prickly pears and everything.'

Mum looked at Ferdi. 'What do you think?'

'Whatever Luca wants.'

'We're going, then,' Mum said.

Dad said, 'It's great that you like the masseria so much! We'll be spending a whole lot of time there.'

There was a silence. Ferdi broke it with a stony, 'Explain.'

Mum and Dad exchanged a look, and Mum said, 'We're moving to Portodimare. Not immediately, but we're moving.'

Ferdi scoffed. 'You're nuts.'

'We are treating you like grown-ups. Try to act the part.'

'Grown-ups don't get a say in where they live?'

'You'll be starting uni by the time we move, and you'll get all the say you want in where *you* live.'

'What about Luca?'

'A change of scenery will do him good.'

Ferdi raised his voice. 'He won't *see* the scenery!'

'And there's a strong local community there,' Mum went on, as if Ferdi hadn't spoken. 'It's going to be safer than a big city.'

'I can't believe this is happening. Did you do any research at all? Everybody says it's easier to adjust to blindness in familiar surroundings.'

'The masseria *is* familiar to Luca!'

'What, because he spent a grand total of *eleven weeks* there his whole life?'

They were already falling into a habit well known to those of us who are blind: the sighted talk of us as if we weren't there.

'Is this all because of me?' I asked, partially because I wanted an answer, and partially because I wanted my voice to be heard.

Dad said, 'No.'

'We've been planning this since Grandpa got ill last year,' Mum explained, with the faintest hint of an apology in her voice. 'The masseria is in disrepair, but it's big, and it comes with land attached. Not a lot, but some: inheritance tax would bleed us dry. Years ago, Grandpa sold it to me and Uncle Mario for a nominal sum. Uncle Mario was not interested in keeping his part, so Dad and I talked, and decided to buy him out. The masseria was already ours when Grandpa died.'

'And we weren't asked what we thought,' Ferdi said.

'To spare you the burden.'

'Let me pick my burdens myself.'

'Anyway,' Dad said. 'The idea is to renovate it from the bottom up. With some serious love, it's going to be amazing: a high-end wedding venue, hotel, and, for us, home. Puglia is coming up! Tourists the world over are discovering it.'

Ferdi asked, 'Renovate the masseria – with what money? Or that's not my *burden?*'

'Okay,' Dad said, in an exasperated voice. 'We spoke to a bank, took a loan against the property. It was already approved when Grandpa passed. It's all done.'

'What about the money to buy out Uncle Mario? Where does it come from?'

'We promised Mario we'd put this house on the market. It'll cover what we owe him and then some. What with everything that happened to Luca, he's been kind enough to wait until now, but… it's time.'

'And you're leaving your job? Both of you?'

'Running the masseria is going to be full-time.'

'You're morons.'

'*You are the moron*, Ferdi!' Dad almost shouted. 'This is going to give us time to care for Luca. Don't you get it?'

Ferdi didn't answer. Nobody spoke until I said, 'I was right, then. It's me.'

'It'd all been decided well before you… visited the doctor,' Dad said. 'It turns out it's an even better idea than we thought. It's all good, boys.'

And they really did believe that it was all good. They started saving, so the week in Portodimare was the only holiday we took that year. The day I remember best is the last one, when I went to the beach, and facing the misty sea thinking, *This is my last time with you.* I had loved to sit on the beach and look at the blue line where water becomes air. I was going to lose the sea, as I'd lost Grandpa Ferdinando, and I wished I could have a funeral for it too.

Ada started out slowly, the bike tilting right and left. It felt like being on a ship caught in a storm at sea; I was sure that we would capsize. But Ada pedalled with a strength I didn't suspect of her, and went faster, until we sped along in a straight line. *Keep still*, I thought. *Keep as still as you can and it's going to be okay.* Every bump of the road came up from the pillion to my coccyx like an explosion.

Suddenly the road became smoother: we were on tarmac. Ada went faster.

The wind rushed to my face with a fresh scent of thyme and juniper, of Ada's skin, of the sea coming closer with every thrust. I felt the speed through my whole body, through my flesh and down my bones, a pure force pulling me with joy. An incline: we were going downhill. Ada didn't touch the brakes. She kept pedalling faster, and faster still. Her shirt was wet with sweat against my cheek. Fear – which never abandoned me for the duration of that first ride – added to the joy.

The wind whistled in my ears. It was a hurricane scent of herbs, girl and seaside, powerful enough to blow my cage away. I felt free as I had never felt since that awful night eight months ago when the final curtain had fallen over my eyes. I had spent the last two years of my life listening to people telling me that I had to take control, that I could live a normal life if only I learnt how, which meant that if I didn't, well, too bad, it was my fault. My life *had to be normal*, goddamn it. I'd spent the last two years minding every step, every routine, always minding the rhythm.

But this. This was punk rock.

I was going fast, living fast. I was smashing my drums. I wasn't in control, just along for the ride, just *there*, and I didn't have a bloody clue what the rhythm was supposed to be. It was awesome.

We rounded a bend, my knee almost touched the pavement, I laughed. Ada laughed too, and screamed, 'Faster?'

'Yeah,' I said.

Her knees came to touch my hand at quick intervals, spinning like tops, pushing harder, and we were still going downhill, so fast now that we could have taken off and headed for whatever countries are hidden in the sky. The roar of a car passed by, accompanied by an angry honk. Ada answered by ringing the bike's little bell and shouting a jolly, 'Fuck you.'

'Fuck you!' I joined, laughing.

A whiff of rosemary came to me, and another smell, stronger and unmistakable, the salty scent of the sea on a calm day, filtered through the junipers and the sea daffodils growing on the dunes by the beach. Ada turned right, and slowed down. The sea, I judged, was on our left; we were on the Litoranea Salentina, a long coastal road. I asked Ada for confirmation, and she said, 'Yes, we're on the Litoranea.'

The sea on our left then, and on our right dunes and sparse houses. The dunes were in full bloom, judging by the smell. 'Which beach are we going to?'

'Do you know the Little Pinewood?'

'Yes.' Each stretch of beach in Portodimare had, and still has, an informal name, not written on any map, but handed down from generation to generation. I'd never been to the beach called the Little Pinewood; Ferdi and his friends had. 'There's no access from the road,' I said, to show off my knowledge.

'We'll walk.'

I knew that we had entered the village when sounds started crowding and the air took on a whiff of people and food. Cars too. Not that Portodimare was a teeming metropolis: in June there was some movement, not much. It only got busy in July and August, and even then it was not exactly central Turin.

Crossing the village took all of three minutes. Ada turned left; fresh sea-scented breeze kissed my nose.

The bike slowed to a halt.

The day before Mum and I moved to Portodimare, Ferdi shaved my head. By then, my descent was done and dusted. I was as blind as a caver who had tripped and broken his light and was now grasping the true nature of darkness. I had to make myself comfortable in the cave, for I would never leave.

I was struggling with learning Braille, using the cane, wiping my arse: the countless new skills my life required. Combing my hair was one too many. I had been told I could learn to keep a hairstyle, but I thought a shaved head would add a touch of toughness to my appearance – a blind man, yes, but not one you want to mess with.

The clunky electric razor droned like a sick beehive on the brink of mass extinction. Tufts of hair ran against my cheek as they fell.

'I wish you were coming,' I said.

'I wish *Dad* was going with you.'

'It sucks they don't give you some space.'

'They treat me like an idiot,' Ferdi said, with a spite in his voice I found disturbing. 'I'd get more work done if they left me alone.'

His exams started at the end of the month. Our parents had decreed he could not be trusted to study on his own, so, while Mum and I would move to Portodimare, Dad would stay with him.

Ferdi said, 'I'm going to touch your right ear, okay? To reach behind it.'

'Sure.'

I was skittish when people touched me without prior notice. I said, 'Can you believe this is the last night at home for me?'

'And how much does *that* suck?'

I couldn't answer honestly, for I was, if not excited, at least curious. I had already lost the place where we grew up. Home wasn't home anymore. It was this maze full of angles, and I thought I might feel less of a failure elsewhere, in a house I was not supposed to know like the back of my hand. 'A hundred per cent,' I lied.

'Uncle Mario will be there.'

'Mum said he's on holiday in Greece. The whole family.'

'I'm going to touch your other ear,' Ferdi said. He bent the cartilage, ran the razor behind it and asked, 'When will they be back?'

'July, at some point.'

'It's you and Mum alone for a good stretch of time, then.'

'Apparently.'

'Try not to kill her,' he said.

I could agree without lying. I was not looking forward to being alone with Mum.

Ada chained the bike and took my arm, the light cotton of her long-sleeved shirt brushing against my skin. In just a few steps the tarmac ended. The wind brought the voice of Lauryn Hill singing a cover of 'Killing Me Softly'; someone on the beach was listening to the radio. Ada said, 'Wait a sec. I want to take off my flip-flops.'

I did the same. My feet sank into warm, pleasantly rough sand. We walked on, arm in arm like old wives, letting the music fade behind us. 'I'm slowing you down,' I said.

'Indeed. I'll be late for the brain surgery I've been called to perform.'

That made me smile. I listened to the waves. They were quiet. 'How's the sea?'

'Blue.'

'You can do better than that.'

'You sure you want me to?'

'Please.'

'Okay, then. Tramontana is blowing, the Northern wind, but it's only a breeze, so the sea is perfectly calm. It is napping in the sunshine. Closer to the shore the water is pale blue. As I speak, I see the sand and rocks on the bottom. There's a bank of fish feeding from a rock. Further towards the horizon, the blue gets stronger, more powerful. It comes into its own, you know what I mean? But even there, even there, I see stars in the water, dots of light dancing on the waves. It's the sun, which reflects not in one point, but in a million. Further on yet, the blue changes again: it becomes softer, but also more uniform, the same blue as the sky. There's not a single cloud to be seen. If you could look at the sea and the sky forgetting all you know, you would think they were one and the same.'

'You like words,' I said.

'I want to be a writer.'

'Writing what?'

'Words...?' She paused. 'We're at the rocks. I'm putting my flip-flops on.'

I did the same. Sand gave way to sharp-edged rocks. I'd cut my feet on those even when I could see, so I negotiated the crossing carefully, testing the ground with my toe before every step. My trust in Ada faltered, for no better reason than fear. When we got to the end of the rocks I felt accomplished, as if we'd traversed an alligator-ridden swamp, and also guilty for my lapse of trust. We took off our flip-flops again, kept walking. I heard voices, not many. They thinned out the further we walked, until Ada said, 'We're here,' and hers was the only human sound left among the waves, the crickets and the occasional demanding call of a seagull.

I turned my back to the shore and took a long breath, to drink in the fragrance of Mediterranean pines. The Little Pinewood was so called because of a private pinewood touching the edge of the sand. Being difficult to reach, this beach would be comparatively quiet even in August. On a weekday in June, it was all ours.

My legs were killing me. I wasn't used to long walks, especially on the beach. I heard the *thump* of what had to be

Ada's backpack dropping on the sand. We took our bottles and drank, and Ada said, 'Swim?'

'I'll test the water.'

I took off my t-shirt but kept my shades on. We moved to the shore, where dry, warm sand became compact underfoot, and cool. Water lapped my feet and drew back, to return and lap my feet again. A sudden fear took hold of me. I imagined getting lost at sea, unable to remember which way was land, my legs and arms getting weaker, weaker, until they finally gave way. There was nothing sensible about that fear, not when there was someone with me, and yet one of the things I learnt that summer is that fear cannot be fought with the tools of reason; fear has its own truth, and it doesn't matter if the truth of the world is of a different sort.

I waded into the water, my testicles retracting at its coolness. When the water reached above my bellybutton, I stopped. Fear was turning into a full-fledged panic attack. I took long breaths, the way I'd been taught would keep attacks at bay.

'Dive in!' Ada said.

'First swim of the season. I'm not risking congestion.'

'Okay, Grandpa. I'm coming.'

I heard her wade closer. I thought she was going to push me in the water, and I was sure, dead sure, that once down I wouldn't be able to come up again. I shouted, 'I said *no!*'

She stopped in her tracks. 'Are you out of your mind?'

'I'm cautious.'

'Twat,' she spat out.

I heard her dive in, her strokes fade into the distance. I poured water over my head and walked back to shore, where I sat. I couldn't see the blue, but I could feel the waves lapping against my legs, and I could lick the salt from my lips, and it was okay.

Ada swam for what seemed like a long time, then her strokes came closer to the shore. I heard the reversed splash of a body surfacing from the water. She sat next to me and said, 'What was that about?'

'Sorry.'

'Yeah, yeah, you're sorry, but what was that about?'

'I can't do it. Diving, swimming – I can't.'

'You can't swim?'

'Not anymore.'

She thought, before replying, 'I can help you if you want. The sea is the same as always and your arms and legs too. The problem's all in your head. You'll get the hang in no time.'

'Can I ask you something?'

'Sure.'

'Why are you so nice to me?'

'I don't know,' she said. 'I wish people were nicer to each other.'

I detected an off-key note, the echo of something left unsaid. I didn't pursue it. I didn't want to intrude, I think, or perhaps I was too pleased with being the centre of attention. In the end, I was a good kid; I tell myself that, had I been one or two years older, I would have asked questions, and done more.

A chorus of drills and hammers welcomed Mum and me. When the car stopped, I thought we were at a service station.

'Do you need help getting out?' Mum asked.

'I'll wait here.'

'We're at the masseria,' she said, after a beat.

I clicked my belt open. 'I know,' I said.

As soon as we stepped inside the entrance hall, Mum said, 'This is wrong.' And a man answered, 'No, it's right, *signora,*' his voice aggressively indolent.

'You shouldn't be doing this wing yet.'

'Nobody told me that.'

'*My husband* told you that.'

'Well, he didn't.'

'I'm calling him.'

I sniffed the air. Quicklime had replaced the ghost of Grandpa's heavy cologne. It was not an unpleasant scent, but not the one I expected.

'Do you want to come with me, or do you want to stay here?' Mum asked.

I didn't understand she was talking to me. The sighted instinctively ask questions when looking your way, to signal they are talking to you. That didn't work with me anymore; when people were talking to me they had to make it explicit with their words. Mum was learning, and she'd almost got the hang of it, but when she was tired, like now, she slipped. She caught herself and added casually, 'I've got to call Dad.'

'I'll come with you.'

She took my arm under hers. I let her guide me straight ahead, then round a bend ('To avoid a pile of rubble,' she explained). I knew we had entered a different room when the echoes changed. We stopped, and I supposed it had to be the kitchen because the phone was there, but it didn't smell how I remembered.

'My God,' Mum said.

I asked, 'What? What's going on?'

'It's a mess.'

I heard her punch numbers into the phone, which had to be on a trolley next to the counter, if the counter was still in its place and the trolley too. Certainly, the telephone had to stand on something.

'It's me,' Mum said. 'We got to the masseria, yes, the travel was okay. It's not okay here though.' She explained to Dad that the builders were doing our living quarters, which they weren't supposed to do until the very end, to leave us time to get acquainted to the new home. 'Yes,' she said, 'yes, I know you told them. Here, talk to the master mason.'

The master – he was called Piero Quarta – had followed us into the kitchen. He took the phone, and in the same tone he had used with Mum he told Dad that no, Dad was wrong, they'd never talked about where to start from. 'Listen, *Dottore*,' he said, 'I don't see why you're working yourself up anyway. We'll just stop and start somewhere else.'

'Yeah, but we're the ones stuck in half-done rooms for the summer,' Mum said, in what had become a three-way conversation.

'So if you don't like it, we finish this wing first. Two months, it's going to take.'

'Are you kidding me?'

'Not much else I can do, is there?'

'We could fire you.'

'Good luck finding someone this time of year.'

In the end, no one was fired. Mum and Dad had to accept Piero Quarta's proposal to leave the rooms as they were. He said, 'But in future please be clear about what you want done and when.'

Thank God the hob and the oven were still in place. After the builders left for the night, Mum fixed a quick dish of fusilli with raw olive oil, finely chopped tomatoes, basil and *cacioricotta*, a seasoned, hardened ricotta. The flavours rolled together in my mouth; their zest reminded me how intensely coloured the pasta was, red with tomatoes, green with basil and snow-white with the tendrils of grated cheese. I wished I could see it.

We had dinner on the arched porch. With the works paused for the night, the soundscape was wonderful: a distant hoopoe was calling with the deep voice of a blues singer, accompanied by a chorus of crickets and the light drumming of sea waves coming ashore. I wasn't sure how I felt about moving South in general, but I did feel pretty good about that moment.

'Earlier, with the builders,' Mum said. 'It was just a hitch.'

That night I got lost on my way to the loo and heard the perfect silence from the countryside, and told myself the same lie, that it was just a hitch.

The sun reached its zenith and made the sand so hot it burnt the soles of our feet. Ada and I took shelter under the pines (a flimsy steel net was all that stood between us and the wood, with holes large enough for two kids to comfortably slip through). We ate with our backs leaning on a slender pine trunk: prosciutto and mozzarella sandwiches, which Ada had brought. The bark scratched my back pleasantly. The balsamic perfume of the trees, the earthy aroma coming from the layer of pine needles on the ground and the brackish tang of the sea all came together to wrap us in a bubble, inside which I felt safe.

I don't remember what we talked about: nothing special, I guess. We read; we would always read when we were together. That first day – this I remember – she had *American Psycho* with her.

'Is it good?' I asked.

'It does deliver on the title.'

'My parents wouldn't let me read a book like that.'

'Mine neither, if I asked.'

I started worrying about how long we had been there, and asked Ada for the time.

'Why, do you have something to do?'

'I need to be home by six. I've got a phone call with my brother in Turin. He has the *maturità* tomorrow.' That's what end of school exams are called in Italy – *esami di maturità*, maturity exams, as if schools could prove that you are mature enough to join the grown-ups. As if any of us ever were. I said, 'Do you have siblings?'

'Nah. Only child. I get all the spoils.'

The bike ride back, uphill, was slower. Ada huffed and puffed all the way, but when I asked her if we should walk, she refused. 'It's good workout,' she panted. We were at the masseria's gate by five-thirty. I said I could take it from there, and Ada replied, 'See you later, then.'

She left, and it was a let-down how she went without fixing a date for next time. While I debated whether to ask, the whir of mechanical wings faded, and it was too late.

Mum gave me a distracted greeting from the garden table. She was shuffling papers, which crackled loudly against the hush of the countryside.

I made an OK sign with one hand. '*Il mare era bellissimo*,' I said, *the sea was great*, a stock Southern phrase Grandpa had taught me, which means, *I had a great time all round.*

'Good.'

'Phone call at six?'

'Phone call?'

'With Ferdi. And Dad,' I added.

'Oh, that one. Don't worry, honey, we already talked.'

'But we said at six!'

'Did we? I don't remember. I had something urgent to discuss with Dad.'

'Can I call again? Just to wish Ferdi good luck?'

'It's not luck he needs. Apparently he didn't get a lot of studying done. You want to do something for him? Let him be. Leave him to concentrate.'

'But, Mum…'

'They'll be here in no time. Honey, go get a shower. I need to concentrate too.'

It was an unfair ending to a great day. I went to bed early, after a dinner during which I was too cross to be civil and Mum too preoccupied to notice. The beach had exhausted me, and I must have fallen asleep quickly, but my sleep didn't last long. Pain woke me up, and if I had to point at a specific juncture in which that summer took the peculiar turn which is still haunting me twenty-five years later, it would be that moment.

I had been dreaming of a cerulean sea, and soft, green algae swaying on rocks like trees in an underwater wind; I woke up and opened my eyes, but the room was too dark to see. I felt for the nightstand light. When I didn't find it, I remembered I didn't have one, and why. In my dreams I was still sighted, so every time I woke up, I went blind again. It took me years to change that.

Going back to sleep was challenging. Before, I only had to lie down and shut my eyes, but now I spent the day attuned to my other senses, which were not as easy to block out: I couldn't just decide to stop hearing or smelling. It was no different than it would be for a sighted person to learn to go to sleep with their eyes open. When I was tired I would doze off as well as everybody, but at other times I would lie in bed and wonder how (or if) I would ever find sleep again. The wondering made me anxious, and anxiety, as it does, chased sleep further away.

Physical pain was thrown into the mix. My back was on fire, and so were my arms. The bedsheets pierced my skin with red-hot needles wherever they touched it. I tossed and turned, uselessly aiming for a position that wouldn't hurt. I was sunburnt, a rite of passage which marked the start of summer. That sort of pain recalled good memories (sand in my toes, sunshine on my face, fridge-cold watermelon), but it was still pain. I gave up on sleep and sat up.

Figments of dream lingered on. I could almost feel the wind, and smell the scent of pines and sea.

Was there a draught in the room? Perhaps; or perhaps it was sweat drying on my skin, giving the illusion of a current of air. I sniffed. I couldn't say whether I was smelling juniper or imagining it.

I sniffed deeper, and I just couldn't say.

The breeze and the scent conjured up the strange suspicion that I might not be in my room anymore, but somewhere else, somewhere in the open. The inside of buildings feels different to the outside. Inside, sounds bounce off walls and the ceiling to come back to you, and smells are neater, with less ragged ends. My room did not sound or smell like a room, but like

Mediterranean scrub, like the blooming dunes on the beach, like a vast open space, as if ahead of me was not the reassuring weight of a wall, but a boundless horizon.

I reached out for my cane, closed my grip around the cork handle.

The capacity of telling the inside from the outside of buildings was the first new skill I had mastered, and I was proud of it in the way people who do not have much hold on to what little they have won. Having that taken from me was upsetting. It might spell trouble with my ears, with my nose, or worse – with my brain.

'Hey,' I said aloud, to check how the sound travelled.

It travelled as if I were in the open, and not the familiar space of my bedroom – and yet, how could I be sure, without seeing? I rested a hand on the mattress, and it was solid. I tapped my toes on the terracotta tiles, and they were solid too. I couldn't help but feel that the bed and a circle of flooring around it had come unmoored from the room, from the masseria, and they were stuck in another place. I was sure that, if I stood up and moved two steps, I would feel dirt underfoot, or sand, or something else entirely, but not tiles. It was silly, I knew it was silly, yet I didn't stand up to check.

I'm afraid of the dark.

I let out a shrill fake laugh. The one thing I could not afford to be afraid of was the dark. 'Is anybody there?' I called.

A voice, as shrill as my laughter, answered, 'No,' but only in my head.

Imagining the voice scared me almost as much as hearing it for real. And perhaps it was fear that made me feel something else: a presence.

Wherever I was, I was not alone.

I put every iota of my attention, every part of my being, into the aural equivalent of squinting my eyes. I detected a faint rustling, a breathing, which reminded me of the dogs Ada had fought off. But then again, when you want to perceive something, you will: senses are sycophants who say what we expect to hear. *It's all in my head*, I told myself. *Just my imagination.*

I didn't scream, though I wanted to. Thick as the masseria's walls might be, Mum's room was close, and if I shouted, she would hear, probably. And she would come, and then – then what? Then I would have to admit I had let my imagination run away with me.

Or my voice would travel far from me again, as voices do in the open, hurled around by the wind, and Mum wouldn't come, and I would know beyond doubt that I was not in my room. And another voice, not Mum's, would answer.

Now that I thought of the dogs, I noticed a change in smell too, a feral note, like fur growing on a wild body. And I knew it was in my head, it had to be all in my head, but knowing didn't help; tangible realities – the walls, the door, the bricks and mortar – didn't feel present, didn't feel tangible at all, while the open space and the rustling, feral creature did. The draught was picking up: that felt real too. It *was* real.

I had to stand up. I had to walk around, sweep my cane on the floor, feel the tiles under my feet and rest the palm of my hands on the walls. But that would be ridiculous. It would be just another call for help, it would be like saying out loud that I was afraid of the dark. I was not a baby. I would stay where I was, just where I was, because I was not afraid of the dark.

Footsteps approached my bed, as real, as *tangible* as the bed and myself.

Tap, tap.

'Mum…?' I said, barely holding my voice from screaming. No. Not Mum.

Tap, Tap. I'd heard that rhythm in the fields.

'Who's there?'

Tap, tap, the steps kept coming.

They halted an inch or two, I think, from my nose. The temperature rose, as if an enormous body before me was giving off heat. I couldn't scream, I couldn't reach out, for I expected talons to rip my mouth, teeth to bite off my hands, so I just sat still, my hand clutching the cane, my mouth ajar.

There was a sound like a growl from the far end of a cathedral. The smell brought tears to my eyes.

Another sound came from very far. A phone ringing. When I realised what it was, how mundane, the growl stopped. I could not sense any presence with me anymore, only a leftover scent.

The ringing grew closer – until that too was cut off abruptly.

A silence, then Mum's voice, 'What are you saying? What happened to Ferdi?'

Her tone was the same as the one she had used with the doctor, when he said I would lose my sight.

'What happened?' I asked.

Mum didn't answer. I had made my way to the room in which she slept, Grandpa Ferdinando's old bedroom, where the only other phone in the house was. Mum and Uncle Mario had insisted Grandpa put a line there after Grandma died.

They were worried for him, all alone in a ramshackle house in the middle of nowhere. He said that he was not alone, you are never alone in the deep countryside.

'Mum?' I asked.

Her breathing was laboured.

'Mum!'

'Nothing happened,' she said. 'He left. Dad saw Ferdi wasn't coming for breakfast, and went to wake him up, and Ferdi wasn't in his room. Or anywhere in the flat.'

Before Grandpa's death, before going blind, I wouldn't have worried, but I had learnt since that bad things do happen to good people.

Mum went on, 'Dad's looking for him.'

'Did he call the police?'

'This is just your brother being your brother, incapable of taking responsibility.'

'Well, you and Dad don't help.'

'Say again?'

'You never listen to him!'

'We would, if he made sense.'

'You're doing it again. You put him down all the time.'

Mum raised her voice. 'Ferdinando has his exams today, and you know what's going to happen if he doesn't sit his exams?' she said, using Ferdi's whole name, which was a sure sign she was furious. 'You know what's going to happen? He'll have to *repeat the year*.'

'Big deal! He's missing, and your worry is about school?'

'He's not missing!'

'How can you know that?'

'Because I know!'

'Like you knew I was okay?'

Mum sucked in air. I heard a stifled sigh, a sniffle, the sounds a person makes when they're fighting tears. I turned my back to leave. I'd won the argument. I would rather have lost.

Ada returned later that morning. I had carried my book under the shade of the carob tree this side of the vineyard, leaving Mum to hover around the phone. I couldn't stand to be with her, but neither did I want to stray too far.

I sat on bare earth (grass is too delicate to survive for more than a handful of weeks in this hot, dry land), and started on Ishmael and his mates. The building noises were louder on this side of the property. After last night, the calls, the clangs and the stout roll of a cement mixer sounded like a lullaby: their music, undeniably human, anchored me to this world and prevented me from getting unmoored. I found it impossible to focus on the story coming through my fingers when the builders' lullaby was reassuring me that no savage beast would hurt me and it was safe to go to sleep. It was a more exciting prospect than whale-hunting.

'Hey!' A voice jumped me awake.

'Ada? Is that you?'

'Yep,' she said. 'I called and called and nobody answered. I was going inside, then I saw you snoozing here. *Moby-Dick* does that, I hear.'

'I didn't get much sleep last night.'

'Why?'

I found myself unsure how to answer. I wasn't going to pretend there was nothing wrong, because the last time I'd ignored a puncture in reality, the puncture had grown into a black hole and swallowed up my world. So, yeah, there had been something wrong even before Dad's call, but where? In my room, or in my head? The implications were terrifying in both cases. 'Sunburn.'

'I was under that impression.'

'Does it show a lot?'

'You've got the colour of someone who is being strangled.'

'How about you?'

'I'm a true Southerner. I can take the heat. I've got sunscreen if you want.'

'Thanks, but I'm not coming to the beach.'

'That line is getting old.'

'For real. It's my brother.'

Ada's voice became serious. 'What's the matter?'

'He wasn't in bed this morning, and we have no idea where he could be.'

I was so used to people saying that everything would be all right, always, that I was grateful when Ada's comment was, 'That sucks.'

'His backpack is missing, and his wallet.' I paused. It felt like a betrayal to confide family matters to a stranger, but I needed to talk to someone. 'Dad's wallet has gone AWOL too. He and Mum think Ferdi did a runner, because of the exams.'

'It does look like that.'

'Ferdi is not the running type.' I knew for a fact that Ferdi hadn't run away, and I didn't want my mind to sort through the implications, to think of what Mum might hear the next time the telephone rang.

Ada asked gently, 'What do you want to do?'

'Go. I'll stay here. I'm not a lot of fun today.'

'You're giving yourself far too much credit.'

'What for?'

'For how much fun you are on other days.'

It almost made me smile. 'You barely know me.'

'And I'm already bored. I can only imagine what your poor family must go through. By the way, I'm not going to talk to you while you're sitting down and I'm standing. It's like being given an audience with Count Fancy-pants.'

'Sit down, then.'

'Or you stand up.'

I pushed myself to my feet.

She said, 'Why don't you show me around the masseria? Before they spoil it completely.'

'They're fixing it.'

'What would you rather be, an ancient ruin or a wedding venue?'

'Well…'

'I rest my case: they're spoiling it.'

I tapped my sunglasses, a favourite gesture of mine, which I thought smooth, a tad world-weary. 'I can't even make my own way round here yet.'

'I believe in teamwork.'

I feel silly now at the thought that I didn't wonder – not for a moment – why this bright, sociable girl insisted on wasting her time with me in a bad mood, when she had a scented countryside, a village and immense beaches to roam and play in. Probably other friends too. Ada hadn't come into being on my moving South, for my benefit only. But we do that; we believe that we sit at the centre of the tale, that we are its indisputable hero, and we are so dazzled by our own brilliance that we rarely stop to consider the lives of those around us, no matter how close they are or we wish them to be.

I said, 'Okay.'

Ada didn't care about what she called *the safe bits*, the lived-in areas. 'They'll be like any other house: telly, table, chairs. Boring.' I couldn't disagree. Same for the rooms in which builders were at work: 'Too late for those,' in her words.

That still left a lot of property, between the neglected parts of the main farmhouse and the outbuildings, which were *all* neglected. I had explored most of those with Ferdi, but not all of them. 'You decide,' I said. 'Where do you want to go?'

'Anywhere. Your grandpa never wanted to show me anything.'

A tuff archway ran along the whole body of the farmhouse on this side, creating a shaded walkway. 'Look at the archway. Can you see a door, roughly two-thirds down it?'

'Two-thirds from where?'

'From left.'

After a beat she said, 'There's a door, yes.'

'Are the builders using it?'

'The scaffolding doesn't go all the way there.'

'Let's go. I'll need your help. I didn't practise the route.'

'Teamwork, brother.'

Ada let me lean on her elbow, and again my hand touched the cotton of a long sleeve, lightly damp with sweat. Out of the shadow of the carob tree the sun was heavy like a mountain toppling on my head. It had to be midday at least, maybe later, and there was no news of Ferdi.

It was a relief to reach the archway and be in the shadow again. 'We're at the door,' Ada said. 'It's old, rotten and half-open.'

'It's stuck that way.'

We insinuated ourselves inside, me first, then Ada, slipping between the wood of the door and that of the doorframe. 'Careful,' I said. 'Last time Ferdi got a splinter in his back.'

It was like crossing a space between seasons, going from summer to autumn; fierce heat and the scent of wild rosemary gave way to an uplifting coolness and the musty, dusty aroma of old things with not much life left in them.

'What do you see?' I asked.

'A tatty table. Loads of cobwebs. Prints in the dust on the floor.'

'What kind of prints?'

'Paws. I don't know. Do I look like a girl scout to you? They're old though. It's so dusty here even prints in the dust are dusty.'

'Can you see a doorway?'

'Yep.'

'Let's go in.'

Past the threshold, Ada commented, 'It's pretty dark.'

'There's a window on our left. The shutters should work.'

I heard her steps go to the window and the wooden creak of the shutter pulled open. A gasp of surprise. 'What the fuck…'

I laughed. 'It's cool, isn't it?'

'It's a *skull*.'

'From the last cow that died in the masseria. Ferdi begged Grandpa to have it.'

'What is this place?'

'What do you see?'

'Said skull on a table, a fitted wardrobe with a 2Pac poster pinned on it, a pile of dank paperbacks and comic books, graffiti on the wall.'

'*Da Klub.*'

'That's what it says. In bright red, round letters.'

'It's our club. Ferdi's and mine.'

'A smallish one, I dare say.'

'It started as Ferdi's lair, a place where he could be alone. *Without Mum and Dad standing on my neck*, he said. One time I had an argument with Dad, I don't remember what about, Ferdi told me, *Can you keep a secret?* and took me here. We did the graffiti together that summer.'

'I like your brother.'

'Yeah, me too.'

'And what do you do in this club?'

'Nothing much.'

'Isn't he going to be mad at you, for revealing it to a stranger?'

If he's ever coming back. 'It's a thing of the past. We didn't use it last year.'

'Why?'

'Because.' I didn't understand Ferdi all that well, lately. Last summer he had barely spent any time at home, always hanging out with a bunch of local kids and his sort-of girlfriend.

'I'm eyeing the books,' Ada said. 'Calvino, King, Fante… *Ask the Dust*, I've been looking for this! Can I borrow it?'

'Ferdi won't mind.'

'Cool, thanks.'

'Take me to the wardrobe.'

'What about it?'

'You'll see.'

We got there, and I ran my hands on the ancient wood, searching for the ceramic knobs to open the doors. It was good oak timber, which was far sturdier than it had any call to be.

'I see a limp football,' Ada started listing, 'a deflated airbed, a spade and a beach bucket with Donald Duck on it...'

'Ghosts of summers past. That's not what I wanted to show you.'

I carefully made my way inside the wardrobe, kicking away the dusty junk. I rested my palm on the wardrobe's back and felt for a seam I knew was there. I found it, pushed the wood backwards and leftwards.

'A secret passage!' Ada said, in awe.

'Let's not get carried away.'

There was a hollow behind the wardrobe, nice to have, but scarcely a door to Narnia: it was nothing more than a tuff niche maybe two metres long, not large enough for Ferdi to stretch his arms inside.

'Grandpa said that *his* grandfather didn't believe in banks. He kept his money in cash, hidden around the house. Mostly here, some – literally – under his mattress.'

'Was he rich?'

'No, he only had a little money, which he blew, anyway.'

'There's something in here.'

'There's nothing.'

'I beg to differ. It's... whoa.' Ada walked past me and inside the hollow. She picked up an object with a metallic sound. 'A hunting shotgun,' she said, in a lower voice.

That took me by surprise. Ferdi and I kept rusty hooks, scraps of metal there – archaeological finds whose function was mysterious to us city boys. They were fascinating, but they didn't *shoot.* I reached out, brushed wood and cold steel, and recoiled when my fingers met Ada's, wrapped around the shotgun. 'Describe it.'

'It's not new. The stock is dark wood, all scratched.'

'Can you see any initials on the chamber?'

'Yes: *F.M.*'

'Ferdinando Mazziani. It's Grandpa's, and it shouldn't be here.'

'Well, it is. With a box of cartridges and a cartridge belt.'

'Ferdi went hunting with Grandpa, something that Dad hated. He was not happy to see his son play with guns. Plus, he doesn't eat game, it doesn't agree with him.'

It wasn't strange that Ferdi had taken the shotgun as a keepsake: nobody would have noticed or cared. What stung was that he hadn't told me.

Ada asked, 'Did you ever shoot?'

'I didn't have time to learn.'

I heard Ada put back the gun. 'We're going to use it before the end of summer.'

'Said the prophetess.'

'Said Chekhov. You find a cool gizmo in a secret alcove, you *use* it.'

I didn't admit to not having a clue what an *alcove* was. We shut the compartment and the wardrobe. Before moving on, Ada walked up and down the room, pulling me with her. She broke into a run and came back. She took my hand and we jumped and stomped. 'To hide our trail to the alcove!' she shouted, laughing. 'To protect our secret.'

By the end we were exhilarated, and I felt bad for having run out of surprises. 'The other rooms are just bare,' I puffed. 'There's some broken pottery, more junk, empty *capasoni.*'

Capasoni, for the uninitiated, are enormous clay jars of a warm yellow colour, as tall as I was at ten, in which wine and olive oil were kept, when wine and oil were still made in the old ways.

'I want to get to the top of the tower.'

'It's a ruin. Literally, it's unsafe.'

'Chicken.'

I let Ada pull me through more rooms, cool and empty, until we got to the door leading to the tower. 'It's the first actual door I see here,' she commented.

'When I was little it gave me the heebie-jeebies.'

'You were afraid of a *door*?'

'Not a door but what lies behind. You noticed it too; there are no other doors in this part of the house. *Why* only this one here? Ferdi explained that it was just that it hadn't rotted as badly as the others, but I thought… I thought it wasn't like that. I thought the door was keeping *something* from getting to us. Something hungry on the other side.'

'And you never opened it.'

'Many times, with Ferdi, and I was afraid every time.'

'Are you afraid now?'

'No,' I lied.

When I turned nine I *said* I wasn't afraid anymore, and I understood why in theory I shouldn't be, but there was just something wrong with one closed door in a place with no doors, and the wisdom of age didn't make *that* any less wrong. Ada's footsteps approaching the door jolted that old fear in me, and that brought back last night's fear too. An absurd thought went through my head – that the night had not passed, and whatever had started was still happening. I was in exactly the same darkness, and even though I was with

72

a friend in my home, I felt an echo of that other feeling, that I was stranded in a place where I didn't belong, touched by an impossible wind. I had deluded myself into thinking that the night was over, but it wasn't, it would never be. I caught a whiff of the feral smell.

Ada cried out.

'Fuck,' she said. 'Fuck, fuck, fuck.'

'What?' I asked. 'What's going on?'

'Oh my God, Luca.' Her voice was breaking up in sobs. 'This can't be true.'

'What?' I almost shouted.

'There's…' She swallowed. 'Behind the door. There's a thing.'

'What thing?'

'A body,' she said.

Fear turned up to full volume, and it was the fear I felt for that closed door, and also the fear I felt when they told me Grandpa was dead, and the fear I felt when I accepted there was *nada* I could do to stop sight loss. It was the fear I felt for the creature in my room, or in my head.

But Ada had overplayed her hand.

I waited for my heart to slow down, and said, '*This can't be true?* Who talks like that?'

She burst out laughing. 'Your face, man. Your face!'

'Ada Guadalupi, you are a horrible human being.'

'Aren't we all,' she said.

The stone staircase was worn, slippery. I climbed carefully, holding on to Ada. We got on top, amidst a niff of bird's poop and a flutter of wings.

The tower was an unassuming affair, a squared structure barely taller than the house, with space for two or three bedrooms, or a suite. Piero Quarta, the master mason, didn't guarantee they would be able to save it. They might have to bring it down and either rebuild it or let it go.

'It's a ruin,' Ada admitted.

'Told ya.'

Breeze and sunshine filtered inside; there were no windows left, only holes in the masonry.

Ada said, 'I don't know about you, but I'm starving.'

'We can go and see if there's something in the kitchen.'

'No need.' She unzipped her bag and pushed an object into my hand. I touched kitchen foil, which I unwrapped to find crusty bread. 'Mortadella and dried tomato sandwiches. Next time *you* bring food.'

'Fair enough,' I answered, happy that *next time* was in the cards.

We sat with our backs to a wall, facing the sunshine and chomping on our panini. I put away half of mine in three bites. It was a rare moment of silence, and thoughts of Ferdi rushed to fill the space in my head. To chase them away, I said, 'It's strange.'

'What's strange?'

'That our families don't hang out together more. Or ever. You'd think they would, with us being the same age and all that.'

She didn't answer.

I went on, 'You said you were friends with Grandpa.'

'I said I knew him.'

'But I didn't see you at the funeral. Or did I? It's possible I didn't notice. That was the day I found out the issue with my eyesight might be serious.'

'I didn't attend. I wanted to, but Mum and Dad…' Her voice trailed off.

'Mum and Dad…?'

'Ferdinando wouldn't want them there.'

Grandpa was a curt man who never missed a chance to speak his mind. He had a lot of friends (on the day of his funeral, the church had been jam-packed, with people standing in the back), but it was common knowledge that he didn't have only friends. It was a boast to him: *If you didn't make any enemies*, he would say, *you didn't do much at all.* I asked, 'Do you know why?'

'Not really. Matters of boundaries, trespassing: old stories.'

'But he was friendly with you.'

'Yeah, he offered me iced tea every now and then. He didn't tell me off when he found me playing in his fields. He was nothing like you.'

I ignored the dig. 'And your parents were okay with that?'

'They're on a need-to-know basis.'

'Is there anything they need to know?'

'What about yours?'

I was going to answer, but a voice from outside stopped me. I must have left my jaw ajar, because Ada asked, 'What's the matter?'

'Shush.'

I stretched my hearing. The voice came from down below and a world away. It was Mum's, calling my name.

I went too fast down the stairs and slipped. My arse slammed on the stone and kept slipping down three or four steps. Ada was merciful enough not to laugh. We got out and turned towards the entrance of the house, striding alongside the wall.

Mum's voice reached me, fretful, angry. 'Luca! Where have you been?'

'It's Ferdi? It's Ferdi, isn't it?'

Mum said, 'Hello, Ada. I am sorry, but it is a family matter.'

'Of course,' Ada said. 'I was going anyway. Luca, I'll see you tomorrow.'

'Mum! How's Ferdi?'

'In trouble,' she said.

Mum refused to talk in the open, where the builders might hear. I had to follow her inside, and it was only after the *thump* of the door closing that she said, 'Dad found him.'

'Is he all right?'

'He was slacking off in a billiards room, smoking with a bunch of no-gooders thirty years older than him.'

'What…'

'The little prince didn't feel like sitting his exams. Exactly as I told you.'

She was lying, and if she thought she had to lie, the reality had to be worse than anything I feared. 'I don't believe you.'

'I'm trying to treat you like an adult, Luca.'

'As if. Ferdi isn't the running type. If you're telling the truth, let me talk to him.'

'This is not the best time.'

I managed to keep my voice level. I knew that if I raised it I would lose what little chance I had to get my way. 'Let me talk to him, Mum. Not for him, for *me*.'

I heard her breathe, then her footsteps and the sound of a telephone handset being lifted.

'Ferdi!' I said.

The voice on the other end was strained. 'Hey, Scrawny.'

'How are you?'

He scoffed. 'Ask me another question.'

'What's going on?'

'I fucked up. I…' He paused. 'Don't turn out like me.'

'I don't believe what Mum is saying.'

'What is she saying?'

'That you ran.'

'That's it. She's right.'

For a wild moment I thought that *he* was lying as well, that there was a family conspiracy to keep from me some truth too horrible for me to contemplate.

Ferdi said, 'I'm sorry, Scrawny. I'm so sorry.'

That was the horrible truth, and I was the one refusing to contemplate it. I had learnt from the best after all. The horrible truth: Ferdi was indeed the running type. The horrible truth: I had been wrong about him. The horrible truth: my rock-solid certainty that I got him and he got me through some mysterious brotherly telepathy had been utterly, utterly wrong. He was a coward, no less than my father, no less than my mother. A cog turned inside me, a match was struck, and resentment flared.

'You're *sorry*?' I said. 'What does it mean, that you're *sorry*? What does it change?'

'Scrawny…'

When I think back to how mad I was, I almost get mad again. I was in the grip of a fury so powerful that it was no different from being drunk in a dump of a bar, eager to pick a fight. When I think back to that, I also feel pity, for Ferdi and me both. I went, 'This isn't something that happened to you, from the outside. This was *your choice*! You chose to party with your mates all winter. You chose to go and play billiards today. You chose all of it.'

'I…'

'You've got everything you need, Ferdi, everything you might possibly want, and this is how you use it? If you're too lazy to do anything with yourself, own it at least, and don't come to me with some bollocks about you being fucking *sorry*.'

I waited for a reply which didn't arrive.

'*Say something!*' I shouted.

Ferdi's voice became belligerent. 'Who do you think you are?'

'Not you, fortunately.'

Ferdi had let me down, and that hurt like physical pain. At the end of the call I was exhausted – my muscles were aching as if I had been running – but the scope of my upset mellowed Mum's. She put a hand over my shoulder. 'Don't be mad at Ferdi.'

'Give me a reason not to be.'

'He's a good boy.'

'You'd say that.'

She decreed we needed to get out, be among humans, so that evening we went to the most popular pizzeria in Portodimare (it had been the only one until two or three years before), The Late Night. It was a stone's throw away from the circular piazza where, in summer, people gathered by night after a long day spent on the beach.

We sat on the veranda, enfolded by the sound of waves and crickets. The tang of the sea mingled freely with the scent of fresh tomato on just-baked pizza. It was a quiet night; real summer would start that weekend, the last one in June, when traditionally the bulk of people moved to their holiday homes from nearby towns. I was relieved. I had never confessed to Mum and Dad that being in a crowd made me dizzy sometimes, like a sighted who is required to have a normal conversation under a strobe light.

'What's going to happen now?' I said, while we waited for our pizza.

'You don't have to worry.'

'I don't worry, but I want to know.'

'Nothing's set in stone. Dad will talk to the headmaster, see if Ferdi can sit his exams late. Given his grades, I wouldn't be holding my breath. He barely made it this far.'

'And if the headmaster says no?'

'Then Dad and Ferdi will come sooner than we expected, and Ferdi will have to repeat the year in the *liceo* in Casalfranco.'

'He's going to hate being here one whole year.'

'I think so,' she said.

I was furious at Ferdi in a way I couldn't fully comprehend. If anything, having him home for one year more should have made me happy. What I couldn't articulate back then was that I resented him for wasting the perfect hand life had served him. I, too, would have to repeat the year, and go to school with smaller kids, babies practically, but I didn't have a choice. It had been physically impossible for me to keep up with homework. In Ferdi's case, the world was his oyster, and he'd cheerfully thrown it away.

I was on my last pizza slice when a piercing voice said, 'Such a handsome young man!' with an undertone I had come to recognise, the implication of which was: *Aren't I nice, complimenting a handicapped boy.* Fingers pinched my cheek and made me flinch.

'Look at him! He doesn't fancy being touched. All grown-up! But you'll always be a child to me!'

I massaged my cheek. I thought, but was too polite to say, that anybody would flinch if ghost hands appeared out of nowhere to nip them.

'And your sunglasses suit you so well! You know who I am, don't you?'

'I…'

'Say my name or I'll be cross,' the voice said, taking that kind of mocking tone which is entirely serious. 'You know *me*! I watched you grow up.'

Which seemed unlikely, considering how little time I'd spent in Portodimare.

'It's Betta, Luca,' Mum said.

I feigned enthusiasm. 'Betta! I was going to say that.' It was impossible to go out in Portodimare or Casalfranco without bumping into at least one person you knew. Mum and Dad found it oh-so charming.

'Sure you were,' Betta said, the implication being, *No, you weren't, but I'm a charitable person and we'll pretend otherwise. It's going to be our little secret, my sweet handicapped boy.* 'And it's *Aunt* Betta! Say it: *Aunt Betta.* Why don't you say it?'

'Aunt Betta.'

'Such a darling!'

Mum and Dad wanted to believe they were as good as locals, though Dad was born and bred in Turin, and Mum's whole family had moved there when she was five, and although the others went to Portodimare when Mum was at university, she never did. As locals, they were supposed to have local friends. Betta and her husband Giorgio were among the very few; my parents met them on the beach in the summer after Ferdi's birth, and they all pretended to share great companionship, my parents entranced by Betta and Giorgio's local knowledge, Betta and Giorgio entranced by my parents' air of city sophistication.

'I have a table with Giorgio, and other friends!' Betta said. 'Why don't you two join us?'

'Thank you,' Mum said, 'but we're going to call it an early night. I've got work to do tomorrow.'

'I heard you were in town! Giorgio thought he saw you at the market. He was right! You should've called the minute you arrived, Stefi.'

'We've been busy,' Mum apologised.

'I'm so thrilled that you decided to make the move at last! We're going to have so much fun.'

Mum laughed. 'When the works are done.'

'Oh, it's so stressful to have works done! Where's the man of the house?'

'In Turin.'

'To stay close to Ferdi during the exams! How sweet. How did the first day go? It's the easy one.'

Mum hesitated, then said, 'We don't know.'

'Swimmingly, I'm sure.' Betta's voice reached a new pitch. 'So you're all alone in the middle of nowhere! Lucky you that Luca stands guard. Do you stand guard over Mum, Luca?'

'Yes,' I said, for want of a better answer.

Mum said, 'We don't miss company, with the builders at work, day in, day out.'

'Do you have plans for this Friday?'

'Not at the moment.'

'It's settled, then!'

'What's settled?'

'I am having a little get-together at mine. I always do at the start of summer. It's a tradition. You must come! Although…' She lowered her voice. 'I've got to tell you, Giuseppe Guadalupi is going to be there too. I am sorry, Stefi, I can't tell him not to come. He's always been invited.'

Mum sighed. 'I'm perfectly fine with the Guadalupis, Betta. Actually, their daughter is Luca's friend.'

'You don't say so! Just arrived in town and already breaking hearts, eh? Already having girlfriends?'

'Luca,' Mum said, 'Betta's talking to you.'

I felt too awkward to volunteer more than a faltering, 'We're friends.'

'Handsome *and* polite! No surprise Ada loves you.' Betta made a little laugh. 'Not in *that* sense! Oh, possibly. What do I know, eh? But tell me, Luca, do you have a girlfriend in Turin? You cannot have two girlfriends at once, young man!' she said, mock-sternly. 'Do you have two girlfriends?'

'I don't.'

'Better for you. You open a new chapter in life, you open it unfettered, that's what I say. Unfettered. You're coming this Friday. Settled, it's settled!'

It took all I had to go into the vineyard again. My only attempt at venturing beyond had been an unmitigated disaster, and I needed to give it another go. On one thing my brother had been right; I didn't want to grow up to be spineless like him. I got up early, had a quick breakfast of milk and chocolate biscuits and headed out, armed with a baseball cap, trainers, a Swiss army knife and water. As I was leaving the grange behind, the rumble of the builders' van came from the drive.

Coming back empty-handed was not an option. I knew, though not in an entirely conscious way, that if I caved in today, I would never try again. I took my sweet time among the vines, enjoying the coolness and the scents, which were riper than before. The grapes too were bigger; it was a wonder to me that things could grow so quickly, so fast, come the right season. When my cane told me I had reached the end, I felt on the edge of a cliff. It wasn't so much a matter of moving forward as of jumping over the edge.

I jumped. I didn't want to (I was afraid of getting lost, of tumbling, of stray dogs), but neither did I want to end up playing billiards on the day of my exams. I would count forty steps, and if I didn't find any clear landmark, I would come back, count five lines down the vines, and start again. That was the plan.

I counted forty steps, I found nothing; I came back.

I moved down the vineyard, counted forty steps again, and again I found nothing. Again I came back, and again I moved down the vineyard, and again I counted my steps, but the bush I found at the twenty-ninth was too nondescript to be of any use. Again I came back.

I was disoriented by now. Not lost – I couldn't be lost in any real sense as long as I knew where the vineyard was – but disoriented. I had turned one way and the other, counted my steps over and over again under a sun growing in strength, weighing me down. I wondered what good it would do to keep going, but keep going I did, and at last I found a workable landmark. My cane touched a root, a trunk; a tree. I rested my hand on the bark, which was rough and thickly textured. I felt for low-hanging branches, and found one. I picked between thumb and index finger an oval, hard fruit, with skin like cloth. I brought it to my nostrils. *An almond*.

I was excited, and also afraid. With an obvious landmark like this, I had no excuses not to strike out further. I used the knife to trace my initials on this side of the trunk, at the height of my face. Later, when I would make my way back here, I would have to know where to turn for the vineyard. *LS*: I carved the initials deeply and made sure my fingertips could sense them. I moved on.

Careful, now. I had learnt from bitter experience that it's impossible to walk in a straight line, ever. An almond tree was a lot smaller than a vineyard, a lot easier to miss on my way back. I decided to count no more than twenty steps. I could only go so far off course in twenty steps.

I walked through the songs of birds and crickets. No dogs, yet. No dogs ever, if I were lucky.

Twenty steps brought me nowhere. I risked five more. Still nothing. I stretched my cane, leaning forward to give it a little more reach, and I got a hit. I got closer. I squatted; my hand rested on a squishy creature which scuttled off at the same time as I recoiled. More tentatively, I put my hand forward again. I touched a rock, warmed by the sun, full of holes and crevices. It would do. I moved on.

While I walked, leaving a trail of landmarks of varying quality (a large rosemary bush, a prickly pear which left thin thorns in my fingertips, like sharp-edged hair), I noticed a breeze. It had been growing for a while, and you couldn't call it exactly a wind yet, but it was picking up. It came and went in gusts, tickling me and bringing me scents of rosemary and laurel; and another smell too.

I stopped dead in my tracks. I sniffed. There was that feral note again, fur growing on a wild body.

'Is anybody there?' I called.

My voice spread in the fields, and a distant barking answered. *The dogs are coming.*

Instinct screamed at me to make my way back, quickly, now. I turned to retrace my steps – and stopped again. I couldn't let the barking scare me off. In order to be free I had to learn more than the lie of the land. I had to learn how to take care of myself. I turned around once again, and went on, pretending not to care about the barking, but with my ears trained on it.

I lost count of my steps. Was this the thirteenth or the sixteenth? I wasn't sure anymore. I had been focused on the dogs rather than my own counting, and I had lost the beat. It wasn't a big deal yet, but it could quickly become one, a small deviation leading me wildly off course. As things stood, it was *really* better to go home. I told myself I had done good work.

My last landmark had been another rock, half-buried in the earth. I wouldn't have considered it workable at the beginning, but my string of successes had made me cocky. Too cocky. I couldn't locate the rock anymore. I counted thirteen steps, and then sixteen, and I went up all the way to twenty, and the rock just wasn't there.

While the barking was getting closer, and the breeze kept picking up.

I wasn't panicking yet, but I was eager to find my way. I used my cane to trace a circle around me, and then a wider one, until the cane bumped into something. I walked to it, bent my knees: it was a rock, but was it the *right* rock? It seemed too small, and, with most of my attention inexorably fixed on the dogs, I couldn't remember whether the jagged end had pointed right or left. And wasn't that end *less* jagged than this anyway?

Stop double-guessing. I decided it had to be my rock and I moved on from there, the breeze undeniably turning into wind. I counted nineteen steps, but the landmark I was expecting to find, a small mound with a spiky shrub on top, wasn't there. I traced circles with my cane. Nothing.

The wind was getting stronger, the barking closer. Grandpa Ferdinando's words came to me – *Praise God, never the wind.* There were angry dogs in the wind. Nature was a smaller affair in Turin; I understood how here it made Grandpa wary.

Get back to the rock. Keep calm, get back to the rock, and start again. Another voice in my head, a mean voice, a bully's voice, added, *If it is the right rock, that is.* I ignored that voice and made my way back, but the rock had disappeared. I traced circles wide and small. No rock.

The barking was closer yet.

'Fuuuck,' I screamed, in rage, in frustration. I repeatedly stabbed the dirt with my cane, as if the field was a vampire and I a hunter. 'Fuck, fuck, fuck!' The wind took my screams away; and when I stopped screaming, I noticed two things. The feral smell was a lot stronger; and the barking was fading. It was not exactly as if the dogs were moving away from me.

It was as if the volume of their barks was being turned down, down – and it was off.

Not only that.

I couldn't hear the crickets anymore, nor the birds, nor the rustle of leaves. I could hear no sound at all. And I felt the purest fear I had ever felt, a fear as pure as I imagine must be the pain of giving birth. I let go of my cane and clapped my hand once. The clap exploded all around me. I started breathing again; I hadn't gone deaf. I realised that I could hear the wind, too, like a large animal blowing in my ear.

I had heard the sound of that silence on my first night in the Masseria del Vento, and now I cursed myself for pushing it aside. What the sighted call *silence* is not silence to me; the world ceaselessly resonates with life, day and night, with things bustling and buzzing energy. But there was nothing here, if not for the wind, gust after gust, and the sounds I made – my heartbeat, my breath, the rustling of my clothes. That was to me what a solar eclipse must be to a sighted: the rise of an abnormal darkness which takes over light. It drove home what an easy target I was.

You came unmoored, the bullying voice said.

I bent to pick my cane up. I had rounded too many turns to be sure, but I remembered that I had been facing the sun, and too little time had passed for it to have shifted position significantly, so I kept its rays on my back as I moved on in what I prayed was roughly the direction of the vineyard.

The silence was not the muffling that descended on Turin on misty winter mornings; on those mornings the music of the world was softer but still clearly audible. Here the music had stopped entirely, except for my steps and the gusts of wind which built up, reached a climax and wound down. I could hear nothing between the tail end of a gust and the vibrato which announced the next one, only my own fretting footsteps.

No; not only mine.

I halted, and listened.

Between a gust and the next I heard the *tap, tap* of the undefinable footsteps. *Tap, tap.* Were they a dog's? They were soft. *Tap, tap.* I could hear them at the end of a gust of wind. Then another gust came, submerging them, and when it was over, I could hear the *tap, tap* again. Closer.

'Go away!' I shouted.

A gust took my voice, and when the gust was gone, the *tap, tap* was not.

I moved as fast as I could in the opposite direction. I would have run if I could. The footsteps didn't seem to hurry behind me, but neither did they stop. *Tap, tap.*

I tripped on a jutting root without falling. I stretched my cane, and there it was: a tree, a large one. *I can climb it.*

I raised my arms but couldn't find any low-hanging branches.

And – *tap, tap* – the steps were getting closer.

I passed my hands across the trunk, which was gnarled and twisted like a giant fossil of a rope, searching for anything that might help me climb. I found something else. I found a void. There was a hollow in the tree. I felt its margins, and, yes, it was large enough for me to get in. *Tap, tap* – the steps were almost with me. I bent and crouched my shoulders and scrambled inside.

A crawler, maybe a spider, fell on my neck. Another walked on one of my legs. I slapped them away with jerky movements, irrationally as frightened of them as I was of whatever was coming. The inside of the tree was like a woody, hard womb I had outgrown, and I moved my legs, my shoulders, to try and find a comfortable position. The steps were so close now I could hear them over the gusts. *Tap, tap.*

And I thought, *You're an idiot. A big, fat idiot.*

I was not in a deep wood or an olive grove. I was in Mediterranean scrub, in a vast plain, and even though I couldn't see the creature that was coming, the creature could see me. It could not have missed the sight of a bony boy entering a tree. I pondered whether I could use my cane, smash it on the head or muzzle that might come through the mouth in the wood, but I didn't have enough space to take a swing.

Tap, tap. That rough, primal smell invaded the tree.

The bloody unfairness again. None of it was fair. It wasn't fair that I got lost in my own home, it wasn't fair that my brother had let me down, it wasn't fair that I was hunted, it wasn't fair that I would never see Ada's face. Fear transformed into anger, and before I could consider the scores of good reasons not to do it, I scrambled out of the tree.

Tap, tap. The steps were here.

I bent on my knees, as if to pick up a rock.

The steps halted. I remained bent, my hands touching clay earth.

Tap, tap. Something came close and then past me; something large and heavy, but which moved gracefully.

Tap, tap. The steps kept moving at the same unhurried pace, going away.

I couldn't tell when I started hearing the crickets, and the birds, and the leaves, but at some point the music of the world was playing again. I inched up. I gave myself time before moving. The step's rhythmic sound was fading into the distance, and I didn't think I would be able to take a step of my own unless it disappeared entirely.

The wind was still blowing in the scorching sunshine, and I was still lost. I could either wait for help or try and make my way back on my own.

The building works, I thought.

I refused to believe that noises so loud could be killed off by open country. I took a breath, exhaled, combed the wind and, sure enough, I found them. They weren't even that feeble; it was only that I had grown so used to them that as soon as they became less than deafening I thought I couldn't hear them anymore. But I could, which meant that as long as the builders were at work, I was free to roam. I could take care of myself in more than one sense, a thought that made me feel elated in a way I hadn't felt since my sighted days. I had explored, and conquered. *Veni, vidi, vici.*

Ada arrived as I was putting the final touches on sandwiches made of thick slices of brown bread, stuffed with tuna in olive oil and spicy salami. She immediately asked me about Ferdi, and I told her what had happened, how cross I was. 'Give him a break,' she said. 'Must be hard as it is, for him.'

When we got to the beach we were both hungry, so we sat under the pines and annihilated our food. The wind had calmed down. The incident of the morning was already acquiring a dreamlike quality. I failed to find the words to tell Ada about it. There had been a hushed moment in the fields and a stray had crossed my way: there was more to it than that, but I could not articulate *what*. 'I used your trick today.'

'You met the dogs again?'

'Yes,' I said, after a hesitation, and almost believed it. 'It worked.'

'Told ya.' I heard the swooshing she made when she stood up. 'Bath?'

'After eating?'

'I swam after eating a thousand times and never died.'

A hand on her arm, I followed her to shore and into the water. I advanced prudently, and relaxed when I had proof that putting my belly underwater was not going to kill me. 'Our families are meeting,' I said.

'What?'

'Tomorrow at Betta's.'

'Your folks are friends with Aunt Betta and Uncle Giorgio?'

'Are they your real aunt and uncle?'

'Nope, but they insist.'

'Same here. You sound unhappy.'

'No, yes, it's just…' She stopped. 'Whatever. Shall we work on your swimming?'

'I'm feeling lazy.'

'The problem is you don't trust me.'

'I don't trust myself.'

'Don't say stuff like that.'

'Like what?'

'Stuff that sounds deep and means nothing at all.'

I flicked my middle finger in the general direction of her voice, and she said, 'Sticks and stones, jackass. Come on, only once.'

'Fine.'

She took my hand in hers. We walked further on. The water rose halfway to my chest, and then all the way to my chest, and there I froze. I couldn't move one step further.

'Let's stay here, where we can touch the bottom,' Ada said, as if she'd meant to do that all along. 'Now. Can you bend your knees? To get the water to your neck.'

I did. As I lowered myself, I felt the coolness of saltwater tickle my body, up to my chin.

She said, 'You could lift your legs, for starters, and float. But I'll have to let go of your hand. I'll be right here, next to you. Is that all right?'

'Let's say so.'

Ada let go of my hand. I lifted my legs, I spread my arms wide, and just like that, I was floating. I was unmoored from the world, an astronaut lost in space – *like two nights ago, like this morning*. My connection to humankind had come loose. I had lost all landmarks, even the most fundamental ones such as gravity, and maybe I could take care of myself or maybe not, but I was still stranded in an endless night where things went bump. Or *tap, tap*.

I snapped my legs down, to touch the sand.

'How was it?' Ada asked.

I said, 'Enough for today.'

'Here's the young man!' Betta chirped. 'The star of the party! Isn't he such a darling, Giorgio? Isn't he such a darling?'

'Such a darling,' a male voice confirmed. 'Hello, Luca.'

'Hi, Giorgio. I mean, Uncle Giorgio.'

Betta pinched my cheek again, and I hated myself for flinching, again. 'Charming, just charming! Your little friend will be here any moment.'

I said, 'Wow,' charging the word with all the sarcasm I could muster.

It was completely lost to Betta, who answered, 'I know!'

From what I gathered, a wrap-around garden surrounded the house. Betta had led us from the front to the back, where the sound of a thousand voices had hit me. She had announced, in a tone which would be better reserved for a grander occasion, 'Giorgio is making pizza!'

It was disconcerting to be thrown into a place I had never seen. At the masseria and on the beach I could draw on memories to form a picture of the space. Not here. Which trees were here? What colours? How were the chairs set? Where was the buffet table? If only I could get a quick glimpse, lift the curtain for a fraction of a second. All those strangers coming too close, introducing themselves, all those incorporeal voices, those ghost hands slapping my back, squeezing my shoulder, those breaths redolent of wine, cigarettes, garlic, made my head spin.

Mum started a conversation and forgot about me. It was part of the strategy she and Dad had adopted; they refused to consider my sight loss as a *disability* – a word they only spoke to deny it, every time spitting it out as if it could bite their tongue – and they treated me exactly as they would have if I were sighted. Like many ideas, it was good only in theory.

Someone stuck a bruschetta in my hand. Now I knew where the smell of garlic came from. Someone else asked me how I was liking my summer, and told me I was a lucky bastard to have all that free time and that it wouldn't last forever, and someone else told me that Grandpa had been a great man, never mind the backbiters. 'Don't listen to them,' one person (I never found out who they were; I can't even remember whether they were man or woman) said. 'Whatever you hear, it's a nasty, nasty lie.'

Metal scraped against brickwork; an explosion of heat hit my back. The aroma of burning wood made its way to my nostrils: Giorgio was throwing the first batch of pizzas into the oven. I turned my head to take in that delicious scent, and felt the heat creep from my back to my face. That made me think. I moved a step back, and the heat became noticeably less intense. Yes, I could make the oven work for me.

I walked around the garden, keeping my focus on the heat slithering on my skin. It took some getting used to, but soon I could tell where I was in relation to the oven, and I could tell, roughly, my distance from it. The heat was a rope keeping me secured to the oven, like the building works did to the grange. It might work even better than those. I conducted an experiment: I picked a random chair, left my plate on it, walked around and then tried to return to the starting point, using the heat to navigate around the garden, the way a sailor used stars on the high seas. I succeeded, weaving a way among people and chairs, and when my fingertips touched the brim of the plate, it was like planting my banner in a new land.

Where was Ada?

Mum and I had got there half an hour late, which was early by Southern standards; people kept pouring in. It felt as if the whole village was gathering, countless bodies in an endless space, everyone except my friend. They were all talking about us, about my family, I mean. I suppose people were more careful around Mum, but they spoke freely around me, as if I weren't there. Blindness has the curious side-effect of invisibility; the same thick curtain that hides others from me also hides me from others. I bear myself differently from the sighted. My reactions are slightly out of tune, so people find my presence unnerving, and rather than acknowledge the unpleasant fact that they are not as enlightened as they think, and a blind person is making them feel ill at ease, they prefer to ignore me altogether.

I caught snatches of conversation about Grandpa, about me, about Ferdi's difficulties. There was one that I remember distinctly, for the importance it took in the light of what was going to happen later. It was an exchange between two men who were standing close enough to me to touch. 'Have you even *seen* the Masseria del Vento?' one of them said.

The other, who was smoking a cigar, ruled in the voice of a world expert: 'It's a wreck.'

'Crazy expensive to fix it up.'

'Do you know what they do?'

'Did: they both retired to work on the masseria. He was an accountant. She was a schoolteacher.'

'They *retired*? Is he rich?'

'Not that kind of accountant.'

The cigar-smoking man sniggered. 'They don't have a clue. Mario was clever selling his part.'

'Mario is a clever man.'

'Very much, I hear.'

'Yeah.'

I didn't give their words any importance at the time. I was barely getting a grip of the notion of *money*, and of the adult meaning of *smartness*. They moved on to other topics, and I kept wandering. I was given a pizza hot out of the oven; I sat on a chair balancing the plate on my knee. I cut a slice. An eruption of delicious lava-hot tomato sauce and stringy mozzarella scorched my palate. I had barely finished polishing off the pizza when I was handed a plastic plate, its centre bent under the weight of food. 'I got you pan-fried aubergines, olives and stuffed peppers,' said the voice of a man, deep, cultivated, a little hoarse. 'There's plenty more.'

'Thank you.'

'The famous Luca Saracino.'

'Why famous?'

'I have heard great things about you.' The voice was teasing, but not patronising. 'I'm Ada's dad.'

'Oh, hi. Good morning. I mean, good evening.'

The weight of a body fell in the chair next to me, with a scented cloud of pipe and sandal aftershave. 'Good evening to you, Luca Saracino. And thank you.'

'What for?'

'Ada told me you met her in your property, and you were very kind about that.'

'*She* was kind to me, actually.'

'That doesn't sound like Ada,' he said, in a playful tone which implied the opposite.

'Where is she?'

'With her mum, talking to yours. They're waving at us, three o'clock.'

I waved back in that direction.

'I'm happy you two got to know each other,' he went on. 'It's only bonkers that we didn't make it happen sooner.'

'Yeah.'

'Although I must be honest with you, I felt relieved when Betta gave you such glowing references. Ada's history with friends is bumpy.' He paused. 'How are you finding living here?'

'I'm getting used to it,' I said.

'Must be hard, coming from the North. This is a land of its own, with its own nature and its own laws.' Ada's father uttered each word as if that was exactly the word he wanted to utter that; and not any other, in exactly the right tone. He knew where he was going, so you might as well follow.

'I'm doing my best.'

'Just as long as you know you can count on us all. *No man is an island*, a poet once said. We need each other.' He paused again, long enough for me to start to think of something to say, but then he said, 'It is no secret that Don Ferdinando and I didn't see eye to eye, and I am not going to offend your intelligence by pretending otherwise, but I am sorry for your loss, Luca, truly and sincerely sorry. Your losses. All of them.'

It was a new, beautiful experience, to hear an adult talk to me without either pity or denial. 'Thank you.'

'When your dad and brother arrive, what do you say you all come over for dinner?'

'I'd love that.'

I heard him stand up. 'Come on,' he said, 'let's join the ladies.'

'What's the deal with Ada's family?' I asked Mum while she drove back home after the party. I was pleasantly dozy. I had stuffed myself with too much food, and Ada had introduced me to people in the crowd by the nicknames she'd made up for them – Betta was Wig, because no way was that her real hair, and Giorgio was Barrel, because he was rotund and unfailingly full of wine. There were Vulture, Candlestick, Zombie; there were Lurch and Mrs Banana. I helped her come up with new names for those she didn't know; we christened a nicotine-smelling man Butt, and a girl Ferdi's age (too self-important to hang out with us) Hyena, for the way she laughed.

Mum said, 'What deal?'

'Something went down between them and us.'

The answer took a while to arrive. 'Grandpa Ferdinando wasn't the easiest man.'

Much as I loved him, I knew he had a temper. Uncle Mario was fond of telling how 'the odd smack' had been part and parcel of his education, and he was better for it. I asked, 'So?'

'They're old stories, Luca, nothing for you to be concerned about.'

'I am curious.'

'You can't chase after every rumour that comes your way. Small-town folks have time to gossip, and the inclination to use it.'

'What did Grandpa have against Ada's dad?' I insisted.

Mum answered with a voice on the verge of exasperation. 'Not only him: Grandpa resented *all* the Guadalupis. The land where they built their house used to be our land. My grandfather lost it at cards. Grandpa must have been your age when that happened, give or take. The way he told it, to him it was inconceivable that a piece of his home had gone, just like that.' I heard her snap her fingers. 'And now it belonged to someone else.'

'It wasn't the Guadalupis' fault though.'

'I know, but it's easier to blame strangers than family. Grandpa remembered the day when the Guadalupis started building their drystone wall as one of the worst in his life. It was the first time he had *lost* something.'

'I think I get that.'

'In time he managed to get over his misgivings and become friends with Pierpaolo Guadalupi, Ada's grandfather, who was more or less his age, but then… they had a major fight, years later. I'm not sure about what. When this story came up in conversation, Grandpa would always refuse to explain. He said that the reason didn't matter. The crux was that the Guadalupis weren't good people and we should leave it at that. Uncle Mario puts it down to money. *It's always about money*, he says.'

'And what do you think?'

She shifted gear, turned right. We were almost home. 'I think it's true that details don't matter. Pierpaolo became a professor of medicine at Lecce university, while Grandpa stopped anything resembling a formal education at fourteen. They lived in different worlds.'

'Grandpa liked Ada.'

'Have you ever wondered why you two never played together?'

It wasn't a real question, and I didn't answer.

'Grandpa forbade it,' Mum said. 'Your dad and I were taking it for granted that we would set playdates, what with Ada being next door, but he ruled it out. His grandson would not hang with a Guadalupi, not now, not ever. This was his house, he laid down the law, and if it wasn't to our taste, we could suit ourselves and not visit.'

'It doesn't sound like Grandpa.'

Mum halted the car, killed the engine. 'Not to you,' she said.

*

By the time Ferdi and Dad arrived, I was perfectly capable of making it to the village and back on my own. It was one of the great triumphs of my life, one I will keep with me until the time I go into that good night. My adventure in the fields had fired me up. Real freedom – real *control* – was at hand; and I wanted it.

Not in the fields, though, not for the time being. I was not going back there, where the sun got stronger day by day, sucking every last drop of water from shrubs and leaves, turning once-soft edges into hard cutting blades. I told myself that it would be a waste of time, that after understanding that I could detect the building works when I set my mind to it, navigating that terrain was too trivial to be worth my time. Of course, it was an excuse that could make sense only to a thirteen-year-old; the builders would leave and I would stay, and the obvious thing to do was study the surroundings while I had that aural anchor to the house. The truth was that something walked in the fields, and I didn't want to walk with it.

I hadn't managed to convince myself it was a dog I'd met, and in the absence of other theories I would rather not have gone there in any sense, for the last thing I wanted was to relive the moment of pristine horror in which all sounds had dropped and I had come unmoored in the wind. Proud as I was of how I had handled myself, standing up to whatever it was that I'd stood up to, I was not itching to do it again.

Besides, the route to Portodimare was of more immediate use; with summer starting for real, the village was abuzz with excitement. It took me three days of Ada's guidance to get a hold of the route. From the farmhouse, straight on the dirt drive to the gate, then right on the unpaved road (lumpy underfoot), until I felt sleek tarmac beneath me and the immensity of the sea ahead, and then right again, downhill, keeping the immensity on my left, and where the first buildings rose to block it, there you go: Portodimare. On the edge of the village was a cloud made of the sweet scent of fruit, the throaty voices of vendors, the smoke of their cigarettes and the heat amplified by the metal of their vans. I realised that moving around here might be easier than in Turin, provided that I changed the way I thought, worried less about exact routines and more about the aural, haptic and olfactory features of the environment. The sensory experience was richer than in a city; not necessarily stronger, but deeper. It held better-quality information.

On the third day I managed to walk without any guidance, while chatting with Ada. When the humming of refrigerators and a vanilla-scented cold current told me that we were passing by Chocolate Delight, one of the two gelato parlours we had back then, I asked, 'Gelato?'

Ada's voice came out astonished. 'You're showing off.'

'No, I'm asking.'

'Then you're paying.'

I *was* showing off, and it felt amazing.

My progress with the sea wasn't as good. I got to the point where I could float without panicking, but I couldn't push myself to do any actual swimming. I was annoyed at myself. I, the Conqueror of the Wild, Vanquisher of Beasts, didn't dare doggy-paddle in calm water, on a sunny day, with Ada by my side.

In hindsight, anxiety was the price I paid for my family's favourite sin, denial. I was more troubled than I cared to admit. When I found myself alone in the quiet of the night, I couldn't tell what I was sensing and what I was making up. Every time the soundscape of crickets and hoopoe waned for a moment,

I thought the silence was back. I had sensed the feral smell in my bedroom before sensing it in the fields, and perhaps there was nothing strange in the tang of a beast coming off the thick stone walls of a farmhouse, but perhaps there was. *This is a land of its own*, Ada's dad had said, *with its own nature and its own laws.* They were all new, all strange, to me; it was hard to say which ones might be just a little stranger than they should be. All considered, though, I was as happy as I had been in months, perhaps years, until Dad and Ferdi arrived.

The rumble of Dad's Volvo rose above Kurt Cobain's voice. I was listening to 'All Apologies' on the grey Walkman that now rests in a box in the basement, buried with other trinkets I have no use for and yet cannot quite throw away. The Walkman had been a present from Dad for Christmas, the tape from Ferdi; one of the rare things they agreed on was that I was going to cultivate a taste in music. I did my best.

It was a dusty late afternoon. Dad had been driving for fifteen hours, and they rolled out of the car with a stale smell of sweat and crisps. Ferdi grunted a curt hello before stomping to his room, chased by the laboured wheezing of a trolley. We hadn't talked since the day he skived off his exams, not even when it was made clear that, no, he wouldn't get a special reprieve and, yes, he would have to repeat the year in Casalfranco. Still, Ada had softened me, and I had been looking forward to his coming. Now my anger flared up again. *He* was the one who needed to be forgiven, and he came here acting the victim? Thanks, but no thanks.

Dinner was grim. I remember Dad saying, in a desperately

happy voice, 'What a perfect night to start a new life.' He was talking like a badly scripted character, which he did when he had nothing to say and yet wanted to talk. He inhaled with a smack of satisfaction. 'Pure air, great food, all as it should be.'

Ferdi kept himself wrapped in silence. Mum made some noise in agreement, and I kept my attention fixed on the flavour of aubergine and tomato that came out as a blessing from the *parmigiana* I was wolfing down.

Dad went on, implacable. 'You've been having a good time, Luca, haven't you? I've never seen you so tanned. And Mum told me you made a friend.'

'Yes,' I said.

'A *girl* friend.'

I hated when adults played chummy to make you feel small. I never do that with my own children. 'She's a girl and my friend, that's all.'

'Ada Guadalupi! I'm glad it's her. It was so silly, that family feud nonsense.'

'I agree,' Mum said. 'The Guadalupis too. They'd be happy to have us for dinner.'

'That's brilliant, just brilliant! We're building bridges, starting on a high note.'

Ferdi said, 'Fucking moron.'

Silence fell over the table.

'Language, Ferdi,' Dad said.

'*A high note?* Is that what you believe, *Dad?*' Ferdi's spite made *Dad* into another swear word. 'Is that what you honest-to-God believe? We're stranded in a ruined farmhouse in the butt-end of nowhere, begging for the friendship of folks that Grandpa *loathed*.'

Mum said, 'You didn't have to be with us after the summer.'

'You two lost our house!'

Mum took the short breath that comes before a snappy answer, then she let it fall. 'No, I'm not going to be dragged into this. You're eighteen, Ferdi. Act like an adult.'

'I don't know where to start. No one taught me.'

Dad sizzled like a hot plate showered by cold water. 'Okay,' he blurted out. 'I didn't want to do this on the first night, I was going to give us all time to settle, but okay, it can't wait, clearly.'

'What can't wait?'

'This summer you'll be lending a hand with the works on the masseria, until school starts.'

'Yeah, no, I'm not working with you.'

'Not with me, with the building crew. On site. You're too cool for school? Fine. You'll see where you end up without a degree.'

Ferdi made a fake angry laugh. 'You never had to do one day of manual labour in your life. Not one hour.'

'And thank God for that. It's time you learn some gratitude too.'

'Guess what? I'm eighteen. You can't make me do *anything*.'

'Oh yeah? Well, if you want to eat at this table and sleep in this house, this is how it's going to be. You think it's beneath you? Suit yourself, and good luck finding better quarters.'

I wanted to be elsewhere. I wanted to be home, in Turin. I wanted to be in the fabulous golden age before I got ill and brought my family down with me.

Ferdi said, 'Mum?'

'We're doing this for you.'

*

What happened next was not a dream and I never believed it was, regardless of what I might have claimed for a while, in the same way that you know, deep down *you know*, that one or two of the insane memories you write off as fantasies must be something else entirely. Ferdi left the table before dessert; Dad, tired from the long drive, had a drop of sweet-smelling Strega, made a bunch of sweeping statements about how grand our life in Puglia was going to be, indeed already was, and went to bed. Mum joined him not long after, which left me on the porch on my own. She left the light on; I knew because it attracted mosquitoes. I turned it off. I wandered inside to fetch my book, came back, sat on our creaky lawn swing. I wished I could still read comic books.

It was the whiteness of the whale that above all appalled me. I rocked the swing with one foot planted on the floor. I was stuck on chapter forty-two, a long, dense essay on the colour white. Having to read it with my fingers was a sick joke. Ishmael went on and on about how terrible white could be, making me want to scream, *Dude, you know what's a million times worse than white? Nothingness, that's what.*

I yawned, closed the book. I didn't feel like going to bed just yet. I loved those hours on summer nights when everybody was asleep and the air was fresh; I made them last for as long as I could. Still do. Rocking weightless on the swing, to the tune of crickets and hoopoe, I was part of a bigger whole, and whole myself. A zephyr ran on my exposed skin like silk.

There was the feral smell, once again.

All my attention rushed to it, like a rabbit who caught the scent of hunters. I sniffed. It was only a note, the faintest whiff, but it was there, clearly there, standing out against the subdued fragrances of the night. Was it getting stronger, or it was me becoming more aware of it? Hard to say.

Tap, tap.

The footsteps came from the vineyard. They joined the rest of the soundscape, this time, which gave them another layer of reality. The wind had built up a little.

'Go away,' I said.

Tap, tap.

There was an unsettling quality to that gait: it had to be an animal's, but which one? It was too loud for a cat, and perhaps too elegant for a dog. Each step fell like a well-rehearsed drumbeat. I'd never heard a walk like that before, but then again, I hadn't heard a whole lot of animals walk before. It could be a goat for all I knew, a devilish horned ram. Or a dumb sheep.

Tap, tap.

There was no doubt: the smell was stronger, the steps closer. Was it coming for me? I thought, *It's okay, don't stress.* I had time to go inside, close the door behind me, lock and double-lock it. I could save face and pretend I wanted to go to bed; it was late at night after all. But I didn't want to. I wanted to spend some time on my own, after an excruciating dinner and before days that were shaping up to be every bit as bad. I wasn't asking much, just to be left alone for a little while, and I couldn't even get *that*.

Tap, tap.

Mum had a camera. She had been taking pictures of the advancement of the works. She and Dad had this idea they would set up an exhibition once the masseria was ready, a visual chronicle of our strong loving family restoring a local monument to its former glory. They couldn't afford a professional, so they took photographs themselves, a lot of them, confident that a bunch would come out good enough. On summer holidays we always kept the camera in the kitchen credenza, and Mum wouldn't change that, I guessed.

Tap, tap.

I stood up, headed towards the front door, slowly, steadily, the way I was learning to walk. I would take a photograph and show it to Ferdi, or Ada, ask them what they saw. Unless I put a name on it, that wanderer would keep its hold on me. I got inside, resisting the urge to shut the door and nail it to its frame. The feral smell was just as strong inside as it was outside. It filled the house like smoke.

Something wasn't right. I stopped. What was it?

I listened to my breath, to my heartbeat. I snapped my fingers, and listened. Sounds did not bounce off the walls as I expected, but rather, they travelled as if there weren't any walls at all, as if I'd ended up, somehow, outdoors. *Just keep walking towards the kitchen.* What I was thinking wasn't possible, and thus, wasn't true.

I walked on, slowly, steadily, ignoring the strange way sounds travelled, ignoring the feeling that I was walking downhill, and for much longer than I needed to reach the kitchen door. At last, the cane touched the door's frame. I swept the cane to search for the other side of the frame; I found nothing at all. Which meant that the first thing I had touched had not been the frame. Was I lost in my own living room?

Was I lost elsewhere?

I tested the thing I had touched with my cane. Moving the cane upwards, I found that the thing was short; it was also large, smooth. The cane swished on it the way it did on slippery surfaces. I squatted, a part of me noticing, without yet taking fully on board, another smell, and a new sound gently rising. I touched the thing with my hands, and it couldn't be, but it very much felt like it was the raised part of a flat rock on the beach, with a fuzz of sea lichen growing on it.

In the air was the sound of the sea, and its iodine scent.

I licked my upper lip. I tasted salt. I heard a sound like a wave returning to the rock; a fine spray of seawater landed on my cheeks.

I was on a beach.

I screamed.

'He'll slow us down,' the master mason, Piero Quarta, said. I had barely interacted with him after the first day, but I had listened to him talk and grown accustomed to his voice, which made me think of wrinkles, like something left in the sun for too long.

'Don't let him,' Dad answered.

The master mason snorted. 'He makes a mistake, you'll say it's my fault.'

'I won't.'

'He hurts himself, you'll take it out on me.'

'Mr Quarta, I can assure you, my son is going to take full responsibility for himself.'

Ferdi was there with them, shuffling on his feet and scoffing at every word.

Piero Quarta sucked from his cigarette, and coughed. 'Training boys wasn't part of the contract.'

'He's going to help you with the job.'

'He'll do more harm than good.'

'I…' Dad's voice trailed off. 'Is that such an issue? More hands on deck. How bad can it be?'

'You say that as if *you* were doing *me* a favour. We'd have to spend half the day minding that he doesn't fall down a ladder, the other half fixing his cock-ups.'

'I can take care of myself,' Ferdi said.

'Ever been on a building site?' Piero Quarta asked.

Ferdi didn't answer.

'Then you can't.'

It was early morning and the sun already beat down fiercely. I sat under the carob tree with my book and a glass of iced tea, which was quickly sliding into lukewarm territory. Dad must have thought he and the builders weren't within earshot, but many things are within earshot when you shut up and listen. I couldn't say I felt sorry for Ferdi. He deserved a slap in the face.

Dad said, 'Surely there are easy tasks for him. Like carrying bricks.'

The master mason chuckled. 'With those arms? One brick at a time, yeah, that's about it.'

'Mr Quarta, help me out here.'

The master mason took a moment before saying, 'I'll let him hang with us. Not for free.'

'Wait, you want to get *paid* to have my son work for you?'

'Sure.'

'I wasn't expecting that, to be honest.'

'Why?' Piero Quarta asked.

In the end Dad agreed to pay, though he managed to convince the master mason to sort out the details later. When

Dad stopped talking I lost track of him: the building noises were louder than his steps, and I only heard him when he was close. 'Hi, Dad.'

'You got me!' he said, as if that was a seriously impressive feat. He sat down with me, and asked, 'May I?'

'What?'

'Oh, sorry. Get a drink of your tea, I mean.'

He'd forgotten that he couldn't point at things and expect me to understand. I said, 'Sure.'

Dad gulped down my tea, let out a satisfied noise and said, 'How are we doing this morning?'

'Fine.'

'Quite a scare you gave us.'

When I'd screamed, Mum, Dad and Ferdi had scrambled down the stairs, calling my name. They had found me trembling in the living room.

I said, 'Sorry about that.'

'Nothing to be sorry about. These big old houses, they take some getting used to.'

Mum had asked what the problem was, and I'd found myself unable to say, *I was on a beach*. By saying those words aloud, I would make them undeniable, and I didn't want them to be. So I'd lied, to Mum and myself both: 'I thought I heard somebody.' I was already in the process of convincing myself that my imagination had worked overtime.

Mum had kept guard over me while Dad and Ferdi searched the room, the kitchen, this whole wing of the house, finding nothing.

'Fucking drama queen,' had been Ferdi's comment, before he went back to bed.

Fucking drama queen. This coming from someone who would rather play billiards than sit his exams.

Dad said, 'You sure there isn't anything else?'

'I'm sure, Dad.'

'You would tell me if…'

'Dad!'

'Anyway, I wanted to say thank you.'

'What for?'

'Holding the fort with Mum all this time.'

'I didn't do a thing.'

'You kept her company. It made a difference. Come with me.'

'Where?'

'Just come,' he said.

I was putting on a show of life as usual. Looking at it from the perspective of now, it was, frankly, idiotic. All I can say for myself is that we all have this thing in common, we humans, that the bigger the change, the longer we take to notice it. We react swiftly to small ripples – a promotion, a new lover – but when a tsunami comes that will upturn our life whether we like it or not, we turn our head the other way and close our ears, as if deep change were a bore who will go away when ignored. It was easier for me to pretend that the salty drops on my face had been sweat rather than admit the stark truth – that they were seawater. Had the events of the night before been more ambiguous, I would have accepted them sooner, but they were radically *other* from anything I considered possible. And the impossible, by definition, cannot happen. I was enough of a child to believe life is that simple.

I followed Dad to the porch. 'On the table,' he said. 'A present for you.'

It was a large, hard object, a wide body with a curved recess in the middle on both sides, and a thin neck. My fingers touched clasps: the object was a box. I opened it and sank a hand inside, to touch strings, six of them. I pinched one.

I said, 'A guitar.'

'A Gibson: the best.'

'This is… great,' I said. I remembered to use my hands, and stuck a thumb up in a gesture of approval.

That made Dad happy.

I remember us trekking to Ada's place like a party of budget missionaries. Dad forged the way, armed with Mum's legendary tiramisu and a bottle of wine, Mum followed with me in tow, and Ferdi sulked in the back. It was a short walk in the opposite direction to the one Ada and I would take to the beach. In a matter of minutes we were making a left into a tiled driveway, and Giuseppe Guadalupi's voice was greeting us.

That voice – I remember it perfectly, in every note and every shade. It etched itself on your memory and became a part of you. It started with a smoothness that cocooned you, and continued in a casually self-assured way, which persuaded you that you were in good hands; the whole effect would have been perhaps too intense, if it wasn't for the ever-present undertone of irony, which hinted at the possibility that everything that was said, and life in general, was but a joke, something to take light-heartedly. That voice was a whole meal, from starters to digestif. Giuseppe Guadalupi was considered the most handsome man in town (he is still remembered as such), one who could have slept with any woman he wished, which made it all the more remarkable that not once did he cheat on his wife, Bianca, as even the most dedicated gossips had to – begrudgingly – concede. But I wouldn't be surprised if his looks were actually average, and his voice alone conjured up the illusion of beauty.

Ada and Bianca came out for a quick *hello*; everybody hugged and kissed everybody else, then they and Mum retired to the kitchen to put the last touches on dinner. I had something to say to Ada. I hoped I would get a chance later.

Us men, we remained on the patio, helping ourselves to soft cherry mozzarellas and home-made chips warm out of the pan, cut the Southern way, thin and wide. Giuseppe poured glasses of cold white wine for himself, Dad, and Ferdi; with Dad's consent, he poured a drop for me too. There was enough wine in my glass for maybe two or three sips, enough to make me feel included. Smooth jazz played in the background, while Dad and Giuseppe exchanged pleasantries and Ferdi stood to one side, conspicuously silent. It was very sophisticated. I felt like James Bond.

'Who's playing?' I asked.

Giuseppe stopped whatever he was saying to answer. 'It's Dizzy Gillespie, *Free Ride*.'

'Great record,' I said, as if I knew what he was talking about.

'Do you like jazz?'

'Yes.' And I did believe it, in that moment: a passion for music fitted a blind boy.

Dad said, 'Luca's studying guitar.'

Giuseppe lightly placed a hand on my shoulder, to signal he was talking to me, and asked, 'Do you have a favourite song to play?'

I was embarrassed as if I had been caught lying, though Dad had spoken, not me. 'Well, I don't know. The thing is, I haven't properly *started* yet.'

'I got him a guitar from Turin,' Dad explained. 'For all the help he's been giving with the works.'

Ferdi scoffed.

Dad ignored him and went on, 'It's a Gibson. The best.'

'For sure,' Giuseppe said. 'Well, Luca, let me know if you feel like learning a few tunes.'

'You can play?'

'I wouldn't go that far. I'm an enthusiast strummer. I can give you the name of a real teacher in Casalfranco for after summer, but meanwhile, I'm here next door.'

Dad said, 'Luca wouldn't want to intrude.'

'It would be my pleasure, as long as nobody's expecting Carlos Santana. Luca, you might want to just hang out on the beach and not with old folks. You don't have to answer now. It is an open invitation.'

I said, 'Thank you.'

Soon there were human footsteps, and an explosive scent of fresh tomato and basil. 'Dinner is served,' came Bianca's voice. She spoke the way she moved, with the same self-sufficient levity as her daughter. Bianca played by the rules of that place in that age – leaving the spotlight to the man of the house – which made it easy to underestimate her. That suited the Guadalupis just fine. Before long I would understand that they acted as a united front, and to fully make sense of one, you had to make sense of the other; and of course you couldn't understand Ada without understanding them both. Ada was more – so much more – than the sum of Bianca and Giuseppe, but there was no doubt as to where she came from.

The table was set in the garden. Two burning mosquito fumigators filled the air with citronella, the scent of summer nights. Bianca made me sit between Ada and Ferdi. I reached out to feel for my glass, when Ada grabbed my hand in hers; moments later, Ferdi took the other one. 'What's happening?' I asked.

'We are saying grace,' Ada whispered.

Giuseppe said, chanting each word like a note, '*Benedic, Domine, nos et haec tua dona quae de tua largitate sumus sumpturi. Per Christum Dominum nostrum. Amen.*'

'Amen,' everybody repeated, my family a split second after Ada and Bianca.

'*Ad cenam vitae aeternae perducat nos, Rex aeternae gloriae. Amen.*'

'Amen.'

Ada squeezed my hand before letting it go. She served me *riso patate e cozze*, a baked dish of rice, potatoes and mussels, seasoned with garlic, parmesan, a sprinkle of black pepper and breadcrumbs all over. It took me back to summers from a past so remote they belonged to another life.

'Funny,' Mum said. 'This was Dad's favourite dish.'

Bianca said, 'I know.'

'Really?'

'It was one of my father's favourites too,' Giuseppe said.

Bianca said, 'As family legend has it, Ferdinando taught Pierpaolo how to do it.'

'It wasn't something we'd do at home,' Giuseppe said. 'Mussels didn't agree with Grandma. The story goes that my father met Ferdinando at a mutual friend's, where Ferdinando had brought his *riso patate e cozze*. They bonded over clandestine food.'

'It's a shame what happened between our families,' Dad said.

'My father was a tough cookie.'

Mum laughed. 'Mine too.'

'Shall we raise a glass to wiser times?'

The sound of food being moved from plates to mouths stopped and was replaced by the notes of glasses tingling. I joined with my sparkling water.

'Cheers,' Ada said.

'So. The big move,' Giuseppe said. 'May I ask the reason for it?'

'A gut feeling,' Dad said. 'Mad as it sounds.'

Bianca said, 'Not at all.'

'We didn't have to *think* about it,' Mum explained. 'When my brother said he wasn't interested in keeping his share of the masseria, the idea just... clicked.'

'We'd had enough of Turin anyway,' said Dad.

Bianca asked, 'Why?'

'Big city life, it takes its toll.'

'I can only imagine.' Bianca sighed. 'And what's the plan now?'

'I'm sure you've heard.'

Giuseppe said, 'We'd rather hear it from the horse's mouth. People say many things and most are untrue, as our families know all too well.'

Dad chuckled. 'I had never been here, Puglia I mean, until I married Stefania. I fell in love with the place after falling in love with her. It's so secluded, so... wild. It's only a matter of time before tourists discover it. And when they do' – Dad made a dramatic pause – 'they'll find us here.'

'A holiday farm, then.'

'More than that! A home away from home, for visitors from the world over, with a swimming pool, a gym, summer schools.

In the first year, Stefania's going to teach cooking classes for local cuisine, and we'll build up on that. Not only a place to stay, but a venue for *experiences*. I met people from Glasgow who've never seen a prickly pear! Can you imagine? They'll love it here. Enormous spaces, bright colours, the best food in the world, wine… Think of the opportunities, Giuseppe.'

'The wild tends to disappear when it is discovered,' Bianca said, in an easy voice. 'Tourists can be a nuisance.'

'Not the ones I'm talking about.'

'You don't need to worry,' Mum said. 'We're not planning to set up open-air dance floors, nothing of the sort. We aim to create an elegant atmosphere: an upmarket venue.'

'Oh, I'm not at all worried,' Giuseppe said. 'Just curious. I didn't realise you two had a business background.'

Dad said, 'We don't! That's the best part. We come to this unfettered by ideas on how we're supposed to do things, so we are free to…'

'… innovate,' Mum said.

'Exactly. Innovate.'

After a beat, Giuseppe said, 'It's an interesting prospect, for sure.'

'It's liberating,' Dad said. 'A dream come true, frankly. We're our own bosses now. We live in a simpler place. I guess this was at the heart of our move: the search for a better lifestyle, for us and the boys.'

'Shit,' Ferdi said. 'You could've asked.'

A silence fell around the table, almost as perfect as the one that had fallen in the fields days before; Ada was quick to suffocate the laughter springing from her throat.

'Excuse me?' Dad said.

'I liked my lifestyle as it was, Dad. Luca too. If you'd remembered to ask, we would've been spared this cock-up.'

'That attitude won't get you anywhere.'

Ferdi raised his voice. 'The one thing Grandpa asked of us was not to hang with these people, and what do we do immediately after moving in the house *he* left us?'

'Ferdi!' Mum snapped. 'Apologise. Immediately.'

'Or what?' I heard him jump to his feet. The outburst had nothing to do with me, but it embarrassed me, nonetheless. I resented him for that. 'Or *what*, Mum? You and Dad blew up our life! *We didn't have to think about it,*' he said, mocking Mum's voice. 'Can't you hear yourself? You don't sound *mad*, as you say, in a cutesy way. You sound mental. Before you do something this big, *you bloody think*!'

'You're one to talk.'

'Fuck you all,' Ferdi shouted, and produced a noise, like a low-key explosion, that startled me. It took me a few moments to understand what it was: he had slammed a hand on the table. When I got it, he had already stormed away.

Dad started talking. 'I am…' He stopped. 'I don't know what to say.'

'There's nothing to say,' was Giuseppe's answer. 'I've heard Ferdi had troubles at school.'

Dad said, 'He didn't *have* troubles, he *made* them.'

'I was a difficult boy too,' Giuseppe said.

'What was that about?' I asked Ada.

The adults were sharing coffee, limoncello and bitter Fernet, leaving us to our own devices. Ada had guided me to a spot in the garden where a hammock hung between two thick-trunked trees. She called it her *reading pod*. 'It's private enough that I have time to switch books if I hear Mum or Dad coming.' Whenever Ada was reading a book her parents would disapprove of, she would always keep another, more suitable, at hand in a bag. She boasted she'd become adept at switching one with the other in no time. 'The trick is to go smoothly about it,' she said. 'You need two moments, like wave and backwash. First movement: you put the book in the bag and let it fall. Second movement: you grab the decoy and take it out. You must be quick, but not hurried, or you'll make a mess of it.' Only she could turn book-switching into a Zen discipline.

Side by side, we sat our bottoms in the hammock and put our feet on the ground, in one of those uncomfortable positions children like to take for reasons they forget when they grow older. 'Your dad,' I explained. 'What was that about, when he said he used to be a troublemaker?'

'Don't listen to him. He gets a kick out of pretending he was such a badass. Dad's notion of *making trouble* is skipping grace before a meal.'

'I didn't know you guys were religious.'

'Your grandpa was.'

'*Praise God…*'

'*Never the wind*,' Ada completed. 'He said that a lot.'

I remembered crosses on walls in the grange when Grandpa was alive, and a Bible, all gathering dust. My family's spirituality was perfunctory at best: Grandpa advised against it, but never followed his own counsel. 'We go to Mass at Christmas,' I said. 'Easter, too, sometimes.'

'We go every Sunday.'

'Isn't it always the same?'

'It's so boring I could hang myself. I get to give it a miss in summer. My parents still go, I don't have to.'

'I like your parents.'

'They're okay,' she said, in a voice that wasn't so sure. 'Yours too.'

'Mine are dumb.'

'Yeah, well.' Ada paused. 'A little,' she admitted. 'Your brother's cool.'

'Are you serious?'

'He cracked me up, before. "*Shit, you could've asked*",' she said, doing a passable impersonation of Ferdi. 'Instant classic.'

'I don't know about that.'

'Why are you so hard on him?'

'He'll have to repeat the year!'

'And you care because…?'

'You don't get it,' I said, with a twitch of resentment.

'Nope, and I'm trying.'

I reviewed my thoughts before putting them into words. 'I turn fourteen in January.'

'Remind me to buy you a present.'

'I was always in class with smaller kids, all my life.'

'That comes with being born in January.'

'Like Ferdi, I'll have to repeat the year,' I said. 'I couldn't keep up with the homework. I'll have to repeat the year and I will be fourteen next January, so I'll be in a class with twelve-year-olds. I'll be going to school with babies, Ada, *babies*. I'm left behind, and I can't do one thing to change that. But Ferdi?

Ferdi fucked up all by himself. He's like, like someone who poured acid on his eyes for a laugh.'

Ada didn't comment immediately; she made sure I had nothing to add. 'I hadn't thought about that,' she admitted. 'It must be hard for you. I'm sorry.'

'But I don't want you to be sorry. That's part of the problem, see? Everybody's sorry for me, for Luca, the blind boy. It's like I'm nothing else but blind. Before this, I used to be a comics fan, I used to draw. I used to be, I don't know, cute or ugly or smart or dumb, but now, all I am now is *blind*. I am not a person anymore, I'm *Luca the blind boy*. I'm this freakish thing I've got no power to define, this... this sob story that makes everybody feel better about themselves and sorry for me, but I don't want people to feel sorry about me. I want people to feel about me just the way they'd feel about anyone else. *Blind* is one of the things I happen to be, it's not... it's not me. Not the whole of me.' I had to stop to catch my breath, and when I did, I realised I'd been steadily raising my voice. 'That came out harsher than I meant.'

'Yeah, maybe I'd bring it down a notch,' Ada said, in her mother's easy tone.

'But you see the point.'

'You made it hard to miss. By the way, I don't see you as *Luca the blind boy*.'

'How do you see me?'

'Dumb. Ugly.'

'That's very kind of you.'

'Your hair is funny.'

'Kinder and kinder.'

'Call me Saint Ada.'

We stood in silence for a while, rocking the hammock back and forth. The adults' busy voices came muffled from a distance, and some animal in the trees above our heads was producing a persistent munching sound. I said, 'Your turn.'

'To do what?'

'Make a confession.'

'Dream on.'

'I told you something I never told anyone!'

'So now you want, what, dirt on me? *Mutually assured destruction*, is that it?'

'Sounds about right.'

'I might do that,' she said after a while. 'Only because you're a sob story and you make me feel better about myself.'

'Jackass.'

'It's Saint Ada here. My acts are nothing but godly. Okay, I'm going to confess one thing, but if you tell anybody, I'm going to kill you.'

'Same for what I told you.'

'No, I mean it, I'm going to kill you as a matter of fact. I'm going to take a kitchen knife and stab you right through the heart, and then I'm going to get rid of your body. I keep a place handy, just in case. I'm a planner.'

'You'll *try* to kill me.'

'Here's another guy playing badass.' Ada sighed. 'Dude, I saw you totally lose it over a couple of rangy strays.'

Before I could stop myself, I was saying, 'I have faced up to bigger beasts than dogs.'

'Meaning?' Ada asked, after a beat.

I scrambled to say, 'Don't change topic. Your secret first.'

'No, you can't just drop something like that and walk away.'

I'd wanted to talk to her about the wanderer tonight, and I needed her help for the next step I'd planned. I had rehearsed the words I was going to say. Now that the time had come, they sounded silly in my head. 'On my first night in the masseria, I heard a strange silence.'

'It's quiet round here.'

'It wasn't only that, Ada, it wasn't just your normal quiet. All noises dropped at once, all of them. I could hear myself and nothing else. I pay a lot of attention to what I hear, obviously, and I never heard anything like that before.'

'Go on,' she said.

I had her full attention, which gave me courage. 'It happened again last week. I was learning my way around the fields, when, *bam*, the silence fell. It's difficult to describe. There was just... nothing. No birds, no dogs, nothing. Or almost nothing. Two noises remained: the wind – strong blows, like a giant breathing in and out, but somehow managing not to rustle one single leaf – and an animal's footsteps.'

'What kind of animal?'

'A big one, from the sound of it. Bigger than a dog, a lot bigger. But also gracious. I don't know. It gave off this acrid smell, not entirely unpleasant like... like something feral made of musk and juniper and skin in the sunshine.'

'I know that smell,' she said.

'What?'

'Keep talking.'

'This wanderer was getting close, and I went and hid in a tree.'

'A tree?'

'A large tree with a hole in it. As soon as I got in I realised it wasn't that bright an idea: the beast, the wanderer, must have seen me, it could smell me too, and I'd done nothing but corner myself. So I came out. By that point the wanderer had arrived.'

'And?'

'And I did as you taught me.'

'You pretended to pick up a rock?'

'Yes.'

'And this big wild beast fell for that.'

'It wasn't afraid. I don't think so. It just went on its way.' I paused. 'It came back four nights ago. Without the silence this time. I was reading on the porch when I heard the footsteps. I think… I think it's personal, somehow.'

'Did you do the rock trick again?'

'Yes,' I said, a little too late.

Ada said, 'No, you didn't.'

'I swear…'

'Don't lie, dude.'

I thought of the impossible beach. I thought of the sweat on my face tasting like seawater. 'It was a dream.' As I said the words, I knew they were another lie. 'No,' I whispered. 'It wasn't. In my dreams, I can see.'

'What are you talking about?'

'When I heard the footsteps, I thought of taking a photograph to show you, so you could describe the beast to me.'

'Smart.'

'Thank you. So I ran inside to get a camera, but then… How can I explain it? The living room became bigger. I know you'll think I just got lost, but no, I don't get lost in the grange anymore, believe me, I can move there as well as anybody. The room had expanded, for real. And it wasn't a room anymore. It was a beach.'

'I'm not sure I follow.'

'I can't say it better than that. I was in my living room until I wasn't, and I was instead on a rocky beach. I didn't see the beach, I was still blind, and that's how I know it wasn't a dream. Because in my dreams I can see. I knew I was on a beach for no other reason that *I was on a beach*. It was simple as that. A wave splashed water on my face. And I let out a scream, and everybody rushed to see if I was okay.'

'Everybody rushed to the beach?'

'No, to the living room.'

'But you just said you were on a beach…'

'Not anymore. I was back home.'

'It's confusing.'

'I know.'

'Is that all?'

'Yes.'

'Heady stuff,' Ada said. 'My confession now.'

I heard the sound of light cloth brushing on skin, then Ada gently took my fingers in her hand and brought them to touch her other arm. 'Here,' she said. 'Be gentle, please.'

I had to stroke her arm with my finger more than once before noticing them: spots slightly warmer than the flesh around them, swollen, with a fissure in the middle. 'What are those?' I asked.

'Cuts. I heal fast.'

'Did someone hurt you?'

She moved back her arm, and I retracted my hand.

'I don't know,' she said.

I stretched my ears for our parents' voices: mundane, monotone, interested in gossip and mortgages, they grounded me to reality. 'How can you not know?'

'In May, we came here for a weekend, to set the house up for summer. I woke up in the morning and found cuts all over my arms. Two weeks ago, it happened again.'

'Did you tell your parents?'

'They noticed the cuts.'

'And…?'

'They gave me the third degree. I made up some bollocks about falling off the bike, and Dad muttered those weren't the cuts you get with a fall. They let it go for now, but, did you ever hear of self-harm?'

'Yes.'

'They think I'm doing that. I heard them talking.'

'Why don't you tell them the truth?'

'Mum is a psychiatrist, Dad's a cardiologist. They'd get sick with worry and not for the right reasons. Their answer would be tests.'

'Tests are useful. Trust me, I know.'

'No.' She paused, rocking the hammock in silence. 'Both times, before going to sleep, I noticed the silence you described, and the smell. And I had dreams of this lonely beach by night, with a large moon in the sky, red like an eye after you punch it, and shadows, shifting shadows, distant, but closing on me. These cuts, Luca, they're not stuff you can test. They're the secret I was going to confess to you.'

'About that,' I said.

Years ago, three men holidaying in the masseria entertained me with stories of an alien race from Sirio which had created humankind in a lab, and had given us weed as a tool for spiritual awakening. These men were highly educated, held well-paid jobs, and shared their pulp cosmology in the tone of someone discussing the weather. I doubt that any of them would have bought it on his own, but together they considered it only sensible. It is easier to believe wild notions when you don't have to do it alone – take one person, and in all likelihood she won't bother to come up with the idea that the Earth is flat; take five, and they might. Belief grows with company: that is the lesson of religions, politics and social media.

I'd walked to Ada's a sceptic and returned a true believer. Before talking to her I hadn't allowed myself to consider the full extent of the oddities I'd experienced. Now I found it inconceivable that I hadn't. Ada had gone through my same experiences, or similar ones anyway, and come out bruised; it was all real, physically real, although, of course, neither of us had a clue to what *it* was.

She came to get me in the morning and we flew to the newsagent in Portodimare, where we pooled our money to buy a disposable camera – one of those plastic gizmos that were the last hurrah of film. The plan was to keep it with me 24/7. When the wanderer came back, or if I happened to stray on the weird beach again, I would take a photograph, and Ada and I could compare notes. I proposed that she could get a camera too, but she objected that we needed to save money for the prints. 'And anyway,' she said, 'if I see the beast, I can just describe it to you.'

'We won't have any proof.'

'What do you want *proof* for? To do what?'

That was a good question. After the newsagent we went straight to the Little Pinewood, which, even with the season getting into full gear, was a far cry from busy. We settled on our towels in the sun. 'Two naked guys at nine o'clock.' Ada giggled.

'No way.'

'Honest.'

The Little Pinewood's seclusion made it, and still makes it, an informal naturist beach. Naturism being illegal, and frowned upon on moral grounds, if we bumped into adults we knew, they'd pretend not to see us. It was heaven.

'We were talking about proof,' I reminded Ada.

She was rubbing sun block on herself – I recognised the soothing sound of skin brushing skin, and the oil's coconut smell. 'A photograph by itself doesn't prove a thing. If your beach is the same I saw in my dream, it's... it's a beach, basically. A photo would be proof of what?'

'A photo of the wanderer, though?'

'It depends on how clear it is, and *what* this wanderer of yours looks like. But even if you took a clear-as-day photograph of a pterodactyl, what would your folks do?'

I thought of Mum and Dad's powers of denial. 'They'd be glad to see that we're playing around with photos.'

'Mine too. They don't trust anything they can't touch.'

'Yours believe in God.'

'With that one exception. No, we're on our own.'

I was not convinced. 'Why only us?' I asked. 'Okay, fine, I agree with you that our parents didn't have the same experiences we did, but what about others?'

'Ferdinando never mentioned a thing.'

'To me neither, but then he wouldn't, would he? Not to children. I could ask my uncle, my cousins. They've been around the grange more than our two families combined.'

'This is so cool! It's like a John Silence story.'

'Who's John Silence?'

'An occult detective: think Sherlock Holmes, only better, because he uses magic. He was created by a writer called Algernon Blackwood.'

'Great name.'

'I know, right? Blackwood was a *real* occultist.' Ada made a pause before adding in the ominous tone of a horror host: 'The guy knew his stuff.'

'I think I heard of him,' I said, though it wasn't true.

I remember my excitement vividly. Ferdi could suit himself with his moods and Mum and Dad with their business; I had plans of my own. I had a friend, a lurking beast, a mystery to solve. Life was electrifying. I had convinced myself that I was going on a real-life equivalent of the comic book adventures I missed reading, and that it would be safe, like those adventures invariably were. I can't find it in myself to blame myself, or Ada, for that: we were still children, for a few weeks more at least.

The matter closed for the moment, Ada stood up and said, 'Come on, let's go.' She could only sit still when she was reading.

'In five minutes.'

'Nope.' She took me by a hand and hauled me up. 'Now.'

She guided me to the shore. Water lapped my feet, then my heels, then my knees, and slapped my stomach. There I stopped, as I'd done every single time. I couldn't accept that anymore. I was an occult detective, a badass adventurer willing to go where angels feared to tread. Ada and I were not easily rattled, we were not cautious. We were the kind of people who leap into the unknown to come back unharmed and, if anything, amused.

I had to outrun my fears. Acting on an impulse, I let go of Ada's hand and threw myself into the water, with my sunglasses on. I took a stroke, then another: I was swimming. I was just going straight ahead, as if I could see, as if nothing had changed since last summer. I was floating. I was flying, suspended in a world fundamentally different from the one I knew. I couldn't hear with water in my ears, I couldn't smell with water in my nose. I was lost again, going ahead blinder than ever before. But it was my choice; I was leaping into this new kind of darkness because I wanted to and not because I had to. I swam out to where I couldn't touch the bottom, and I felt elated, free, and taken care of. The sea held me like a crowd does a rockstar, or a parent a newborn baby. I changed swimming into paddling, only my head above water. 'Ada,' I called. 'Ada, where are you?'

'Here,' her voice came, from my left-hand side. She was laughing.

I dived in, let the water submerge me completely, and swam to her.

Around two weeks, or a little more, must have passed before I managed to snap the negative I keep between the pages of *Moby-Dick*. Obviously, I don't care about the print, but the film had been there with me when reality broke down, and by holding it I reach out to the boy I was. You never know when you will need a talisman.

Those weeks are a marmalade of conversations, flavours, scents, all jumbled together in my memory. It is a mystery how we never manage to pack as much living into winter as we do into summer, when apparently we idle around doing little else than play and rest. Days last for ever, but they end too soon, as if each of them were a whole life lived, from birth to death, to rebirth the next morning. Winter hours might be busy, but summer hours are bottomless.

I swam every day. It was the first sport of any kind I did since the curtain fell, and I had energy to spare. The soreness in my muscles after a long swim made me feel human again. I didn't see much of Ferdi. We were civilised with each other, barely. We exchanged words over meals and when strictly necessary, but by and large we ignored each other. He would spend the bulk of the day with the builders, then he would go to the beach, and he would be out late at night with his friends. I never heard him slip back into his room before the early hours of morning. If he was old enough to earn his food, he was old enough to do as he pleased with his free time. He showed up at work on time, unfailingly, and our parents had to bite back their reprimands.

They were too busy, anyway, to mind him. They had works to oversee, decisions to make. New habits to create for the family. The house kept changing around me; doors that existed the day before were nowhere to be found after a night's sleep, walls appeared, hallways vanished, and I could not be certain if the routes I learnt today would still be viable tomorrow. I was living in a liquid world; the masseria shifted and moved all around me like a boundless sea, with no walls, only waves. I was coming to terms with that.

Sometimes Dad would drag me with him on his errands, because, he believed, I needed to get on with learning the family business (he spoke as if he were an old hand at that). He wanted me to assist him with his pep talks to Quarta, which he invariably thought had gone pretty swell. I remember one particular excruciating occasion when he took me to a tile shop. He wanted my help to pick tiles for one of the bathrooms.

'How can I possibly help you with that?' I asked.

'Why shouldn't you?' he answered, in the can-do voice he had borrowed from American films.

We spent what felt like entire geologic epochs in the shop, with him describing tile after tile, asking for my opinion. Conversations stopped around us; strangers commented on how cute we were, what a nice scene we cut, complimenting my strength and my dad's unconquerable spirit, I wanted to beat them all with a large hammer and feed them to the dogs. I wasn't any help with deciding which colours and materials would give floors the right rustic vibe, so all that was left for me to do was shuffle on my feet uselessly, make the noises I knew would keep Dad happy, and wish for it to be over with soon.

Time in summer takes on a ritual quality, in the way any action repeated more than once becomes a venerable tradition, something *you used to do in the summer*. When I think back, it seems to me that I used to go shopping with Dad regularly, that there were hundreds of those agonising trips, rather than the handful there must have been.

That wasn't the only tradition originating in July of '96. Another, more pleasant, started with me taking my brand-new guitar in its brand-new case to Ada's place, on an afternoon filled with the eager scent coming before a summer rain. I turned into Ada's driveway while the first fat drops started to fall. I was wearing cargo shorts; I always did now, the camera tucked in one of the oversized side pockets. Secrets are the most exciting thing you can have.

'In the nick of time,' Giuseppe Guadalupi said when I came up to the house. Ada popped in to say hi, and returned to read outside, under a lean-to roof, where, she explained, she could enjoy the rain. Her father and I went to his study on the first floor. 'Opposite Ada's room,' he said, in good humour. 'Go figure.' He opened the door, letting out a cloud of leather, pipe smoke, and the same strong aftershave his skin exuded. 'I arranged for us to sit by the window. I like summer rains too.'

'That makes three of us.'

Following the pelting of rain, I got to the window, beneath which I touched a wicker chair with a soft cushion on the seat. I sat, put the case on my knees, opened it to take out the guitar.

'I laid out some snacks on the table,' Giuseppe Guadalupi said. He picked up an object (his own instrument, I figured) and sat in front of me. 'Iced tea too. Ada tells me that is another shared passion.'

'That's true. Thank you.' I tested the coffee table, touched a ceramic bowl full of *taralli*, another with olives, a little dish for the cores, two squared chunky glasses, an ice-cold bottle.

Giuseppe Guadalupi started strumming. 'How are your parents?'

'They're good.'

'Ferdi?'

'Well.' I wasn't sure what to say. I was angry at my brother, but I didn't mean to come out as judgemental, and uncool. I opted for, 'He's fine.'

'Can I see your Gibson?'

'Sure.'

He put his own guitar somewhere to pick up mine. 'And do you mind if I tune it?'

'You'd do me a favour, Mr Guadalupi,' I said, addressing him formally, in the third person.

'Friends call me by my name.'

'Giuseppe.'

'That's better.'

I listened to him tune the instrument; at intervals he would let out a satisfied noise, until he said, 'Here. It is ready.'

I reached out and found smooth wood. I was almost afraid to take back the guitar, to spoil its newfound perfection.

'Let me repeat it once more,' Giuseppe Guadalupi said. 'I am no music teacher. I tried with Ada, but it didn't catch.'

'She says music doesn't do it for her.'

'Which begs the question: Is she really a daughter of mine?' He chuckled. 'That's a great guitar you have there, Luca. Your father is a man of taste.'

'He must have had some help.'

'I thought he was musical.'

'He thinks that too.'

'Right,' Giuseppe Guadalupi said, embarrassment shading his voice. 'Let's begin, shall we? When I learnt, I started by practising scales. We can do that, or we can skip directly to songs if you prefer.'

'What's best?'

'The first way is the proper one, but in practice, it is more fun with songs. If you catch the bug, formal practice will follow naturally.'

'Let's do songs, then.'

'Okay. Simple ones, that is, the only ones I can play decently. "Eleanor Rigby"?'

'Sure,' I said.

We got to work, rain in the background. My fingers were clumsy; they couldn't press on the position markers decisively enough, and they couldn't find their way quickly enough (or at all). The strings cut into my skin. Giuseppe Guadalupi came behind me, took my fingers in his own to guide them to the right place, and when I tried on my own and missed the mark, he gently took my fingers again and put them in place. He said I had to get a sense of the guitar's neck, that my hands, not my brain, were to learn how to move along it. He said sight is useless anyway to playing guitar. I trusted him completely. He was in this respect the polar opposite of his daughter: while Ada had an ever-present edge to her – you knew she would have your back, but you also knew she would get you into trouble to begin with – her father, like all capable doctors, gave you a sense of being in safe hands.

'That's good!' he said. It was an overgenerous assessment: after an hour of attempts, I had managed to string two chords together, badly, playing the song's opening chorus, more or less, that heartbreaking reminder of the lonely people among us.

I waved my hand, cracked my fingers; they had gone stiff.

'Tired?' he asked.

'A little.'

'The first weeks feel like punching a wall: your hands bleed and the wall doesn't show so much as a scratch.'

'No, it was fun.'

'You're being polite. It takes practice to make it fun, a lot of practice and then some. Mind,' he added, 'there is nothing wrong with being polite.'

'I know about practice.' It occurred to me then that the way I learn how to navigate a new environment is similar to the way a musician learns how to play a new song. I made the comparison aloud.

'Clever,' Giuseppe commented. 'I hope you don't mind me saying so, Luca, but your experience of the world is nearly impossible to imagine for me.'

'It was nearly impossible to imagine for me too, until not so long ago.'

'Adjusting must have been painful.'

Adjusting must have been painful. Had he done nothing else, Giuseppe Guadalupi would have had me with those five words, which recognised my pain, and allowed me to express it. 'I'm still in the process.'

'You make it seem easy though! You come here on your own. You find windows and chairs without hesitation. I'm impressed.'

It was a sincere compliment, delivered plainly, without any trace of ready-made compassion. 'Thanks,' I said.

'If you set your mind on learning guitar, it's going to be a cinch after what you've done. *You* will be giving *me* lessons before next summer.'

A strange lump came to my throat, not exactly happy, not exactly sad. I wanted to say something which would show Giuseppe Guadalupi how much I appreciated what he was doing for me. 'I cannot understand what problem Grandpa could have had with you,' I blurted out.

Giuseppe held his breath; the patter of rain had stopped too. The room emptied out and I was alone. Then time flowed again. 'Frankly, Luca, me neither. I suspect he couldn't let go of the issues he had with my father.'

'What kind of issues?'

'Your family doesn't have its own version of the story?'

'If they do, they never told me.'

'Then it wouldn't be right for me to tell you ours.'

'Please. I can do my thinking for myself.'

'You put me in a tight spot here. I know very little, and that little was filtered through Dad. Whatever I told you, it would be misleading. And...' He paused. 'The last thing I want is to drive wedges in your family, Luca. Do you know what I mean?'

'We're good at doing that without any help from others.'

Giuseppe opened the window. The rain had left the air clean and crisp like a t-shirt fresh out of the drawer. 'I don't think Don Ferdinando was a bad man,' he said. 'He was a man of another time: his South was different to ours. You find it lonesome now, you should have seen it the way it was. A lot of people couldn't read; many didn't speak Italian. To this day we are not the biggest fans of laws, but back then? The central government and its rules didn't even come into the picture, not when it mattered. The South took care of itself. There were two centres of power, and they were the Church and old surnames. Your mother's surname is old, Luca. Your family used to have land. It was one of the local powers, a long time ago.'

'I know that.'

'That power had almost all vanished by the time your grandpa was born, gone with the land. And my surname, it is old too, it is local, but we were never rich or influential. Things went the other way for us, my folks went up as yours went down. My grandfather made some money – not a lot, mind, but enough to buy a small plot of what land you had left, and build a home there, when Don Ferdinando was but a child.'

'May I say something?'

'Of course.'

'No offence, but I heard that your grandfather didn't *buy* the land. He won it at cards.'

'See? My family say one thing, yours another. I wouldn't swear on my version, and I'd suggest you be wary of yours. We will never know. What is certain is that the land did exchange hands, and the relationship between our families was shaky at best because of that. But then your grandfather and my dad became friends, like brothers if you want to believe the old-timers. And they remained such for a good many years.'

'Then – what?'

'Ask five people in town, you will get seven different answers. As far as I understand, they were drawn apart by the one thing that always draws men apart in the end.'

'Love?'

'Money. Dad's version was that Ferdinando...' Giuseppe paused again. 'That he was using the Masseria del Vento for certain unlawful activities. Dad objected to that, and your grandfather made the point, not entirely incorrect, that it was easy for my dad to judge, sitting as he was on a nice little income that would keep his family well-fed through the worst of winters. Before you ask: Dad wasn't forthcoming with details about what Ferdinando was contriving in his farm. My guess – and please take this with a pinch of salt – is that it was involving some kind of contraband.'

'Grandpa wasn't a criminal,' I said, though I wasn't so sure.

'It was a different world, Luca, truly and utterly different. There are countless old stories in this country, and if some have been let fall by the wayside, so be it.' I heard him stand up. 'Enough with ghosts: the living are worthier company. Let's go and bother Ada, shall we?'

The guitar lessons with Giuseppe became a cherished ritual. I would go to his place most days, spend some time with him, and go back home feeling stronger. We would play, and talk; he asked about my life in Turin, about my plans for next year, and he actually let me speak, and rarely offered his opinion. He was almost as good a listener as Ada – the polar opposite of my parents, who heard my voice but didn't listen to my words, because they were older and wiser, and had accomplished so much in life. Giuseppe Guadalupi offered me more than guitar lessons; he offered me, for the first time in my life, a model of the man I might want to become.

I had, and blew, my first chance to ask Uncle Mario about unusual goings-on in the masseria at around the time I took the photograph. It could be the previous day, or the day before. I remember for sure it was on the morning in which the movers' lorry arrived from Turin with everything we owned, jewels and trinkets and all, thus marking the finality of the revolution in our lives.

A car's rumble rolled in when the movers had just emptied their coffee cups and were setting off to work. Mum said, with a spring in her voice, 'It's Mario!' and Dad proclaimed he was going to put a fresh pot on the stove. In Turin we were not used to people swinging by unannounced; Grandpa taught us that when that happens, you make them coffee. Dad had taken the lesson in the same way he took every bit of Southern lore, as a picturesque rule to apply rather than a way to live.

Uncle Mario's car groaned with relief when he climbed out of it. Everything about him was large: he had an enormous belly that he let children play like a drum, a booming voice, an uproarious laugh, a villa overflowing with friends and acquaintances and second and third cousins which he seemed to produce at will, like a magician extracting an endless supply of bunnies from top hats. He would eat for three and pay for everyone. The old-fashioned sharp cologne he wore, after Grandpa, was the stuff of family legends: Uncle Mario claimed he had bought the leftover stock when the producer had gone out of business, and he prayed it would last him until the time he shuffled off this mortal coil. To this day I couldn't say whether that story was true or not, but I swear I only ever smelt that cologne on Grandpa and him. Blind or sighted, it was impossible not to notice Mario as the biggest, loudest, liveliest presence at any table. Dad treated him with what he believed was subtly humorous contempt, as he did with men he felt threatened by.

'Stefi!' Uncle Mario called to Mum, his voice rising above the builders' ruckus and the movers' noises. 'Is this a good moment? I can come later if it's not!'

'It's always a good moment,' Mum said, which was true. She was happy in her brother's company, happier, I came to understand in time, than she was with Dad.

'Hello, Aunt Stefania,' a honed female voice said. 'Hello, Luca.'

'Maddalena?' I asked. 'Is that you?'

'Yes.'

Maddalena was Uncle Mario and Aunt Gemma's teenage daughter, a girl a year younger than Ferdi. She had a brother, called Ferdinando too, four years her senior, who went to law school in Lecce like his father before him. He counted among his numerous accomplishments the founding of the local Rotaract Club. Maddalena and Ferdinando were the epitome of perfection in my mother's eyes: well-behaved, properly dressed, they had top grades, never spoke out of turn and were unfailingly devout.

'Devout? When was the last time *you* went to Mass?' Ferdi asked once, after Mum had sung the well-known litany of our cousins' virtues.

'I don't have time,' Mum answered. 'What I am saying here is that Ferdinando and Maddalena respect their parents.'

'We respect ours, by *not* being devout, just like you.'

Mum's best attempts notwithstanding, Ferdi and I got along well with our cousins. I suspected Ferdi had been making out with Maddalena in a past summer, but I was too shy to ask, and it was out of the question that the truth would out on its own. Fools who might start to hazily entertain the idea of spreading gossip about our cousins would find themselves impaled, burnt and forgotten before they had time to put their tongue to work. Maddalena and Ferdinando took after their mother, the beautiful and terrible Gemma Dicastri, and after their father too.

'Wait!' Uncle Mario said. 'I'll give you a hand with that!'

There was a grunting and a grinding.

'What's going on?' I asked.

'Dad has grabbed a couch,' Maddalena's voice explained. 'And now he and a mover are hauling it out of the lorry... hauling it out... and it's out.'

'The friendliest couch I ever sat on!' puffed Uncle Mario. 'Be careful with that, it doesn't look like much, but it's where buttocks go when they go to heaven,' he said, presumably to the movers. 'Give it a go before you leave and you'll see what I mean.' Then to me, 'Luca! You're tanned. We're gaining the true Southern colours at last.'

'Sit down,' Mum said, laughing. 'Carlo is making coffee.'

'I'll go help him.' I heard Uncle Mario's steps disappear inside, his voice calling my father's name.

Soon we were all sitting on the porch, with coffee, apricots, watermelon and peaches. Dad said that Ferdi was at work, to which Uncle Mario commented, 'You did it, then.'

'For his own good,' Mum specified.

Uncle Mario had brought us presents from Crete, where he had been renting a family home: jars of honey, bottles of ouzo and a big amphora – thoroughly modern, not one of those faux-classic kitsch horrors – which Gemma had eyed in a Rethymno workshop and everybody agreed was a thing of beauty. I keep it in the living room, and often receive compliments for it.

Mum asked, 'How's Gemma anyway?'

'In a bad mood about Ferdinando leaving.'

'Where is he going?'

'Oxford. He's staying with a family there, studying English.'

'*Oxford.*' Dad savoured the sound of it. 'That is nice.'

It was only another summer school of English, of course, and it could have been located in Oxford or in a nondescript Essex town and it wouldn't have made a lick of difference, but that word had a ring to it, *Oxford*, an undeniable magic. I could hear the scales in Dad's mind weigh Uncle Mario's Ferdinando, who was rubbing shoulders with the great minds of the age in an august city of learning, against our own Ferdi, who was laying bricks in our dusty backyard.

Maddalena must have detected that too. 'Getting to more interesting topics,' she said, 'is it true what they say?'

'What do they say?' Mum asked.

'That Luca and Ada Guadalupi are best friends.'

The question made me feel put on the spot. 'Who's *they*?' I asked.

'Oh, just about everybody.'

'But I don't know anybody!'

'They know you,' Maddalena said, managing to make it sound like praise. 'You two have been seen together.'

'We are friends,' I admitted. 'As a matter of fact, she'll be here any minute.'

'To go to the beach,' Dad explained.

Maddalena clapped her hands once. 'Marvellous!'

Uncle Mario said, 'So peace is made between the tribes.'

'Are you aware of any reason why it shouldn't be?' Dad asked.

Uncle Mario pondered, then said, 'I'd have made an opening myself, but it was a delicate matter on a lot of levels, what with my father being his stubborn self in the face of that awful tragedy. God bless the children for doing what we can't.'

I said, 'Tragedy?'

The others blinked out of existence, then Uncle Mario said, 'Ouch! Sorry, Stefi, I was taking for granted that Luca knew.'

I felt an emotion akin to panic. In my experience, when adults kept things from you they did it because those things would hurt, and they were under the illusion that by hiding those things they'd keep you safe, which was never the case. 'I knew *what*?'

Mum said, 'We had to tell him sooner or later.'

A shout came from deep in my throat. 'Stop pretending I'm not here!'

A shuffling of bodies, a dragging of chairs, a clinging of cups. Dad said, 'Don't be like your brother.'

I found the willpower to conjure up a half-hearted *I'm sorry*, and repeated the question: 'What's this tragedy?'

Mum said, 'Ada had a sister.'

I was going to answer, *No, she's an only child*, but as my lips parted I registered the tense Mum had used, *had*, and I froze.

'She died before Ada was born. She was… Mario, do you remember how old the girl was?'

Dad said, 'Five.'

'Four,' Uncle Mario corrected him. 'But it doesn't matter.'

'Do you want to tell the story?' Mum asked. 'You know it better than me.'

Uncle Mario lowered his voice, nuanced it with a note of respect. 'Not much of a story,' he said. 'The Guadalupis had this big, *enormous*, black dog, a sweetie by everyone's reckoning. Akela, he was called, like the wise wolf in *The Jungle Book*. He'd never hurt anyone, never got nasty. Little children would ride him like a horse. People joked that if a thief tried to sneak past Akela, Akela would jump on him – to lick his face off. You've seen that kind of dog: bumbling gentle giants.' Uncle Mario paused to grab something from the table and bite into it with a crunchy noise. He swallowed and said, 'When Bianca found she was pregnant again, she and Giuseppe had a private celebration in the garden, here, in their summer home. There were no warning signs. The child must have touched him in the wrong way, or it might have been the excitement, nobody knows, but Akela snapped. All of a sudden. They say the child was pulling his ears, as she'd done countless times, when Akela turned, and didn't lick her face off, no, he *bit* it off. There was screaming, I imagine. What I heard is that it wasn't just a bite, no, Akela clenched his jaw around her head and didn't let go. Giuseppe tried to pry them apart, but the dog was far too strong. Bianca got hold of the knife she had been using for cutting the bruschetta bread and sunk it into the dog's neck. It was messy, and – too late. By the time the ambulance came, dog and little girl were both dead. Hell, probably the girl was already done for before Bianca even got to the chopping board. And that's all there is to the story.'

A big black dog.

'Didn't Bianca almost have a miscarriage?' Dad said.

A big black dog.

'Almost,' Mum said. 'But it turned out fine – that, at least: they were blessed with another girl. With Ada.'

A big black dog.

Uncle Mario said, 'Luca, can you believe that some folks, not a lot, but some, blame Giuseppe and Bianca? Dad was the most vocal of them. Said they shouldn't have let a little girl play with that colossus. If you ask me, that's bollocks, and excuse my French. It was rotten luck, with no reasons behind it, no meaning, and it couldn't have been avoided any more than being struck by a bolt from the blue can be avoided. Children play with pets and it's fine, more than fine, ninety-nine per cent of the time. Dad let me mess around with *billy goats*, let alone dogs, that old plaster saint. Remember this, Luca: It's tempting to call another man the cause of his own tragedy. It takes out the sting of fear. Blame the victim and you can go on believing that tragedy couldn't come your way, because you're careful, because you're quick-witted. Because you're *better*. Truth is you're not. Nobody is. We're all frail, all the same.'

A big black dog.

A beast had been killed in those fields thirteen years before; a beast wandered in the same fields thirteen years later. In my mind the dots were joined.

A thick hedge had grown between Ada and me; I could barely hear her talk from behind foliage. I was studying this new space in which I found myself, all too conscious that I could stumble upon thorns any moment. When we went to the beach that day, when we swam together and when we got gelato from Chocolate Delight, every word she said came to me from an unexpected angle, as if spoken in a language slightly askew, which I got, but not completely. What I had learnt, not even about her past, but her family's, had caused a shift in the way I understood Ada Guadalupi. I had to make peace with the fact that I barely knew this girl, that we were not old mates; we were not a tried-and-tested detective duo. We were Eleanor Rigby and Father McKenzie.

'Are you all right?' she said.

'Sure, why?'

'You're acting strange.'

'I'm not.'

She hadn't exactly lied, but she hadn't trusted me with her whole story either. I wished I could find a way to tell her that I knew, that we could talk. A hundred times I found myself on the verge of speaking out, and a hundred times I kept mum. We had stilted conversations, wooden interactions. We reached one of those mutually unsatisfying agreements by which she pretended to believe me that nothing was wrong, and I pretended to believe her that she bought it. She must have made the same connection I had, between her sister's murder and my encounters, but if she hadn't broached the subject, I wasn't sure I could. Death, no matter how old, never ceases to be a big deal.

So I found myself alone at dusk, dragging my guitar in search of a place where I could practise. It was that indefinite hour when the weight of the day is lifting up: the soundscape of sunshine is winding down and that of the moon hasn't ramped up yet. I was downcast, but there was also a degree of mannerism to my getting around: I acted the part of the mystery man rambling at sunset, a lonesome cowboy with dust on his boots and a ballad in his heart, though my boots were actually flip-flops and I couldn't get through a basic tune to save my life. The detective, the artist, the dutiful son, that summer I was trying on identities for size. The guitar was a prop; I acted for an audience of foxes, cats and owls, and for my mind's eye.

I settled under the carob tree, tried a few chords, got frustrated. The wooden jigsaw of the bark was unyielding against my back, roots and rocks jutting out to stab the fleshy parts of my legs. I couldn't play like this. I was cursed with an impossibility of ever finding the right conditions to practise: it was too hot, or I didn't have time, or I couldn't sit comfortably. So far music had turned out to be just something new I could suck at. There was an undeniable romance to the general idea though – the blind musician, the softly-spoken aloof guitarist. I stood up and headed to *Da Klub*. I hadn't tried playing there. I hadn't returned since the day I had shown it to Ada.

I stopped at the door; someone was inside.

The grudging dragging of feet, the resentful breathing, the anxious sucking from a cigarette and the blowing out of smoke like a weight let fall: those sounds were Ferdi. The smoke was tobacco and another substance, much sweeter, which I couldn't yet name as skunk. For the briefest moment I felt the urge to go inside and let bygones be bygones, but when I thought of the awkwardness that would follow, I turned my back. Anger was turning into a habit.

I swept my cane on the dirt. If I wasn't going to be in the same room with Ferdi, I was going to get as far as possible from him, where he couldn't hear me practise. I wouldn't give him the pleasure of sniggering at me from his safe seat in *Da Klub*.

I reached the vineyard; I entered.

It was pleasant walking there. Sunshine had slow-cooked the grapes during the day, and with the air getting cooler they released a sugary scent to get drunk on. The vines were growing in size and strength with the progress of the season; their coarse leaves crowded the corridors between lines, tickling me. I stopped in my tracks. I took a lungful of the scented air, and kept it inside before letting it go. I understood why Grandpa would stay here, even alone, rather than move into town with Uncle Mario.

When I took the next breath a different kind of sweet scent had sneaked in, disguising itself behind the grapes. It was the same sweetness I had sensed at the door of the clubhouse, laced with a faint, not disagreeable, memory of tobacco.

'Ferdi?' I called.

The answer was Ferdi's dragging of feet, his sucking from a cigarette. Leaves rustled when his body, heavier, thicker than mine, moved them apart, coming my way, in the same furrow.

He couldn't not have heard me. He was pretending not to, and I was sick of people pretending.

'Ferdi!' I said.

He grunted an answer, not quite words but almost, as he did when he was in a bad mood; and he almost grunted in the right voice.

I repeated, 'Ferdi…?'

The sounds behind me kept coming closer, those sounds which were almost, but not quite, Ferdi.

I felt a jolt of terror. 'You're not my brother!' I shouted. 'Who are you?'

The feral smell burnt bright.

I immediately let go of my guitar, and squatted as if to pick up a rock. The sounds didn't falter, and the wind rose.

I turned my back, dashed as fast as I could the other way. So far the wanderer had seemed to ignore me, but this time, this time it had tried to *deceive* me, and to what ends?

There was nothing but open fields in the direction I was going.

I took a left and squeezed between two vines. The jagged edges of the leaves brushed against my skin. I squeezed between two more, then another two. With one hand I swept the cane, with the other I moved aside grapes and offshoots. A twig grazed my cheek, a grape burst between my fingers, and this stupid image came to my mind that I had squeezed an eyeball, that the grapes were all eyeballs, swelling, getting ripe on the gnarled branches of age-old vines. I suppressed a retch, which left an acidic feeling up my throat and in my mouth. The rustling and stomping fell into step with me, picking up when I picked up, slowing down when I went slower. It was less like Ferdi's step now and more like the relentless *tap, tap* I'd heard in the fields and on my porch. The wanderer knew I was the mouse in this game.

I had felt so smug, drafting plans with Ada in the padded safety of the Little Pinewood, where it took nothing to be brave. I heard surf and smelt seawater. I had nowhere to go, nowhere to hide, and nothing to fight the wanderer with.

I had the camera though. Its hard edges pressed against my leg from the side pocket in the cargos. I stopped. I turned.

Going against everything that my heart and brain were screaming to me, I brought my hand to the pocket, extracted the camera, and pointed it ahead of me. My legs were aching to take me away, and the wanderer was coming. I could not be sure there was enough light for the cheap camera to take a clear picture. I engaged the flash with the thumb, the way Ada had shown me.

I heard a cracking and a rubbing when a body much thicker than mine broke out of the same vines through which I had swished a moment before.

All sounds came to a halt.

I pressed the camera button, with the click of the shutter, the whir of the flash. Next there came a snarl, and the camera was slapped out of my hand. I peed myself a little, backed off. Something pushed me backwards. I had always envisioned the wanderer as an animal, but the way I was pushed, the pressure on my chest, it felt human, and in the endless time I took to fall, I thought that it could be my brother, that it had always been my brother.

I fell on soft sand. I swung my cane in front and above me with an inchoate war cry. And the smell and the sounds transformed again, until they were nearly Ferdi, and they swirled and churned, and for a heartbeat they were Grandpa's cologne, they were the jangling of the massive bunch of keys he kept fastened with a snap link to a belt loop. They faded to nothingness, and I was alone.

I gasped for air; a brackish scent invaded my nostrils. Waves were gently coming ashore. I was sitting on sand.

I was sitting on sand.

I was not in the vineyard.

I sank my fingers down and brought up a handful of grains of sand, held together by dampness. I scanned the surroundings with ears and nose. The wanderer was gone; or it was keeping out of reach. I heard waves returning ashore. I got on my feet, too puzzled to remember to be afraid. I tapped my cane and it sank into sand. I swept the cane for the camera, but didn't find it. A cool breeze blew.

There was sand in my flip-flops, sand stuck to my hands and to the backs of my legs. I headed towards the gentle sound of waves, until I reached flat rocks, a little slippery. I took off the flip-flops to get better purchase with my naked feet, and walked on cautiously. I almost slipped on seaside lichen. I advanced slower still, testing each step for the slick lichen. I reached the shore.

Swash and backwash sounded like a healthy little girl breathing in her sleep. I dipped a toe in the water, and found it delightfully lukewarm, the way seawater gets right after sunset. I was going to sit on the rock and dunk my feet, but I stopped midway through.

What *was* this water anyway?

The sea, a lake, a pool, something else entirely; I couldn't be sure. Had I been sighted, I still wouldn't know: the fluid in which I'd dipped a toe could feel like my sea, smell like my sea, sound like my sea, it could taste and even look like my sea, but that didn't make it my sea. Nameless predators could be lurking there. The fluid itself could be a predator, alive and hungry; it could swallow me whole.

Hadn't the wanderer masqueraded as Ferdi, just a moment ago?

I stepped back. The rocks could be hungry too; the wind could be hungry.

Every part of my body deemed that I was on a beach, no different from any beach on a calm day after sunset; the seagulls cried their last calls, the crickets warmed up for their nightly concert. If this was a beach, its only remarkable feature was its being empty of any human-made sound, but even that wasn't necessarily odd, depending on how long after sunset it was. A secluded stretch like the Little Pinewood could empty out quickly, people wanting to go home to shower, eat, and get ready for a night out.

'Is anybody there?' I called.

My own voice startled me. Only the wind answered.

I had no food, and worse, no water. The air was fresh now, but next day the sun would be fierce, and I'd dehydrate quickly. A part of me laughed at those narrow-minded fears: I was stranded in an impossible space and the first thing I worried about was breakfast. But – how can I explain? – even though I was acutely aware of the extreme strangeness of it all, it was a theoretical awareness. What I sensed on my skin, what I felt with my body, was a beach. Almost.

A discordant note was getting in, one which I could not quite place. It was like listening to a well-known song, from a well-known vinyl you have owned for decades and of which you have studied every scratch and every quirk, and suddenly noticing a word in the song has changed. Only one word, and you are positive it is not your memory playing tricks, but the word has changed and you cannot demonstrate to yourself it was different before. This is how the beach was not entirely a beach.

I walked back to the point where I had fallen on my bum, and further on, until sand became more compact underfoot, the way it did on the dunes on which bushes and flowers and low, knobbly trees grew. My hands touched vegetation of some sort, often spiky, sometimes smooth, and my thin flip-flops walked on something like ragged pebbles. I bent to pick one up, and I brought it to my nose. It was a pod of sea daffodil; Grandpa would scoff at the tourists who mistook those large black pods for charcoal. I marched on, surrounded by a rising scent of juniper, and I got to a place where the ground became hard-packed.

I squatted, rested my hands on the ground. It was dusty, bumpy. I walked on, almost on all fours, touching the floor with my hands at intervals, until I got to sand again, with vegetation growing on it. I gave it some thought, and decided the dusty strip might be a road, though unpaved. I stretched my ears for cars, but didn't hear any.

I heard something else, from my left.

It was distant, barely audible – a sound of fiddle, and drums, and voices singing words I couldn't discern. They had the cheerfulness of carrion birds partying over carnage. They filled me with dread. They gave me that sinking feeling, like the mouth of a pit spreading out on the top of your belly, that feeling you get when you wake up to a presence in your home and hear an intruder work the handle of your bedroom door. The thought of joining in the revelry made me think of spying on my parents having sex, of trapping a cat's tail under one foot and kicking it to death with the other, of smashing a hammer on a baby's head. It was wrong on a fundamental level, beyond any rules and laws and opinions. Whatever happened to me, whatever I did now or later in life, I did not want to join in the revelry.

I turned in the other direction, and walked down the road. The track went up and then down, and when the revellers' tunes couldn't reach me anymore, it was like breathing again after holding your head underwater for almost too long. Another kind of melody came from my right – smooth jazz.

I knew where I was.

I walked further on, until my cane found a certain column and a certain creaky gate, and I turned right, onto the driveway of the Masseria del Vento, home.

'Oh my God, Luca!' Dad's voice was thankful and angry. 'Where were you?'

I was shaking so violently my legs gave way.

I lay in bed for three nights and three days.

I have the vaguest recollection of that time. I ran a fever; Giuseppe Guadalupi was in and out of my room, taking my temperature, applying *bagnoli* – rags folded and soaked in water and vinegar – on my forehead, whispering prayers to Saints Cosma and Damiano when nobody was listening. I felt hot and stuffy and also cold and shivery, my chest sweating while my teeth chattered. I was fed broth and water, and I did manage to get up from bed when I needed the loo, although the journey was as perilous as it was exhausting.

As always, I was sighted in my dreams. I recall separate images: a sea the wrong shade of blue, an orange in the sky which was not the sunset, sand fine and white. I recall the masseria as it was when Grandpa was alive. The feral smell came and went. Ferdi did too, bringing me food, changing the water in my glass, or just staying in the room, a presence of nervous steps, sweat and stale cigarettes. I thought that Ada visited as well, but she flew in from an open window, and I could clearly discern the fine features of her face, her curly hair floating around her head like the rays of a black sun, so I knew it was another dream.

In the animal kingdom (and beyond, perhaps) humans are the boxers who can take it. We are not especially strong or quick or swift, we are nothing much really, but when they knock us down, we get back on our feet; we might take some time, and yet we always get back on our feet. In the millennia we've been around on this much older planet we have gone through famines, wars, epidemics, earthquakes and world-shattering volcanic eruptions, and every time we ended up with our face in the mud, every time, without fail, we got back on our feet. In the course of our lives, as individuals, we are hit by defeat and illness and heartbreak, and what we do is count our wounds, heal what we can, grieve what we've lost and get back on our feet. The unthinkable happens; we take its measures; we adapt; we move on.

On the fourth day, I woke up feeling fine.

A presence was with me. 'Ferdi?' I called.

My brother answered, 'Scrawny! How are you?' and it was really him.

'I'm okay, I think.'

He hugged me, and didn't let go for a long while.

Things had changed and they hadn't. I had lived through an event larger than my imagination and no less strange than death, and the world was unmoved. Reality was thin ice and it could crack again any moment, but while I trod carefully, everybody else was a fool stomping up and down. No human being could witness what I witnessed and go on with their life as they did before, a little scared perhaps, a little inspired, but fundamentally the same. No, that event, and what followed, defined the rest of my life more – a lot more – than blindness ever did. How could it not? I was never the same after hearing the revellers. Even if I wanted to, I couldn't be.

There was only another time in my life when I felt like that: last year, the morning after Mum died, when I woke up with my heart in tatters to a world that had not taken notice. Sparrows were chirping, newspapers were out. The season hadn't turned overnight. It was obscene. Things change and they don't; after you leave, another person will sit down and get coffee in your special place at the bar. There will be queues on Judgement Day, and folks complaining they would do a better job of it.

Most of us just while away our time on Earth in a soft stupor, without ever having to question, and I mean *seriously* question, what we know to be true, plain and obvious. Such notions became moot to me when I sank my hand into damp sand. I have met through the years a few stragglers like me, people who have tasted a deeper tang of reality. I have heard their often ridiculed accounts on podcasts. You don't get to go home after that, after learning that the world is a flimsy wonder, easily undone, for you have no home to go back to. You may think you do – you may try and act as if you do, but you don't. You know, with a certainty which is not faith but the stark understanding of a fact, that what you thought were the solid stone walls of your house are *trompe l'oeil*, that the laws of nature are a children's game, and even though you might never sense again that deeper tang of reality, it is always there, just out of reach, like the most perfect pear on a branch you will be able to touch next summer, when you'll be taller – if you survive until next summer, that is.

I didn't walk on solid ground anymore.

Nobody does; to say the contrary is a dangerous lie.

'We were worried,' Giuseppe Guadalupi said.

My parents had often pronounced themselves worried about me or Ferdi, but they would infuse the words with the cutting quality of a threat. 'I'm worried for you – so behave, or else.' Giuseppe meant exactly what he said, and I loved him for that. The time I spent with him, with the excuse of our guitar lessons, had become precious to me. Giuseppe was safe, Bianca was safe, even their house, a proper villa with walls which did not change, was safe, unlike the Masseria del Vento, with its ever-shifting boundaries. 'I know.'

'It was my decision not to let Ada come and see you. She will never forgive me, I'm afraid. I didn't want her to see you like that.'

'Like what?'

There was the scratch of a match, and pipe smoke filled my nose with its round mature scent. 'I never doubted you would make it. You are hardy.'

I was pleased he thought me *hardy*. I strummed on my guitar, drawing out a sound like a cat being sick. It was my first lesson since – since whatever had happened to me. 'But if it were another in my place,' I said, fishing for compliments, 'you wouldn't be so sure.'

'You're out of the woods now, and I can speak freely: no, with another one, I wouldn't have been so sure. High fever, loss of consciousness, you were not in a good way.' He inhaled from his pipe. 'Bianca and I were afraid Ada might catch whatever you had. My gut feeling was that it was nothing viral, and I think I was correct.'

'Just heatstroke probably.'

'It wasn't heatstroke.'

I pinched my guitar's strings. 'What are we doing today? Another go at "Eleanor Rigby"?'

'May I ask you something, Luca?'

'Of course.'

'Is there anything you're not telling us?'

And that was the problem with Giuseppe, that is always the problem with people who listen, and observe: they learn more about you than you are comfortable sharing. 'Why are you asking?'

'Why aren't you answering?' Giuseppe said, as a friendly tease.

I came very close to tell him everything then; to unburden myself. I trusted Giuseppe Guadalupi at a fundamental level, because, I understand now, he was a grown-up in a way my father had never been. At the end, the reason why I didn't talk had nothing to do with him and everything to do with Ada: the wanderer was ours, a part of our private world, and to involve others before talking with her would be a betrayal. 'I have nothing to say.'

'When you change your mind, remember, Bianca and I are just next door.'

It was a thought that gave me strength.

Eight days had passed since I had entered the vineyard armed with my guitar and my camera, not a century, only eight days. July had inexorably slid into August, the height of summer, the early days of its decline: the season peaked on the night of the fourteenth, the vigil of the Feast of the Assumption of the Virgin Mary, and on the fifteenth, the Feast proper. I felt strong, and from the next day I would be allowed to the beach again. Meanwhile Ada and I were heading to the vineyard.

We passed the building site, said a quick hi to Ferdi. He tried to start a conversation, but Quarta called him, and he had to go. Ferdi hated every second he spent with Quarta's crew, and the feeling was mutual. 'I'm so happy you guys made peace,' Ada said. 'Feuds are stupid.'

'I took a photo,' I said.

'You mean…'

'Yeah.'

'Luca, that's awesome!'

'And then I lost the camera.'

'How?'

I tapped my cane on the outermost vines. 'The wanderer slapped it out of my hand. I was here, in the vineyard.'

'Was it scary?' Ada said, after a moment.

'Terrifying.' I paused. 'What came afterwards was way worse though.'

'Do I want to know?'

'I need to talk.'

Ada took my hand, put it on her elbow. 'It was a figure of speech. *Of course* I want to know,' she said, as she walked into the vineyard.

I went with her. It was the last thing I wished to do, even in the height of day, even with the ruckus of the works anchoring me to home, but I needed to get the camera back. There was a photograph in it that Ada needed to see, and that I needed to hear described. 'Keep your eyes peeled,' I asked. 'With a bit of luck, the camera will be here somewhere.'

'I don't think the builders stole it.'

'It might have ended up somewhere else.'

'Stop hinting at the story and tell it already.'

I did. I told her the whole story, as I remembered it, fishing for words, going back and forth, correcting myself. It was hard to constrain my memories within an orderly narrative, and to discern between facts and fever dreams. I threw around words like 'beach', 'sea daffodils', 'dirt road', but I wasn't sure then, as I am not sure now, that such clear-cut labels didn't conceal more than they revealed. We let our language grow around the most humdrum aspects of life, and then, when we stumble upon the extraordinary, we use language to pare it down to the commonplace, to what we are comfortable with. I threw around words like 'revellers'.

A cold wave crashed through my body, from head to toe. Those were not fever dreams; those were the fever dreams' *prima causa*.

Ada said, 'And then you got back home?'

'Yup.'

'Just like, walking?'

'Yup.'

'Fuck. I understand why you got ill.'

'I'm thinking my family deserves to know.'

'They won't believe you.'

'I've been running scenarios in my head, and, admittedly, in all of them they pack me off to see your mum. She's a shrink, right?'

'That she is.'

'Your dad might give me a chance, don't you think?'

'What's the point?'

'The wanderer attacked me, and what if it attacks our families next?'

'The wanderer doesn't care about them.'

'How can we take that for granted?'

Ada snorted. 'Well, if you talk to any of them, leave me out of it.'

'Why?'

'Because it's a terrible idea and I want nothing to do with it.'

'But…'

'Just leave me out of it, okay? Is that too much to ask?'

'Chill, it's fine, if that's what you want. At least you believe me.'

'Wait a sec.'

She walked ahead, picked up something, came back, handed it to me. 'Is this your guitar case?'

I ran my hands over the large object. 'Yes!' I said. 'It totally slipped my mind. I dropped it when I met the wanderer. This was the spot, the exact spot it happened. I went straight on for, say, ten metres, and turned left.'

'Through the vines?'

'Through the vines.'

Ada sighed, and we ventured in a tangle of leaves and grapes. Their touch on my skin made me halt. I wanted to puke. The wanderer was chasing me again...

'Luca?'

... I was utterly powerless...

'Luca, are you okay?'

... and I was coming unmoored, floating to a place very far from home.

'Luca!' Ada called for the third time, raising her voice.

'I'm here.' I was back to the present, to my friend. 'I got carried away.'

'This thing scared you stiff, huh?'

'Do you believe me? You didn't answer.'

We walked on. 'I've got the cuts,' she said.

'About that.'

'About that, what?'

'You could have told me.'

'What're you talking about?'

'Your sister.'

Ada's steps slowed down. It took a while for her to say, 'I didn't take you for a big mouth.'

'My uncle told me about her.'

'That's fascinating. It's almost as if people in small towns can't mind their own fucking business.'

162

'Ada, why did you keep it from me?'

'Because it was my business and I wanted to.'

'A dog killed your sister. I told you a giant beast is stalking our fields, and you told me you woke up with cuts on your body, not once, but twice. Don't tell me you didn't put two and two together, because I won't believe you. If the wanderer's Akela…' I let my voice trail off.

'It could eat my face as it did the little angel's?' she asked, angling for a fight.

I shouldn't have answered, but I was thirteen. 'Yes!' I said. 'That.'

'And you'll be coming to the rescue, *hop hop!* on your white stallion?'

'I can help you out.'

'Who do you think you are?'

'All you have.'

'Did I ask for your help? Because I didn't,' Ada exploded. 'I never asked you fuck all! You, or anybody else.' She took a breath. 'Look: Do you remember what you told me about people seeing you as *Luca the blind boy*? Do you remember that? Same goes with me. I'm *poor Ada who lost a sister*. Over and over and over again, I'm *poor Ada who lost a sister*. And the funny thing is, I don't give a damn for my sister. She bit the dust before I was born! *Obviously* I'm sad that a little girl died, and so gruesomely too, but little girls are going to glory all the time. They're being stabbed and shot and thrown off balconies now as we speak, and I'm not responsible for them. I'm not supposed to feel bad personally for each and every one of them. This is no different to me. Do you get what I mean?'

I did; and I felt closer to her for that. 'Remember to look for the camera.'

'It's the same bright yellow as Tweety's arse. If it's around, I won't miss it.'

I chuckled. 'See, we look after each other.'

'I was lying just now.'

'About Tweety's arse?'

'My dead sister. It's not true I feel nothing for her. Actually, I hate her guts.'

'That's… strong.'

'Oh, yeah? She was beautiful, and smart; she spoke her first word at ten months. Can you believe that, *ten months*! Oh, the things she would have done, *had she been given time by our Lord*, in the immortal utterance of Auntie Betta. And she was good with animals, well, not so good towards the end, clearly, but nobody says *that*, and she was obedient, and Don Alfredo, the family priest, was crazy for her, and everybody was crazy for her 'cause she was perfect, Luca, just fuckin' *perfect*. I'll never be like her. I can't be like her. I've got too much of a heartbeat to be perfect.'

'You're good with words.'

'Well, she was better. Before she died she'd already written a sequel to the *Divine Comedy*, the little fucker.'

'What was her name?'

'Your uncle didn't tell you?'

'No.'

'See what I mean? He pities me, *the poor Ada*. He and everybody else.'

'I'm not following.'

'Ada.'

'Ada, what?'

'My sister, she was called Ada.'

That took me by surprise.

Ada went on, 'Mum and Dad couldn't get over their grief and they said, *You know what, let's have another go with the bun we've got ready in the oven.* Makes sense, right? The first Ada had been on the meh side all in all, a wonder, yes, but short-lasting, so they'd try again, with a sturdier specimen. That's what I am: another go. The supermarket glass you drink from, after you smashed the fancy crystal in the sink.'

'It is a little weird,' I admitted after a while.

'My folks are weirdos.'

'You seem tight.'

'We *are* tight, doesn't make them any less weird.'

'I think they care for you very much.'

'I know they care for me, yes, I know. They worry for me, they only want what's best for me, they want to help me reach my full potential *yadda yadda yadda*. Great. But they never agreed to buy me a puppy.'

'What do you want a puppy for?'

'I like dogs.'

'It's understandable if they don't.'

'Again, I know, it makes sense, perfect sense, they've got a truck full of trauma et cetera. Still, at the end of the day, I'm the one who doesn't get the puppy.' She stopped, and the sound of her breath descended. She had bent onto her knees. 'We struck gold, Luca. I spy with my little eye Tweety's arse sticking out of the soil.'

We finished up the roll of film. Ada took photographs of me pretending to play the guitar, dragging it around. 'For the cover of your first album,' she said. I took photographs of her: she would talk, and I would point the camera at her voice and snap. The fruits of prickly pears, she said, were ripening in a riot of colours, and we took photos of those too. We took photos of us together in funny poses, funny to us, that is. She left in time to make a run to the village and leave the camera at the shop before it shut, to have the film printed, the sooner, the better.

The next thing I did was a mistake. I caught up with Ferdi.

I waited for the end of the day's shift, plodding through *Moby-Dick* under the carob tree. I heard the builders pack their stuff and exchange what I thought must be goodbyes – I didn't speak the local dialect at the time, so I couldn't be sure. Ferdi's voice was the only one pronouncing words intelligible to me. 'Scrawny,' he called, exhausted, as he came closer.

There was an awkwardness between us. We hadn't wasted time on sentimental blabber – we were not wimps – and we simply pretended the last few weeks hadn't happened. Neither of us was a good actor.

'How was your day?' I asked.

He quaffed some drink. 'Go with another question.'

'Okay, I was wondering – do you have any plans?'

'I was thinking the beach. It can wait if you want to hang out.'

I said, 'Just a walk. It won't be long.'

'Where?'

'Up the road.'

'I'm not coming to the Guadalupis',' Ferdi said.

'No, really, just a walk.'

'There's nothing there.'

'Please?'

It didn't take a lot to convince him; like me, he wanted to spend time together. The sun was still on a warpath when we got out of the gate. The dirt track sent memories up from my feet and through my spine; it was utterly mundane underfoot, but so it had been on the night I had come back from that other place.

'Ada's an okay kid,' Ferdi grumbled. 'I don't want you to think I've got beef with her.'

I asked, 'What about her family? I'm not being weird, just curious. Why are you so set against them?'

'I don't know,' he said after a pause. 'It doesn't sound right that Grandpa dies and we switch to being best buddies with his enemies. The way I see it, it's a matter of respect. Our folks and the Guadalupis *exchanged keys*, Scrawny, like good neighbours. We gave Grandpa's enemies the key to his farm, and how's that right?'

'I'm getting the vibe that Grandpa was a hard case.'

'He was,' Ferdi admitted.

'I didn't realise it until recently.'

'When I was little, Grandma smoothed him around the edges. He got crankier after she died. He was a good man, only… set in his ways, you know?'

'He was friends with Ada.'

'Sure he was. She's okay.'

There was no scent of juniper in the motionless air, or sea daffodils. I discerned a brackish note, but no stronger than at the masseria.

I said, 'Do you ever feel guilty about what we're doing? The renovation works. It's as if we're cancelling Grandpa from the face of Earth.'

'We're not doing anything, you and I. It's on Mum and Dad.'

'I'm sorry you're stuck here, Ferdi.'

I heard a shoe screech against the ground, and the rolling of a rock just kicked. 'Yeah, well, at least you're not alone, in the butt-end of nowhere.'

'Speaking of which, would you tell me what you see?'

'Fields as far as the eye can see, with brushwood, bushes, drystone walls. A reddening sky.'

'What's ahead of us?'

'More of the same. Why you ask?'

The soundscape was the same as always; the dirt track was a dirt track. 'The night I fell ill – something happened.'

'I knew it,' he said, his voice tensing. 'I bloody knew it. Did someone hurt you?'

'I'm going to tell you, but you have to promise you will really listen to the words I say, you will give me a chance. For real.'

'I always do,' he answered, and perhaps he was implying that I hadn't done the same with him, and perhaps he was right.

'It's important,' I insisted.

'Scrawny, you're scaring me.'

'Good.'

I told him everything I could, from the silence that fell on the first night, to when I crashed in front of Dad. I left Ada out of it: her cuts, my suspicions about Akela, our secret plot. I skipped all of that, albeit reluctantly.

When I was done, Ferdi said, 'I don't know…' He stopped. 'I don't know where to start.'

'Start by saying you trust me.'

'Always! Don't be afraid, Scrawny, if this wanderer thing comes back, I'll take care of it.'

'I don't think you can.'

'Try me,' he said, in a tone which was only half-joking.

'We must talk this through, not only you and I, but Mum and Dad too.'

'Sure, but first, give me some time to take it in, okay? It's a lot.'

I agreed.

Ada's voice came out of her throat like a raw sound of nature, gushing out of earth and sea. She had a way with words, but it wasn't only what she said, it was the way she said it. When she described the prickly pears, I could see them in my mind's eye. That quip about Tweety's arse? Instant classic.

My penis stiffened.

I was in bed, at night, and Ada was curling up with me, her chest against my back, in my imagination. She had accepted my story for what it was, no questions asked. She had confided her best-kept secrets to me. Her shampoo was vanilla and coconut. My penis throbbed. I brought a hand inside my boxers.

I had discovered wanking before curtain fall, and perfected the craft with dedication, on images of Cindy Crawford and Naomi Campbell while I could still see, and later on memories. At school, we all became interested in masturbation more or less overnight. One or two wisecrackers had joked that I was going blind after wanking too much, and I'd pretended to laugh with them. I had never wanked to the one near-girlfriend I had; it had not occurred to me that I might wank to a real girl. It had not occurred to me that I might wank to a girl I had never seen. For the whole of summer Ada had been leading me into new territories, love or lust, I couldn't tell, and I was deep into them. There was no way back.

When I kissed Ada's lips they had a marine, salty taste, which tingled my tongue. Her voice was the susurrus of young olive trees. It was almost real. It was almost good enough.

And, in the turn of one night, there was another mystery in my life: I could not figure out what pulled the strings of my body when Ada pronounced certain words and when the scent of her skin came to me. It was a mystery I badly wanted to explore, but Dad had other plans.

Dad would not let my lack of enthusiasm deter him from his mission to make me part of *the business*, so it came to pass that on an afternoon I would have happily spent on the beach with Ada, bouncing half-serious theories about what the photograph would show and secretly studying my feelings for her, or playing guitar with Giuseppe in his pipe-scented office, I found myself stowed inside a sweltering car with Mum and Dad, bound for Uncle Mario's home. The car had not been washed in a while; a memory of sweat haunted it.

It was not clear what Uncle Mario had to do with *the business*, even less so what my function was supposed to be, but then this last bit was never clear. Dad enquired perfunctorily about my guitar practice, and when I answered that I couldn't do any if he forced me to go with him on his little missions, he gave me one of his stock answers: 'Don't be like Ferdi.'

I felt I had to defend my brother, and said, 'Ferdi is working hard.'

'So are you,' said Mum, a comment which had nothing to do with the point I had just made, but she wasn't listening. They were distracted, more so than usual.

Uncle Mario's house was not far from the centre of Portodimare. I remembered it as a bungalow surrounded by a large garden, an unassuming holiday home in which outdoor spaces were much larger and better loved than those between walls. Since my sighted days I had associated that garden with the delicate, rose-like scent of geranium, Aunt Gemma's favourite flower. She planted geraniums everywhere, and wore the flower's essence as a perfume; geranium was her signature. A woman like her needed one.

'Stefania!' Aunt Gemma's voice welcomed us. 'It is so lovely to get to see you at last.' She made an effort to put warmth in her words. I heard the effort.

'We are going to see each other a lot,' Mum said, feigning enthusiasm.

There was an age-old rivalry between the two, an unspeakable secret everybody knew. Mum could not forgive Gemma for being glamorous (Mum held a Calvinistic suspicion of glamour), and for taking away Uncle Mario; Aunt Gemma, I suspect, found Mum too dull to have a right to exist.

'We have already started,' Gemma said. 'And how are you doing, Luca?'

She hugged me; a tactile woman, she never missed a chance to hug. The silk of her top, or dressing gown, caressed my face, and the geranium on her skin smelt good. 'Fine,' I said.

'Mario is working. He will join us in a minute.'

'We're in no hurry,' Dad said, always accommodating when Aunt Gemma was around. 'Maddalena's on the beach?'

'With her friends, yes. She has so many I lose count.'

We sat in comfortable chairs, at a table set with aromatic white wine for the adults, Coke for me, and nibbles – cured meat from Martina Franca, green olives from Fasano, *taralli* from a famous baker in Lecce. Aunt Gemma only sourced the best food. She couldn't cook, not beyond the essentials, and Mum never failed to remark that it is one thing to purchase, but another to make.

Apparently, Aunt Gemma's Ferdinando was getting on swimmingly in Oxford. Apparently, our Ferdi, too, was getting on swimmingly at the masseria. 'It's character-building,' Mum explained. 'You can see the results already.'

I just sat in my place, happily forgotten, listening to the grown-ups talk of the Guadalupis, of that year's best stretches of beach, of what to do on the Feast of the Assumption of the Virgin Mary, until Uncle Mario's voice boomed, 'Sorry I kept you waiting.'

'No, Mario,' Mum said. 'Thank you for taking time to do this.'

A chair moaned and cried when Uncle Mario let himself fall in it. 'I should be on leave. *I am* on leave. But lawyers are like doctors and priests, we never rest.'

'Clients in troubles?' Dad asked in a knowing voice.

'Clients *are* troubles. I've spent the last hour talking a guy out of suing his twin brother over some teeny-weeny sum their dad left them. It wasn't for the money, the guy said, it was for the principle of it. They all say that. I convinced him the inheritance wasn't worth the hassle of a legal case.'

'Mario goes against his own interests if it's the right thing to do,' Aunt Gemma said.

Mum commented, 'He was like that since we were children.'

Uncle Mario put away what sounded like a prodigious quantity of wine. 'Money tearing families apart, that's never a happy sight.' More wine was poured. 'What can I do for you?'

'It's a silly thing,' Dad said. 'I wasn't going to trouble you, but Stefi insisted.'

'Better safe than sorry. Tell me.'

Mum said, 'A couple of weeks ago, a council surveyor came round for an inspection. Routine stuff, we thought. It lasted twenty minutes, if that. He took a few pictures, talked to builders, got coffee with us and left. We'd completely forgotten about him, until we received this.'

A bag was opened. A piece of paper was taken out of it, and exchanged hands.

There were a few minutes in which all I could hear was food being munched and wine being swallowed. 'I see,' Uncle Mario said.

'You see there is a mistake,' Mum said.

Dad chipped in, 'I was on the phone with the council yesterday. They refuse to hear reason.'

Uncle Mario asked, 'Why do you say there is a mistake?'

The piece of paper changed hands again, from Uncle Mario's to Dad's, and Dad said, 'They say here that the staircase on the back, the one that goes up to the roof terrace, was built without planning permission, and they want to fine us for it.'

'Yes, I just read.'

'But your surveyor guaranteed the staircase was legal when we bought your part of the grange.'

'To the best of his knowledge, it was.'

'*Quod erat demonstrandum*,' Dad said. 'A mistake.'

'Who's the council's surveyor? Is he a Dr Giovanni Ranieri, by any chance?'

'Yes.'

'Pay the fine,' Uncle Mario said.

'I won't pay seven million lire for someone else's mistake.' It was a large sum, roughly equivalent to five thousand euros.

'Nobody's mistaken here. I guarantee you that my surveyor was right, *to the best of his knowledge*. Unfortunately, new information must have come up, and the council must be right too. It happens, with works as important as yours. Pay the fine.'

'Yeah, no, that's not going to happen.'

'You're going to live here, run a business here. You want to be on the council's right side.'

Mum asked, 'Why were you asking for the surveyor's name? Do you know him?'

'Yes. Yes, I know him. I know him enough to tell you: pay the fine.'

'How much would it cost to appeal?'

'I wouldn't charge you a penny, it goes without saying, but there would be court costs. Then, when you lose, and you will lose, you'll have to pay for the council's court costs too, and their lawyer.'

Dad's voice came again, lower, conspiratorially. 'Can't we just... you know?'

'I know what?'

'Stir this up out of court. With Dr Ranieri direct.'

'I would never suggest you bribe a civil servant.'

'You're not *suggesting*, I get it, you're not saying one thing, but if you gave us his number...'

'Darling,' Aunt Gemma's voice came, imperious, 'the fine *is* the bribe.'

Uncle Mario sighed. 'If we need to spell it out, yes, that's how it is. Someone at the council is squeezing you for money. They found an irregularity, or made it up, as an excuse. Whose pockets that money is going to line, that's another matter.'

'One more reason not to pay,' Dad said. 'I'm a fighter, Mario, you know me. I don't cower.'

'I'm not going to tell you two how to run your business, but if I were you, I'd pay. I have been you, in fact. And I've paid.'

'What can they do, if we don't?'

'For starters? They can stop the works.'

'They're welcome to try. No offence, but if you don't want to defend us – and I understand it, I understand that there are local checks and balances you've got to consider – I'll find someone who does.'

'Perhaps I wasn't clear just now. The council *has the authority* to put your works on hold while you're in court, and they're going to use it. They won't *try*, they'll just go and do it. They might stop you for *years*, and definitely until the winter.'

'They're going slow as it is!'

Uncle Mario ignored him and went on. 'You'll probably have to pay your contractors anyway, because it's not their responsibility if they can't work, and they will argue that they won't find other clients at such short notice. Which you know is bullshit and I know is bullshit; what they'll do is get your money and work off-the-books on another site, but you cannot argue *that* if your builders take you to court. You signed a contract with them, if I remember?'

'Yes, as our architect told us to.'

'We advised you not to,' Aunt Gemma reminded my parents.

Mum said, 'We're doing everything above board. That's how we like it, Gemma.'

'You were asking whom to bribe just a minute ago,' Aunt Gemma chirped.

'The council is doing everything above board too,' Uncle Mario said. 'The mayor of Portodimare does everything above board, like his father before him: elected above board, both of them, every time. The only lawyers who'd take you on are second-rate shysters, because it's plain to see you don't have a cause. Pay this seven million, Stefi: it's a piss in the sea compared to how much you've got tied up in the masseria. Or go to court and you'll spend more than double that. Is cash flow tight right now? Tell them. They'll be open to talking instalments, work something out with you. Dr Ranieri is a reasonable man.'

'*A reasonable man?*' Dad snapped. 'Is this still the council we're talking of, or the mafia?'

For the first time Uncle Mario sounded exasperated. 'Bloody hell, it's people,' he said. 'People, you know? Like you and me.'

Bianca and Giuseppe Guadalupi ambushed me in their house when I went for my guitar lesson. I had done my best to ignore the signs that my parents were planning something (Ferdi fading into the works again, Mum and Dad not leaving me alone); denial runs strong in my family. I was excited for the next day, when Ada and I would finally go to the shop and get the printed photograph of the wanderer. I was excited for the print and I was excited that I would spend time with Ada. We had skipped some days, lately, and it was like skipping meals.

'Hello, Luca,' Bianca said.

Her voice sounded uncannily like that of an older Ada who had travelled back to 1996 from thirty years in the future. Bianca played the same notes as her daughter, with less raw power, but adding nuance and depth.

'Hi, Bianca.' The sounds and smells that were Giuseppe stood close to her. I was learning. 'Hey, Giuseppe,' I said, to show off.

'Good to see you, Luca.'

'Where's Ada?'

'In her room, catching up with summer homework.'

It was unusual that she hadn't come to say hello.

'Come, sit,' Bianca said. 'There's iced tea.'

That was unusual too. I did as I was told.

'Did you have time to practise?' Giuseppe asked.

'Not with Dad pestering me all the time.'

'Happens.'

Bianca said, 'Without beating around the bush: your parents wanted us to have a chat with you. I hope you don't mind.'

That whole summer had been a learning curve. The penny dropped at once: Bianca was a psychiatrist, and what could my parents want from a psychiatrist? Ferdi had stabbed me in the back. I felt anger, worry, resentment, and mostly I felt stupid. 'Sure,' I said.

'It's about what you told your brother.'

'I thought so.'

'Don't hold it against Ferdi,' Giuseppe said. 'He's worried for you.'

'When folks want to do as they like, they say it's for others.'

Bianca asked, 'Would you mind repeating to me what you told him?'

'I don't need a shr—a doctor.' I struggled to keep my words polite.

'I'm asking as a friend.'

'Would you at least respect my intelligence?' That straightforwardness was new to me, and satisfying. 'Everything I told Ferdi – it did happen. For real.'

'I don't think you're lying,' Bianca said.

Giuseppe added, 'None of us do.'

'Okay,' I said. 'Whatever.'

I related my story, more succinctly than I had to Ada or Ferdi. Mundane tales grow in the retelling, prodigious ones shrink: repetition turns silly anecdotes into epics, but makes gaudy baubles of miracles. I was getting used to calling the place I had stumbled upon a 'beach', as if it were just that, and the more I tried to convey the strangeness of the wanderer's gait, the more doubtful it sounded that a city boy was in any position to dictate how animals should walk.

'It is an amazing story,' Bianca commented, and sounded sincere.

'But you don't believe a word I said.'

'Before, I didn't think that you were lying. Now I am positive that you aren't.'

'Yeah, but you think I've got, what, hallucinations?'

'I'll be square with you and say that yes, I absolutely do. But I'll also tell you that it doesn't mean what you think it does. There are too many misconceptions about what hallucinations really are, and what they point at. My go-to example is Charles

Bonnet syndrome, which comes to some patients after they lose their sight. Have you heard of it?'

Syndrome. The word had on me the effect headlights have on a rabbit – it clubbed me with fear and pinned me to the spot. *Syndrome* meant bad things happening to your body. I had been there, I had done that, and I had come out of the other side disabled. 'No,' I said.

'You can think of vision as a two-step process. Step one is straightforward: light reaches you, physically touching receptors in your eyes.'

'Which, in my case, broke down. I know.'

'Marvellous. But step one means little, on its own. It is in step two that magic happens. In step two, the brain uses the information received with that light to create fully-formed images, like an artist who takes colours from a palette – a touch of blue here, a smudge of green there – to make a painting. We have a naive illusion that we see the world as it is, but no, all that we are able to see, all that we will ever be able to see, is an image of the world which we make in our brain. Same goes with all our senses: we hear with our brain, we taste… you get the gist. Saying that the whole world is inside us wouldn't be far from the truth. The external world does exist, of course it does, and it provides us with building blocks – light, vibrations – which our brain uses to create an inner model. But then, what we call *reality* is only that inner model, which stems from objective reality. But it is not an exact copy. Do you follow me?'

I said, 'Except, our brain might get the model wrong.'

'Exactly,' Bianca said. 'Our brain is like an obsessed artist, addicted to making this model, and if there are hiccups with the supply of building blocks, well, it can get creative.

Normally sight loss is caused by this or that damage to the eye, but the part of your brain that was in charge of vision stays in ship-shape condition. With Charles Bonnet syndrome, it keeps painting in the dark, so to speak – with the result that sightless people may see things. It is not that they *believe* they are seeing things; they are *actually* seeing things. Their brain is painting images for them exactly as it would do when it had light to go on, as mine is doing right here, right now. Those images are *real*, but they do not correspond to objective reality. People seeing them do not have any psychological issue, well, no more than any of us does: their brain is taking time to adjust, to recalibrate itself, and in the process it is creating phantasms. The worst you can say is that it is trying too hard.'

'But I didn't *see*,' I protested. 'I didn't see a thing.'

Bianca answered, 'We can hallucinate with all our senses, using more or less the same areas of our brain that we use when actually sensing. This is what makes hallucinations so scarily convincing. When you pet an actual dog, a part of your brain lights up. When you remember petting a dog, it is another part that lights up. So far, so good? Now, when you *hallucinate* petting a dog, the first part of your brain lights up, not the second. The dog feels real because your brain is making up the real model of a dog for you. The dog feels real because it *is* real – for you.'

'I was not hallucinating.'

Giuseppe asked, 'How can you be sure?'

'Are you saying I might have this Charles Bonnet syndrome?'

'Oh, no,' Bianca said. 'Charles Bonnet causes visual hallucinations, by definition. I was using it as an example to illustrate how one can be sane and yet sense things which are not objectively there.'

'Sane, yes,' I said. 'Healthy, no.'

Giuseppe shuffled on his chair the way he did when I made a smart remark.

Bianca said, 'You went through so much, Luca. An adjustment period is to be expected.'

I knew what was coming: the rest of summer ruined, August spent hopping between hospitals and clinics, having my blood taken, my body prodded, and, the worse part by far, the wait for a diagnosis. 'What tests are you getting me to do?'

Giuseppe answered, 'None,' sending a rush of gratitude through my body.

'Only if you promise you'll be responsible,' Bianca added. 'I gave you a frame for your experiences. You're clever. You're young. They might never return now that you know what they are. Or, if they do, you might be able to recognise them.'

'If they keep up, though, and they don't get any less convincing, you go to Bianca and tell her,' Giuseppe said. 'It was hard work to convince your father that we can trust you on this.'

'You can,' I said, almost before he had finished speaking.

'At the first sign of trouble, you come to me immediately,' Bianca said.

'Yes.'

'Don't betray our trust, Luca, I'm begging you, don't.'

'I trusted you, Ferdi.'

'Scrawny…'

'Fuck you and shut up.'

We did this on the porch, on a damp day with the wind of Sirocco blowing. I had stormed back home to find Ferdi gone to the beach, Mum and Dad busy indoors with papers and phone calls. I heard their voices ebb and flow without paying them too much mind, and sat on the swing to read *Moby-Dick* while waiting for my brother. I wasn't after my parents. It was Ferdi's head I wanted.

'Listen, Scrawny…'

'Are you deaf or what? I said, *Shut up*.' I paused to give him a chance to disobey, and when he didn't, I went on, 'You asked me for *time to take it in*, and this is what you do? You go and tell on me?'

'I did it for you.'

'Oh, please, you sound just like Mum and Dad.'

'Remember the mist, Luca? How spooky it was? You saw it because you were *going blind*. The mist was a symptom of a damn serious condition.'

We were raising our voices. 'And now I've got symptoms of what, brain cancer?'

'How can I tell? Say you do and we catch it too late because I didn't speak up.'

'Then I'd snuff it and it'd be my bloody business. It's not your life. It's not your call. It's mine. Thank God Giuseppe Guadalupi is a better mate than you, or I'd be looking at spending the rest of summer around doctors. Do you understand what you did to me?'

'I convinced Mum and Dad to have your eyes tested.'

'So what? What good did it do?'

Ferdi took a moment or two to reply. 'It might do some good this time. Scrawny, I could still be open to the possibility that there's an animal at large: a panther escaped from a private zoo, that sort of thing. But the beach? Do you sincerely believe there is one person in this world who would hear the story of how you went there and back and not worry for you?'

'One person in the world, yes – *you*. I trusted you, Ferdi. And I trust myself. I know what happened.'

'But you don't! How can you? You couldn't even *see*—' He stopped abruptly.

I let his last words linger.

I said, putting all the coldness I felt into my voice, 'This is it, then. I couldn't see the wanderer, I couldn't see the beach, I couldn't see where I was. I cannot see a fucking thing, not ever, and what does a blind man know? One who cannot *see*?'

'It's not like that.'

'You just said it.'

'Well, yes, then. If you want me to say it, bang on, it is like that. You ask me to believe a crackpot story and you give me *nothing* to hold on to. Put yourself in my shoes.'

Many years later, I can finally do that. I came to understand that to the sighted, sight never ceases to be the only sense that truly matters. It is written in the Gospels that when Saint Thomas saw Jesus Christ come back from the dead, he had to touch his master's ribs to believe the miracle, but going by my experience, I'll bet the contrary happened. A sighted could stick a hand down a crocodile's throat and not realise he's one sudden movement away from becoming Captain Hook until he *sees* the crocodile. I would be lying if I said I don't miss sight – I would pay good money to spend an afternoon just looking at the blaze of a poppy field in May – but I appreciate how it can limit your world. It gives you so much that you forget there is much more to be had. Sight is like an overbearing mama, of the kind so common in this corner of the world, who feeds her children great food and great wine too, who cleans up after them and tells them they're strong and smart, and the children are too satiated to ever make the painful effort of growing up, so they are still children at forty, well-fed, yes, possibly even content, but capable of survival only within a very narrow set of conditions.

My own mother, who didn't count overbearingness among her faults, came out before I could answer. 'Hi, boys,' she said. Our shouting had flown over her head. 'I had a long talk over the phone with Bianca Guadalupi. Luca, I know you'll be upset…'

'Nope, I'm not doing this.' I took my cane and went inside, to my room. I didn't come out for dinner, didn't come out at all until Mum and Dad had retired to bed and Ferdi had gone out with his friends. Then I returned to the porch, and enjoyed the cool night air and the solitude, and read a little. The wanderer did not visit. The countryside listened.

When we went to collect the print, Ada and I walked, rather than cycled, to slow down the journey and make a ritual of it. On the way I complained about how I had been treated, and she said, 'This is when you learn why to lie.'

Ada Guadalupi was the same as always, only more so, which made her a completely different girl. A tectonic shift had occurred within me, so now when she talked I didn't focus so much on the words she spoke as on the marvellous new things we had done in my bedroom, in my imagination. I couldn't help but wonder how it would feel to run my palm (my lips!) down her backbone. Maybe by doing so I was spoiling our friendship. Was I? I had as many questions about her as I had about the wanderer, all vying for attention, raising hell, covering the one thing I should have noticed with their silly clatter – that Ada, the real Ada, the Ada who was with me in flesh and bones, was sad.

I said, 'I was a hundred per cent sure I could trust Ferdi.'

'My old folks grilled me.'

'How come?'

'They weren't convinced your hallucinations were new to me. Still aren't, but they let it go for the time being. They'll have another go when I least expect it. That's how they do it.'

'Sorry for dragging you into this.'

'Told ya. Good job you kept my name out of your story.'

I felt a stone with my cane, and one step later I kicked it in anger. 'Moron.'

'You mean you or your brother?'

'My brother.' I thought about it. 'Me too.'

'People don't listen.'

'You do.'

'If not for my own experience we might be looking at a different scenario.' She paused. 'I overheard Mum and Dad talk, after the grilling. Well, I eavesdropped. Mum's worried. She was saying that you've been hallucinating with all your senses at once, well, all four of them, and that is Not Good.'

'Not good how?'

'The words she used were *full psychotic breakdown*. I looked them up in her books and, not to put too fine a point to it, they're a long-winded way to say one's sectionable. She hopes it won't get to that, but she's fetching the meds today to have them at the ready. The minute you're back with another reality-bending story, she'll have you start popping pills.'

'We're on our own.'

'We're on our own together.'

Bianca Guadalupi's theory was sensible. It was in fact the only kind of theory a well-adjusted adult could deem sensible, but this is the problem with adults who adjust too well; they forget that while theories need to be sensible, the universe came up with dodos and black holes. Reality is a loony. Four years earlier, the idea of reading with my fingers would be fantastically strange to me. Now it was my everyday. Had I not already lived through one revolution, perhaps I would have listened to common sense. But I was done with that. I do not put much stock in common sense – I would rather all my senses be extraordinary.

The photography shop was a tiny building on the edge of a public garden which nuns planted with eucalyptus trees a long time ago, when there was a working convent in Portodimare. It faced the village's central square. The shop is long gone now, but the trees remain. I often go there to stretch my legs, and every time I stroll in that marvellous eucalyptus scent, I slide back to that day in August, as if I were still young, still there with Ada at the long-gone shop's door, where we stopped to take a moment.

'Ready?' Ada asked.

'Let's roll,' I said.

It was hugely anticlimactic. The guy at the till handed Ada a fat envelope, took our money and that was it. If he had glimpsed anything astounding in the prints, then he could hide his shock.

When we came out, Ada said, 'He lacked all the context.'

'Look at the photo, Ada.'

We sat on a bench among the eucalyptus trees, at some distance from the shop. I heard her shake the envelope. 'This is momentous.'

'Just go and open it.' I didn't know what *momentous* meant.

'We should pop open a bottle of champagne, like when they launch boats.'

'Ada!'

'Okay, okay. Jeez, chill.'

I heard her pry open the envelope, extract the prints, shuffle them, chuckle once or twice – and suddenly stop.

'I'm looking at it,' she said, in a low voice. 'I'm looking at the wanderer.'

I strained my senses for the silence, for the steady *tap, tap* and the feral smell, but none of that could burst out of a photograph. 'And?' I asked.

'And it's…' She paused. 'It's not an animal, Luca. It's a man.'

It's a man. Those words made me want to stand up and run. *It's a man.* Beasts might attack you, yes, but at thirteen I was old enough to know you can't call them evil. People, though? 'It didn't *sound* like a man.'

'It looks like one. Although…'

'Describe him, Ada, please.'

'It's not the greatest pic. It's all blurry, and you shot against the light. But anyways. He's got black hair with white in it, coming from under a flat cap, and a beard, same colours. Age-wise, I'd say late-fifties to mid-sixties. Strong, tanned, wrinkly, you know the type, one who works hard in the fields day in, day out. Not a giant, but you could build a motorway on his shoulders.'

'What's he wearing?'

'Shoes are not in the frame. You cut it at the knee. He's got brown corduroy trousers, and he's shirtless, skin glistening with sweat. I could draw each muscle and sinew. But it's his face that…' She paused. 'I don't like his face.'

'What about it?'

'It's…' She paused. 'It's…' she tried again, and again she paused. 'It's *righteous*,' she said at last. 'It's the face of a man who would do anything, to anybody, in the name of his personal definition of a greater good.'

'Anything more specific?'

'I'm working with a crappy photograph here, not a feature film.'

I had been so looking forward to knowing what the wanderer looked like, and now that I did, I also knew that it didn't matter. As Ada had predicted, the photo proved nothing. We could show it to our families and they would concede not all was right with the masseria (there had been a stranger, after all, in the vineyard), but they'd never consider accepting my truth. The wanderer's face was no more key than its feral smell, its out-of-tune gait. 'I'm at a loss,' I admitted. 'Thanks to Ferdi, I'm going to have to watch my words. We can forget about asking questions.'

'Yeah, we have to keep a low profile,' Ada said. 'But you have a gun, right?'

It took us three or four days to get the gun and go after the righteous man. I was more wary than Ada, although she had been spot-on at every twist and turn. It seemed to me that she still treated what we were doing like a game – the young detectives, kids fighting monsters, patterns well known to an insatiable reader like her. She had not stumbled on the beach yet, or heard the revellers' strains. In those days of dithering, I realised I had become the talk of town.

Humans are to hearsay what dry brushwood is to flame, more so in August, when the sun scorches humans and brushwood alike, making them willing to catch fire at the smallest spark. I never knew where the spark came from: Ferdi might have spilled the beans to some girl after a beer too many, or Mum might have confided my problems to Aunt Betta, or perhaps Dad had a spot of brotherly talk with a new friend at a bar. I am inclined to believe it wasn't the Guadalupis, for Giuseppe and Bianca were discreet to a fault, and Ada – well, as I finally managed to realise, Ada didn't appear to have any friends. At any rate, every last person in Portodimare, old or young, knew one version of my story, and the versions varied wildly. I heard them all, I think, or most of them, thanks to my special power of invisibility. At the grocery shop, at Chocolate Delight, when Uncle Mario took us to his favourite fish restaurant by the harbour, on the beach: folks talked behind my back, even when my back was not far from their lips. Wherever I went, a flurry of rumours followed me, like mosquitoes on the hunt.

A disturbingly high number of people believed I had been found kneeling at the Devil's feet, or at the feet of a devil's idol anyway, and the priest had been called in. I heard someone consult Portodimare's priest himself about a variant of this story, in a bar where I was having a cappuccino. He neither confirmed nor denied. He decreed in his most ominous voice, 'The youngsters are especially vulnerable to Satan's lure,' before finishing his coffee with a slurp and the chime of cup hitting saucer.

Many knowingly argued that without a pair of good old eyes I couldn't *really* know where I was, ever. 'That boy can't tell an apricot from a watermelon,' a man explained, with the pain of someone who would rather not waste his time pointing out self-evident truths. 'He cannot be trusted on anything he says.' Others compared me to Art, a boy from Casalfranco who had run away from home, sending the town into a frenzy, only to return seven days later admitting to having played a prank. Both attention seekers, he and I.

Surprisingly, my association with Ada did not help my cause with younger people. 'He hangs with Ada Guadalupi,' a girl said, making a bad job of whispering. 'That explains *everything*.' A snotty-voiced boy who was leaving church with a group of friends monologued on the fact that you would think that well-respected folks like Giuseppe and Bianca would deserve better luck, but no, God gave them a daughter like Ada and a neighbour like me. 'It is said in the Bible that the Lord,' he concluded to a chorus of approval, 'disciplines the ones He loves.' It beat me what Ada could have possibly done to get the exalted rank of biblical scourge. I did not much care. Kids' general dislike of her was a boon, for it cut down the competition. If nobody else understood the wonder of Ada, I did. The challenge was finding a way to let her know that.

A different take came from an unexpected quarter – Aunt Betta. She dropped in the masseria for coffee, and when Mum went to put a pot on the stove, Aunt Betta whispered, 'I believe you.'

I didn't reply, not to get in trouble.

'The Lord took your eyes and gave you a more powerful Sight,' she went on undaunted. And she added, for my benefit, 'I read in a book that He does that.'

This was a minority theory, but one that did the rounds: the sightless one who receives a psychic gift, a trite cliché, which appeared well grounded because it was well known. Tiresias, anyone? When you are different, so many well-meaning people will zone in on your one difference and make of it the whole of you.

One night Dad joined me on the porch. I was reading a chapter on the representation of whales in art, one more passage that played like a sick joke in my head, when I heard him come down the stairs. I thought he had gone to bed. I almost would have rather heard the righteous man's *tap, tap*.

'Hey, kid,' Dad said. It was his latest fad, this calling me *kid*.

'Dad.'

He came and sat next to me on the swing, with a sigh of rusty springs. 'I couldn't sleep,' he said.

'Happens.'

He inhaled profoundly. 'I see why you like it here. The fresh air. The solitude.'

'The solitude most of all.'

'Yeah.' He didn't catch my drift.

'How are you?' he asked.

'Fine. Why?'

'You and your brother, you're always *fine*, aren't you?'

I wasn't sure which words he was expecting from me, so I didn't say any. The hoopoe's call filled the silence.

'Between you and me,' Dad said, after a while, 'what's the situation with Ada?'

'Dad…'

'Did you smooch?'

'Dad!'

'Just asking.'

'We're friends, Dad. *Friends*, have you ever heard of that?'

'*Friends* is where you start from.'

'It's all there is.'

'So how come you spend every hour of the day together?'

'It's not like I know many other people,' I said, on the defensive. I immediately felt like a traitor for putting it that way, as if I would get rid of Ada when better options appeared. I couldn't imagine a better option than her.

'You will. New school in September! In small towns, new friends flock to you.'

I thought about Ada, who seemed to be quite lonely. I thought about the boys outside the church. 'I suppose.'

'But this girl's special,' he said. Suddenly a punch hit my shoulder. I recoiled. A fraction of a moment later I realised it was Dad punching me lightly, in a gesture he must have thought as chummy. 'Kid, you should see how she looks at you!'

'Yeah, I should *see* it.'

That cut him off. 'You know what I meant,' he mumbled.

Dig out your own eyes, I thought, *and be haunted by a monster, and travel to another world and back, and be threatened with drugs when you ask for help, then you will know what I fucking mean.* 'I don't want to talk about Ada. There's nothing to say.'

'I didn't mean to talk about Ada either,' Dad said. 'Not really. You and I didn't have time for a proper chat, after your episode.'

I was going to answer, *It wasn't an episode*, but luckily I caught myself. If I defended my story, that would demonstrate that I was nuts – and if I didn't, it would be like admitting it. Walls encroaching on me from all sides. I resorted to a non-committal, 'You've been busy.'

'Ferdi did the right thing. You know that, don't you?' He had a dangerous tone.

'Probably.'

'I have to ask: Do you believe what you told your brother? Do you really?'

'I was ill,' I hurried to say. 'I might have dreamed the whole thing. I think I did.'

'Did anything happen, Luca? Anything at all, that you might be covering with this fantasy?'

'No, Dad, nothing happened.'

'Good,' he said. 'Good.'

He didn't talk for a while, then said, 'Mum and I are doing the best we can.'

'I know,' I said, although at the time I didn't believe it.

'Adjusting to a new life, it's hard. You were right, we've been busy, and if you've been feeling sidelined, it's normal. You don't need to call for our attention though. You've got it, always.'

I bit back my answer and said, 'Thank you.'

'You sure you don't want the medication?'

'Dad…?'

'You should know there's nothing to be ashamed of. When you come down with a cold, you get aspirin. When you have other issues, you get—'

'I don't need meds,' I said.

'Giuseppe convinced us to wait, but you're not his son, you're mine, and I worry. If a pill can make you better, why not?'

That was my father through and through: always looking for the magic solution, the snap of fingers which would make all badness go away. He *wanted* me on meds, sedated, not a problem anymore, and if he wanted that, he would get that. For the first time in my life, I was genuinely afraid of him. 'It was an episode,' I said. 'Only an episode.'

'You sure about that?'

I yawned. I had to remove myself before I panicked and said something I would regret. 'I'm asleep on my feet,' I said. 'Better go to bed.'

I went to fetch Grandpa's hunting shotgun from the secret compartment in *Da Klub* on a damp, warm night. Sirocco blew from the sea and made the air thick with humidity; I plodded on the bottom of a swamp. I didn't like to be out and about on my own. I went all the same because Ada had argued that it would be inconceivable to smuggle out the gun during daytime, in plain sight of the builders, and once again she was spot on.

I remember a nervous walk to the creaky door under the archway, my senses painfully stretched towards the smallest trace of any presence. I didn't doubt the righteous man was prowling. Or my father: he would take my night stroll as a sure sign of illness, which would give him permission to stuff happy pills down my throat. Sirocco's dampness makes your problems heavier.

When I got inside, I breathed in the cooler air with relief. I smelt the ghosts of Ferdi's sweat and cigarettes, with the sweet skunk undertone. I half-dreaded, half-hoped the shotgun wouldn't be where Ada and I had left it, but no, it hadn't been moved. I took it, and took Grandpa's cartridge belt as well, which I slung around my shoulder.

I had some troubles on my way back, a heavy gun under one armpit, a heavy belt over a shoulder. I didn't know if the shotgun was loaded and I didn't know how to check. I walked carefully, jumping every time it moved against my side, afraid I might shoot myself and die stupidly. I left the shotgun leaning against a tree on the opposite side from the farmhouse – not a perfect hiding place, but it only had to make do until tomorrow morning. I left the cartridge belt too, and made my way back home, a part of my attention on the route, a part on the countryside.

Once I read in a book by a French philosopher, Gaston Bachelard, that our first house is forever inscribed in our body, physically, tattooed in a muscle memory of gestures and routines. I have not one, but two, first houses – the flat in Turin, in which I learnt how to live as a sighted, and the Masseria del Vento, the place I still call home, where I was initiated into my new sightless life. The farmhouse and the surrounding fields were inscribing themselves in my body. In June I got lost on my way to the bathroom. Two months later I only needed a part of my attention to move around the property. When I considered that, I imagined myself taller, and the grip of Sirocco loosened.

Ada had planned what she called *a scouting expedition*, the reasoning being that if the righteous man was at least partially flesh and bones, he might have an abode – or a lair, or a nest – not far from our houses. Which left a lot of ground to cover in our endless countryside. 'But then, we have time on our hands,'

Ada pointed out. Time to spend in empty fields with the girl I, perhaps, loved. The shotgun was for self-defence. 'Yes, I can use it,' she said before I could ask. 'Ferdinando taught me.'

You should see how she looks at you, Dad had said. If only. 'He never taught me.'

'Did you ask?'

'Dad wasn't so keen.' We walked into the vineyard. 'You spent an awful lot of time with Grandpa. Any story worth sharing?'

'Let me think… Oh, yes. I was nine, and there was this boy I liked in Portodimare, a husky guy, five years older, who came from Rome with his family. Curly hair, square jaw, the works. The boy didn't even know I existed, which made me feel terrible. Ferdinando took time to listen to me being a baby about it. He didn't do anything practical, he couldn't do anything, but he was there, with iced tea.'

'What was the boy's name?'

'Patrick. His mum was American. They've not been back since, now that I think of it.'

'It's possible Grandpa shot the whole family for breaking your heart.'

'I wouldn't put it past him.'

'Were there other boys?' I asked, faux-casual.

'Hundreds. I made a checklist with all the names of suitable, dick-equipped humans in a twenty-mile radius and made a point to go through them. It's hard work but I'm getting there.'

'I wasn't implying anything.'

Ada chuckled. 'Did you ever have a girlfriend?'

'There was this one girl,' I said. 'She was at school with me, same class.'

'Give me a name. I like names.'

'Ginevra. She was cute.'

'*Was?* She dead?'

I hadn't thought about Ginevra in a while: her face popped back to my mind from some dreamlike place. 'No, she's still cute, I guess. Widely considered the cutest girl at my old school.' I said that with some pride; I wanted Ada to know that cute girls did find me attractive, and she could too.

'How come she wasted time with you, then?'

'You do,' I said.

She tapped on Grandpa's shotgun. 'I'm your bodyguard.'

'She liked comic books.'

'A *girl* reading comics? Dude, you're making her up.'

'Not the American stuff. Mangas, mostly.'

'Ah, okay. So what happened with cute, arty Ginevra?'

I briefly pondered whether to lie. 'Absolutely nothing,' I admitted.

'Not a peck?'

'We didn't even get to the stage of holding hands.'

'So you were the perv stalking her and making up dirty scenes in his mind.'

'No, no, it wasn't like that. She enjoyed talking to me, I enjoyed talking to her. It came easy. We spent whole afternoons together. Then my sight went downhill, and I had to leave school. They didn't have a special needs teacher handy, and besides, we were moving South. It was pretty obvious I'd have to repeat the year.'

'You didn't call her?'

'She called me, once or twice.'

'And you never called back.'

'It was all too much.' I hid behind a platitude not to tell Ada the truth, that I had been embarrassed. Embarrassed that I didn't notice if globs of sauce landed on me when I ate, embarrassed that I couldn't tell whether my hair needed combing and that Mum had to comb it for me, embarrassed that no one told me when I left my jeans' zipper open. Embarrassed that I had stumbled out of tune with time and space.

'You pulled a disappearing act on gorgeous Ginevra.'

'The world pulled a disappearing act on me.'

We came out of the vineyard. 'First stop, the hollow tree,' Ada said. 'You lead the way.'

The plan was to go back where I had first heard the *tap, tap* and faced the righteous man – as good a starting point as any. I navigated to the first landmark, the almond tree, easily enough. I tested its trunk with my fingers.

'What are you looking for?' Ada asked.

'My initials.' I showed her where I'd carved them. 'I used them to sign out the tree.'

'You're smarter than you look.'

'I am a man of mystery.'

What was next? A peculiar rock, twenty-one steps from the tree. That too was easy to find. What came after that, the rosemary or the prickly pear? I started stumbling. I wasn't so sure. The sun had burnt plants and bushes, making the land as uncompromising as it had ever been. Where my hand would touch leaves only a month earlier, now it got stabbed, if I were not careful, on spikes and thorns. I picked a direction, almost randomly.

Tap, tap.

I had not come back to these fields since the day I had faced the wanderer, and it was so odd to think that almost a whole summer had passed. It was so odd to think how much had changed in a matter of weeks. I wasn't afraid of getting lost anymore. I was afraid of less definable possibilities.

Tap, tap.

Memory was a different inflection of reality. There are moments like that in all our lives, moments so deeply etched in our mind that they are always present, never past. You are forever giving your first kiss and forever answering the phone to be told your mother's dead, as I will be forever lost in that field, with all sounds dropping away except the wind, and the *tap, tap* rising in the silence. It was still happening on the day I searched for the hollow tree with Ada. It is still happening now, while I dictate these words to a state-of-the-art laptop.

I asked, 'Do you see a hollow tree?'

'I don't think so,' Ada answered after a long while. 'What kind of tree would that be? Apart from hollow.'

'The kind with jutting roots and a knotted trunk.'

'There's one like that ahead of us.'

It was not hollow, and the roots were not thick enough. I said, 'Okay, let's try a different angle. Another landmark of mine was a half-buried rock. From there, I remember how to get to the tree.'

'There are more half-buried rocks than soil.'

We checked one and then another, and I was positive I had found the right one, but it wasn't. I was positive the hollow tree had to be close, but Ada couldn't see it, and in the midst of that expanse of Mediterranean scrub, she must be able to see a large chunk of land. 'Maybe it's not here,' she said.

'I *know* it is.'

'I mean it's not *here* the way the beach is not *here*.'

That struck me. I wished I could say it was not possible. 'What do we do, then?'

'I'm thinking,' Ada said. 'We're not far from the Yellow Chapel. Let's say a half-mile, cutting through the fields.'

'What's the Yellow Chapel?'

'It's a chapel. It's yellow.'

'And what has it got to do with us?'

'I know everyone who lives in the hood. The righteous man does not count among them. The Yellow Chapel has been abandoned for a million years. It has a history of being a squat. A place for satanic rituals too, they say, though it's bollocks. It's worth checking out. If you've got anything better, I'm all ears.'

I had nothing better. 'You lead the way,' I said.

I followed Ada through spiky bushes and lonesome trees, breathing in sandy dirt that grated on my lungs like nails on a chalkboard. By that point in the season, the sun beat relentlessly on every form of life. We walked in silence for a while, but to Ada silence was a mistake to put right, so she said out of nowhere, 'I'm going to ask you a question which is probably ghoulish, but I've got to ask. You're free not to answer. I won't hold it against you.'

'Go on.'

'How were the first days? When you got blind.'

'Why do you say it's ghoulish?'

'You suffered and I'm here asking for the icky details. That's a textbook definition of ghoulish.'

'It's human, I think.'

'Humans are ghoulish.'

'And why do you want to know?'

'It's an experience I haven't had.'

Ada Guadalupi was the best listener I'd ever met. She did not jump to interpret my thoughts in the light of her own, or offer solutions, and she didn't start talking the moment I paused to catch my breath, no, she was curious about what I had to say, and effortlessly asked the right questions, because she honestly wanted to hear my answers. She spurred me to put into words thoughts I had not fully formed before.

'I was dumber,' I said. 'For a while. I didn't understand people. I couldn't always get the words they said, and when I did, I often couldn't tell if they were being serious, ironic or what.' I paused. 'I couldn't see their lips, their gestures, which made it harder to understand what they said. I hadn't expected that. I had expected to be clumsy, or, or unable to watch TV, but not that I'd get worse at *talking*. There were plenty of tasks like that, tasks for which I'd been leaning on sight without even knowing. And that was before it all went dark.'

Ada handed me a bottle of water. I drank, thanked her and said, 'I was in the shower. Blindness had been snowballing. It started slowly, and it picked up more and more, from a leisurely stroll to warp speed. It took years, then months, then weeks, then days, like a funnel narrowing to a single moment in time. That moment was under the shower. I was already blind. I could see light, broad shapes, little more. Side vision was gone. I was able to read from very close, with effort. TV, Game Boy – forget it. The majority of blind people stop there, or at an earlier stage: blindness is on a spectrum, and those at the very end, like me, those who cannot glimpse any light at all, are rare.'

'Okay, okay, you're special. Enough with the boasting and get on with the story.'

'So, I was in the shower,' I said. 'I was soaping my hair, and I shut my eyelids to stop the shampoo from running in. I felt a pinch behind my eyes, which was not unusual; I often suffered a little pain there. When I opened my eyes again, it was gone. Not only the pain: all was gone. The shower curtain, the tiles, my hands – all. The funny thing is, I didn't notice immediately. I didn't think, *My eyes are open. I should be able to see.* I went on as if nothing had happened, like when a guillotine's blade severs a head and the head still blinks after rolling on the floor. But when I did notice… I'm not sure if I can explain. I shut my eyes and opened them again, many times, frenetically, as if I could fix them that way. My head spun, and I remember thinking, *I'm falling.* I was falling down the darkest pit in the world, and I could scream all I wanted, the fall would never end. What I didn't realise was that I was screaming *for real*, and a moment later Ferdi burst in shouting my name, *Luca! Luca!* He asked what was going on, and I said, *I'm falling, Ferdi,* and he reached me in the shower, completely dressed as he was, and held me.'

'Your brother knows how not to be a dickhead when he wants.'

I was done with cutting Ferdi slack; I ignored her comment.

She said, 'We're almost at the Yellow Chapel, FYI.'

'Thanks.'

'Was it hard to cope?'

'I was scared stiff. For around two weeks I only left my bed to go to the loo. In practice very little had changed; I'd been walking with the white cane for months. Mentally, it was a whole new level. I call it *darkness* for lack of a better word, but it's not correct, what I see isn't darkness, it's… nothing, absolutely nothing. I couldn't…' I paused, searching for the right words. 'I contemplated killing myself,' I said, in a low voice. 'I was thinking, *the easiest way is out*. In a video game, when you screw up and your energy bar is low, you know you could go down any moment. Playing stops being fun, and there are gamers who find it easier to forfeit one life and have another go. Same thing: I thought, *I can't fix this mess, let's get it over with*. The idea didn't even make me sad, it just… stood to reason.'

'I know the feeling,' Ada said. 'What made you hold on?'

I hadn't known the answer to that question until I had to give it to her. 'I thought, *Fuck reason, I want to live.*'

'The Yellow Chapel. We're here.'

I stopped. 'How does it look?'

'The usual.' I heard Ada's hand clench the forestock, and the shotgun cut the air while being raised. 'I'll go first.'

I followed her inside.

August is the least interesting of months, for everything smells scorched. While in the dead of winter you still have the fragrance of chimney smoke to keep you company, August leaves no quarter. I was grateful for the ghost of a scent of flowers and frankincense that came off the chapel's walls. I sniffed for the feral smell without finding it. I asked, 'What do you see?'

'Rubble, more rubble, dead spiders, centipedes, also dead, a tacky painting of the Virgin Mary, an inverted pentagram covering her face.'

'Wait—what?'

'Don't start peeing your knickers, it's a billion years old. The kids who painted it moved on to mortgages and beer bellies.'

I swept my cane on dust and discarded cans. 'Anything else?'

'It doesn't look as if anyone has been sleeping here recently, or hanging here, or invoking old gods.' The Southern countryside is dotted with lonesome chapels, barely big enough for two or three people to stand shoulder to shoulder, and some are abandoned, some aren't. Ada's voice travelled as voices do in small rooms. I thought I could detect disappointment.

'It was a wild guess anyway,' I tried.

'Yeah.'

'Shall we regroup?'

'I suppose.' She paced up and down the chapel, and said, 'When I needed to unwind, Ferdinando made me shoot bottles, cans.'

'So?'

'There's beer cans all over the floor. Must have been left by long-gone Satanist groupies.'

'I can't shoot,' I pointed out.

'Not yet.'

She picked something up, then walked past me and outside, brushing my shoulder with the shotgun she held on hers, and I could do nothing but follow. I heard her steps move away, then a cling of tin hitting wood. 'I placed a can on the trunk of a fallen tree, and we're going to shoot at it,' she declared. 'When I say *we*, I mean *you*.'

'It is physically impossible.'

'You can hold a shotgun, you can squeeze a trigger, hence, it's physically *possible*.'

'But…'

'It's going to happen, Luca. Live with it. We can make a man of you yet.'

I heard a decisive *clack*, echoing like a slap. 'Starting with the basics,' she said. 'You open the shotgun in the middle, like this, to put the cartridges in. Here, I'll show you.'

'Really?'

'Trust me.'

She touched the back of my hand with the palm of hers, and made me shiver, in a way I had never experienced before. I let her guide my hand on the metal and polished wood of the shotgun. She was close; I could have kissed her. I thought of doing that, and I thought of turning my head too much or not enough, and kissing the air, like an idiot, and ruining all my chances forever after. 'Here is where you stick the cartridges,' she said, when my fingers touched two twin cavities in the metal. 'Wanna try?'

'I'm going to kill myself. Or you.'

'Sweetie, you can't kill a thing while the gun's open.' She handed me the shotgun. I familiarised myself with it, brushing its whole length with my fingers. They trembled, I didn't know whether out of fear or excitement.

'Here,' Ada said. 'A cartridge.' She handed me a cylinder with a metallic tip. 'Put it in one of the holes. Keep the metal end upwards.' I did as she said, and succeeded on the first try. 'Beginner's luck,' she commented, and handed me another cartridge. I had more trouble with this one, but managed to stick it in as well.

Ada walked to a position behind my shoulders, and pressed more closely to me than before, her chest against my back. She took the back of both my hands in hers. I let my muscles go limp, so that she could handle me like a puppet; she made me grip the shotgun's stock with one hand and the forestock with the other, and motioned to show me how to keep one end still, while sharply moving the other upwards. I did as she wanted; the shotgun locked. Now it was in one piece. Now it could fire, and wound.

'It's an old gun, this one,' Ada said. 'Kicks like a mule. So hold on to it.'

'This isn't a good idea,' I said, the first words I'd spoken in a while.

'Nope,' she agreed. 'Keep your fingers away from the trigger. Legs springy but firm, shoulder-width apart.' She helped me put the shotgun in position, the stock against my shoulder. She repeated, 'Pay attention or it's going to kick you in the face.'

Gently, she guided my index finger onto the safety, then made it run along the trigger guard, and finally inside the guard, against the trigger itself. We'd never been so close. *If only she could never stop touching me*, I thought, *if only we could keep repeating this moment for all eternity, I would be happy.*

'Hold on to it,' she insisted, for the third time, 'and fire.'

Ada stepped back and stood quiet, leaving me with the gun, alone. It was a nerve-racking thing, to shoot in the darkness, trusting her there was no one I could hurt. Trusting her; that was the key.

I pulled the trigger, an explosion punched my eardrums, and the stock kicked hard, just like a mule, but I managed to keep hold of it.

'Again!' Ada shouted.

I fired before she finished talking. I heard her laugh in the explosion.

My ears rang. It was like being newly blind, unable to discern what was going on around me. When the ringing subsided, Ada asked, as from a distance, 'Funny eardrums?'

The mixed scent of gunpowder and girl was the best thing there was. I'd smelt and touched Ada's skin more than I had any other human's, that was a bare truth, and everything about it was enchanting. 'Yes.'

'It gets better when you get used to shooting. How did it feel?'

'It felt powerful. *I* felt powerful.'

'I know, right? Take a gun in your hands and you're in charge. You get to decide who lives and who dies.'

'You're a good shot.'

'No, I'm abysmal, so as a matter of fact I mostly decide who lives, but it's the principle that matters. Apropos of that – we're ready for cans, I reckon.'

'There's no way in hell I could take aim.'

'No, but *we* can. I give you instructions, you follow them to the letter, and fire when I say so.'

'This is not going to work.'

'We're not paying for the cartridges.'

Once again I loaded the shotgun, this time without any help from Ada. I locked it and pushed the stock against my shoulder, savouring the simplicity of the gestures. I disengaged the safety. I gently ran my index finger from muzzle to barrel, all the way down to the trigger guard, and carefully put it inside, to rest upon the trigger.

'Point the shotgun upwards,' Ada said. 'Now move it to the left. Not like that, I mean *your* left. Right. You went too wide –

come back a little. Up again… Hang on, you're lowering the gun! It's heavy, yeah, but come on, act macho just this once. Good. Better now. A little more to your right. Go.'

I pulled the trigger, the fields exploded.

The next morning I came round to a disconnect between my sweaty skin and the quiet in my ears: the heat said it was well into the day, while the soundscape spoke of an earlier hour. I listened to birds and dogs, rather than machinery. Far away, an angry voice, Dad's, all but shouting into the phone. The thick walls muffled the words.

I dragged myself out of bed and to the window. I slung the shutters open. The sun shone on my face the way it did at around ten, when the builders would normally be heavy at work. I yawned, headed down the stairs. I could make out Dad's words now; they were to do with the masseria. He pronounced a name that rang a bell, Dr Ranieri, attached to a protest: 'This is completely unacceptable.'

I was tempted to run back to my room, but I was hungry and I had a right to breakfast. In the kitchen my theatrical welcome was a receiver being slammed on the phone cradle. Dad and Mum were both exuding anger. 'What's the matter?' I asked.

'The council,' Mum answered, at the same time as Dad gave me his answer: 'A fucker.'

There was an awkward silence, then Dad said, 'Sorry.'

Mum explained: 'The builders didn't show for work this morning.'

'I had to call the master mason,' Dad continued. 'He said

he's received a letter from the council which advised against continuing the works until further notice.'

'Were you talking to him now?'

'No, I was on the phone with Dr Ranieri.'

That's where I'd heard the name: at Uncle Mario's. He was the guy fishing for money. 'Did you pay the fine?' I asked while I opened the fridge to get some milk.

'I said it's not going to happen, and it's not going to happen. The South is a wild country, kid. You've got to learn to stand your ground.' On that one thing my father was right, of course: he should have learnt. But he was one of those soft men who mistake bluster for strength.

I fetched a box of biscuits. 'Uncle Mario saw this coming.'

'It's your home too,' Mum said. 'It wouldn't hurt to show some interest.'

I did not answer. I had already talked too much. It was imperative that I didn't draw Dad's attention to me. That he didn't have any excuse to do what he wanted to do.

He said, 'I convinced Dr Ranieri to pay us a visit. We're talking this out in person. Mum and I want you and your brother to assist.'

Despite my best intentions, I said, 'Ada's coming by.'

'The beach can wait, for one day.'

'But, Dad…'

'You'll be grateful when you're older.'

I'm older now, and not grateful.

There were mysteries to investigate with Ada, cans to shoot at, and instead I was stuck at home waiting for a town clerk. I had to call her. When Giuseppe Guadalupi picked up the phone, I mumbled half-hearted words about resuming guitar lessons sometime soon. It was a confusing exchange. I resented him as much as I missed him. He handed the call to Ada, who, after I explained the situation, said, 'I get it. No big deal.' She didn't mind my no-show. Why didn't she mind? I would have minded. That, too, piled on to worsen my mood.

The day dragged on like torture administered by an indifferent Inquisitor, with Mum and Dad pretending to plod away at meaningless tasks, Ferdi holing up somewhere, and me laying around listlessly on the porch unsure of what to do with myself, until finally the soft purr of an expensive engine pulled up the driveway, and died. A car door clacked open. A person in hard-soled shoes dismounted.

'Good afternoon, Dr Ranieri,' Dad said in the stiff tone which marked him taking the moral high ground. 'We were expecting you earlier.'

'I didn't have to come at all. I'm here as a personal favour.'

'Should I say thank you?'

'Oh, there's no need for that.' Dr Ranieri laughed. 'It's a small town. We look after each other.'

Dad's voice came out less secure, more perplexed, when he said, 'Coffee?'

'Beer would be great. Only if it's cold.'

'Luca, would you go and get two bottles, please? Some water too. And call Mum and Ferdi.'

Dad wanted me to perform. Lo and behold: I was normal enough to find the fridge and siblings! I was a refurbished boy, as good as new.

In a matter of minutes we were all gathered on the porch, and I couldn't shake off the sensation that we were the guests and Dr Ranieri the kindly host who was giving us a hearing.

Dad went on about the approaching grape harvest, and the year's yield of olives, as if he knew the first thing about the land. Dr Ranieri didn't talk as much as listen, until Dad said, 'Coming to business.'

'Yes,' Dr Ranieri said.

'Could you explain to me what this is all about?'

Dr Ranieri had a friendly tone when he said, 'Perhaps you should? You were the one asking for this meeting.'

'The fine.'

'What about it?'

'Our surveyor said…'

'Didn't we square it over the phone? There was a misunderstanding, in good faith, it goes without saying.'

'And we have to pay *seven million lire* because of a misunderstanding?'

'It's the law.'

'Spare me. It's extortion.'

The season of Dr Ranieri's voice turned from summer to winter. 'That is not a word I would throw around lightly.'

'It is the only word that applies,' Dad said, and in my mind's eye I could see him puff out his chest like a cartoon rooster.

The other man sighed. 'Extortion is when your car blows up, when your animals get poisoned, all of them, when your house catches fire if you don't do exactly as you are told. That is extortion, Dr Saracino, and I'm not going to lie to you, it does happen, unfortunately. This? This is the law. It *protects us* from extortion.'

That man had the gall to come into our home and threaten us. It would be many years before I had a chance to make him pay, but pay he did, for I have a good memory. Dr

Ranieri walks meekly these days, and never fails to buy me coffee when he crosses my path. His was the first name I wrote on my list, before I even learnt that no one can grow older without building up a list.

At that moment, it was clear that we could not oppose him, that he had power and we had not, and that was that. When you turn your back to reality, reality doesn't cease to exist; you can shape it, like a dream, only when you are lucid enough to see it for what it is, exactly like a dream. I had learnt that lesson, my parents had not yet.

'We are not going to pay,' Mum said.

'Then you are not going to continue the works, and I won't deny it: I for one will be disappointed. I was looking forward to seeing what you would make of the Masseria del Vento. It's a beautiful old building.'

'We weren't clear,' Dad said in his tougher voice, which only Mum took seriously. 'We are not going to pay *and* the works are going to continue.'

Ferdi made a sound bursting with contempt.

Dr Ranieri said, 'You tried, and I had to order your builders to stop. They won't start again unless I give them the all-clear. The master mason is an old friend of mine, an honest man, keen on the law. And to be clear, what you've been doing here, continuing the works even though you'd been expressly forbidden to do so, that would make you liable for another fine. Are we asking you to pay that, on top of the previous one? We're not. Nobody is interested in making your life hard, blowing this little misunderstanding into an out-and-out conflict. We're not against you, Dr Saracino.' He reverted to a formal Southern courtesy that was anything but friendly.

'We're doing our best to help you out, if anything. But the law is the law.'

'We're not afraid of escalating,' Mum said. 'Of writing to the mayor.'

'My cousin, you mean?'

'Bastard,' Ferdi muttered under his breath.

'Excuse me?'

'I said—'

Mum interrupted Ferdi. 'We're locals too, Dr Ranieri. You know my brother.'

'I'm here thanks to him. I'm not a GP, I don't do house calls, but Mario's a good man, well-liked in town. And your father, he was a legend. Hate him or love him, you won't meet a soul in town who didn't respect Don Ferdinando. Yes, you're basically locals, which makes it all the more surprising that we must have this conversation.'

'I'm sure Mario has his own connections.'

There was a beat of silence; then Dr Ranieri said, 'I've heard what you paid him to buy out his share of the masseria.' He chuckled. 'That was *quite* some price. More than twice its worth.'

Mum swallowed whatever she had been on the brink of saying. *More than twice its worth.*

'Mario, too, is an honest man,' Dr Ranieri said. 'He's got children to provide for, two of them, and a beautiful wife with expensive taste. He's not going against the law for his sister. I don't think so. He's too smart for that. But let me tell you, as a friend of the family, that you're taking this whole matter the wrong way; we're all in it for the long run, you, the council, everybody. Your brother, obviously. Sign a cheque now, I will deposit it in the council's account soon as I can, and tomorrow, first thing in the morning, you'll have your builders start again. This is but a hiccup. We can leave it behind us and go out for dinner, with the families. I harbour no hard feelings.'

'What I do harbour—' Dad started.

Ferdi cut him off. 'Oh, for fuck's sake,' he said. 'Get the chequebook.'

Mum and Dad had to pay. Of course they had to pay. No other outcome had ever been on the cards, as actual locals would have known from the get-go.

I remember Mum's long phone call with Bianca Guadalupi, a conversation on house prices in the area, and I remember how crestfallen she was when she hung up. Dr Ranieri's every word was true. Mum and Dad hadn't checked the local market, like they hadn't checked the surveyor's work, because Uncle Mario was taking care of the pesky details of their grand plan, and who can you trust, if not family? Fleeced by her big brother, her favourite person alive, the one who'd protected her from all evils when she was little. Had it been Dad stabbing her in the back, Mum would have suffered less. Had it been me or Ferdi, I suspect she would have suffered less.

We had dinner under a cloud of grief. My parents were defeated on every level. Short a good chunk of money, duped by the person they'd been counting on to start building their dream Southern life, they found themselves financially trapped in a country with arcane rules far beyond their comprehension, with their two sons, one a good-for-nothing who held them in contempt, the other a sightless nut-job. They'd been so proud of their hard work, their achievements, and it had come to this.

When Dad tried – 'It's not always smooth sailing' – I heard (and it stunned me) doubt in his words.

By night Ada returned to my room, in my fantasies, to soothe me and make me feel better. I was lying in bed spent and dripping with sweat, my right wrist aching, when an otherworldly voice broke through the hush. It came and went in waves. It was like the keening of a child whose head was being submerged in water, then given enough time to catch a breath before being submerged again. I trained my ears on the sound. What was familiar about it?

I climbed out of bed and followed the thread of the keening, along the corridor and up a staircase, making my way between cobwebs and dust to a ruined part of the masseria which had been left untouched. Over the grime, over the dampness, over the dried-up bird poo, I detected a distinct tang in the air.

Dad.

I stopped. Dad was hiding in a disused room, crying his heart out.

That set me off-balance. I didn't know Dad had it in him to cry. The thoughtful thing to do – the decent one – would have been to approach him, talk to him, go as far as give him a hug if he consented. My feet didn't move. Dad was capable of true feelings: that was yet another exotic territory for me. I needed time to get to know it at my own pace.

I left him alone. I tiptoed back down the stairs to the safety of my room, and perhaps I wished for the righteous man to come.

In the hours I spent tossing and turning in bed, wide awake, I came to the conclusion that it was time for a man-to-man with

Uncle Mario. Getting to his home on my own would not be easy; I had never gone there on foot. What in June would have been a daunting task was now an interesting prospect.

The next day, the road to Portodimare was busy with cars, mopeds, bikes. Summer was peaking; the last time Ada and I had been to the Little Pinewood you could almost have called it bustling. Unusual accents lifted from bars and tobacconists, the air heavy with exhaust and sweat. There was a happy buzz, a heady buzz. It was a welcome change from the grange.

It was the tenth of August, the Feast of San Lorenzo, when the Perseids meteor shower is at its most spectacular, they say, and if you only raise your head up to the sky you will be graced with shooting stars. That night teenagers would light fires on the shore and wait for dawn, looking at the stars, smoking weed, playing bad music, whatever might lead them to making out or to die trying. From then until Ferragosto, the Feast of the Assumption of the Virgin Mary, on the fifteenth, it would be one uninterrupted party. Afterwards, it'd be a matter of cleaning up and tucking in for the turn of the season. August is a month of two halves; the first is an orgy, the second a death sentence.

I got to the general vicinity of Uncle Mario's house, took a right from the main road, and walked on slowly, scouring for familiar voices among those coming from the front gardens lining the street on both sides. I found none, went back, started again on a different street and kept going until I heard my cousin Maddalena's sweet-sounding voice call my name: 'Luca!' When she wanted, she could give you the impression that seeing you was the finest of treats. She said, 'What are you doing here?'

I felt for the metal gate, then for the handle. 'Is Uncle Mario in?'

'Sure. Dad!' she called. 'Luca's at the door.'

'My favourite nephew, back from the dead!' Uncle Mario's jovial voice boomed.

Aunt Gemma came out too, made a fuss, but soon she and Maddalena, with their perfect social graces, understood that I wanted to be left alone with Mario and went out to look at a purse or a sarong or something they had seen in a shop.

'Down to business,' Uncle Mario said.

I drank from the delicious lemonade Aunt Gemma had poured me. A hint of her geranium scent lingered on the brim of the wet, cold glass. 'Is it that obvious?'

'For one who knows you.'

'Did you hear what they say about me in town?'

'Difficult not to.'

'I'm not a Satanist, Uncle.'

'I somehow suspected as much.'

'But I stand by my story. One hundred per cent.'

'And here's me, wishing they were only rumours. But, no. My favourite nephew is cuckoo.'

'Is there anything I should know about the masseria?'

'What can I say? No, I never saw any ghost or ghoul. And your mum asked me to go to her immediately if I noticed you poke your nose that way.'

'You won't though.'

'And why is that?'

'You shafted us, Uncle.'

'Excuse me?'

'I know what you did. I know we overpaid for the masseria.'

'Do you want a peach? I've got two on my plate.'

'Thank you.'

He handed me a smooth-skinned fruit. 'Was it Dr Ranieri?'

'Yeah.'

'This explains your mum's frosty tone on the phone this morning.'

'You're the person she trusted more in the whole world.'

'I named a price and your parents accepted it. I was happy to sell, they were happy to buy. I didn't force anyone to do anything.'

'Please. You knew Mum would accept any price you named because she trusts you. And because she and Dad are too arrogant to bother with research.' I bit into my peach. 'Oh, I get you, believe me, I do. They're full of hot air, those two, and it must've been so tempting, to shaft them and laugh behind their back. But here's the thing, I'm not like them. And I'm going to grow up here, in this place.'

I heard Uncle Mario munch. 'Your tone is not great.'

'You're thinking something along the lines of: *How cute. My handicapped nephew is playing tough guy.* But think about this, if you really are smarter than Mum and Dad. It took me, how long – a few weeks? – to learn how to move around the village as well as anyone sighted, born and bred here. A few weeks, Uncle. Imagine what I could do in a few months, in a few years. Imagine what I might be capable of doing by the time I grow up. Imagine who I could *be*. And then ask yourself: Do you want that man, the man I'll become, to have forgiven you by then – or not?'

The stone of Uncle Mario's peach fell onto a ceramic plate. 'Are you sure you are your father's son?'

'Can I ever be sure?'

He laughed. 'Okay,' he said. 'We have an understanding. Just so you know, it's not because of those ominous-sounding threats you just made, but because it's pretty obvious that you can take care of yourself.'

'You believe my story, then?'

'That's immaterial.'

'Okay, let's leave it at that. So, in the name of this understanding that we seem to have, are you sure you've got nothing for me?'

'Do you want to know if I believe in ghosts? I don't. But the South has changed drastically in the last thirty-odd years. When I was your age, the world, this corner of the world, was stranger than it is now. Folks had their ways, and their ways were old. Your mum and I grew up on stories of this woman who knew how to sing the Psalms to make girls pregnant, a man who could remove – or cast – the evil eye. On the eighth of December we would dine on nine different courses, no meat allowed. Snakes might be the Devil in disguise, and Saint Paul handles them. Et cetera. You know what I'm talking about. Some of these traditions are still around. By and large they're around in that guise, traditions, quaint and lovely, while when I was little they were the hard facts of life, everyday life. Some favours you asked of friends, others of saints, and that was the pragmatic thing to do. Our family wasn't any more superstitious than others, or any less. We had our own stories, our own ways, just like any other. We had an ancestor who'd talk to the Virgin, a second cousin who played drums to exorcise the spider's spirit, a simple nugget of wisdom handed down through the generations.'

'Which nugget?'

'You know: *Praise God, never the wind.*'

'I thought it was Grandpa's.'

'No, it's been in our family for ever. Our ancestors put a lot of effort into wiping out all their money and land, but they couldn't bet a sentence in a card game. It's not much of an inheritance, but there you go. Growing up in that context, it was only normal to have some… experiences, occasionally.'

'Like what?'

'Like experiences that all children had, back then. We had no TV, no video games. Our imaginations were easily excited. I remember one time I was looking in a mirror, I might have been five or six, and I noticed that the figure looking back at me was… slow. I'd raise my arm, and the figure, too, would raise its arm, as it should, but not immediately. No, it would raise its arm a fraction of a second too late. As if it wasn't a reflection, as if it was a *thing*, mimicking me for its own amusement.'

'And you didn't do a thing about it?'

'Do what about what? I told Mum and Dad, and they said what they always said when Stefi or I went to them with this or that children's story; they said to praise God, never the wind. All we had to do was say our prayers, ignore the strangeness, and the strangeness would go away.'

'Did it work?'

'Every time. The ignoring part more than the praying, I dare say.'

'I thought you'd be more open-minded. You guys are religious.'

'We go to Mass,' said Uncle Mario. 'The Church is great and powerful. God? I wouldn't know. Praise God, never the wind, and better praise Him in public, for God might not take notice, but people will.'

'Grandpa didn't give a hoot about what people thought.'

'The Guadalupis did, and see who was living in the crumbling farmhouse and who had the nice villa.'

'About that – what beef did Grandpa have with the Guadalupis? Everybody's got a different story. You're his only male heir, and you were close to him until the end. If anyone knows, it's you.'

Uncle Mario chuckled. 'You're a tad too young for some stories.'

'I wasn't too young to be dragged from one end of Italy to the other, and to have my family ruined by my dearest uncle.'

'Your parents are not ruined.'

'They will be soon, won't they?'

'When I say you're my favourite nephew – it's for real.'

'I know.'

Uncle Mario shifted in his chair. 'What the hell, you can take it in your stride. When they were young, Dad and Pierpaolo Guadalupi had a business together: a smuggling business, small-scale. Don't judge Dad for that, please. He had a wife, a baby – me – and very little in terms of money. Nobody should have gotten hurt. They imported goods from Eastern Europe, cigarettes mostly, and cartridges too, maybe the odd shotgun. They did the supply runs on Pierpaolo's boat and stored the goods in the Masseria del Vento. The reasoning was solid. There's more than enough land there to serve as storage and marshalling yard, the sea is a stone's throw away, it's a perfect hideout. It was easy money, and good fun. Pierpaolo didn't need the cash. The way Dad saw it, his mate was in for the romance. I get that. Ours is a beautiful sea to sail, night and day, and the law, well, the law is a beautiful thing to break. *Law* is what we call the rule of the crooks who won the last round.' Uncle Mario was talking in a low voice. Someone from the street cursed loudly, covering his words. He waited for the cursing to subside. 'It was a good partnership until it wasn't.'

Grandpa had been, among other things, a smuggler. It fit. 'What made it stop working?'

'This is strictly confidential, Luca. I'm trusting you're old enough to understand and respect that.'

'Go on.'

'Pierpaolo shot two people dead.' Uncle Mario stopped there.

I supposed he wanted to gauge my reaction. I asked, 'Why?'

'He and Dad were coming back from a supply run on a full-moon night. Not the best of ideas, to make a run on a full moon, but those two were young hotheads, not seasoned criminals. It was a summer night, warm and nice. They docked at the usual spot, came on land with their cargo, no hiccups. Only, there was a couple on the beach. Young, very – not much older than you and Ada. Buck naked. Those two idiots had seen the boat approach and just stood there to see what was what. They were curious, can you believe that? *Curious*. They thought they had a good hiding spot among the rocks. When Dad found them, they hadn't even bothered to put their clothes back on. Dad gave them a good scare, a slap or two to the boy, some harsh words to the girl, and if it were up to him, he'd have left it at that. Pierpaolo though – he went ballistic. He started worrying they'd seen his boat, they'd know who he was. Mind, he was obsessing over nothing: those two poor bastards were pissing themselves with fear, *literally* pissing in the case of the boy. If they blabbed, they'd have had to explain what they were doing on the beach by night, and that'd've ruined the girl's life infinitely more than an accusation of smuggling would Dad's. The girl's father might have killed the boy – easily. Smuggling, though? It's small beer. If the Carabinieri gave a damn – and it was a big *if* – it'd have been a matter of cutting them in on future runs. Annoying? Yes. The end of the world? Definitely not. It was one of those situations that look bad at first but when you think them through are nothing to lose sleep over. Dad explained this to Pierpaolo, and Pierpaolo seemed to listen. Emphasis on *seemed*. Dad was still talking when Pierpaolo took a gun and shot the kids. Two shots, two dead bodies.'

'Dad and Pierpaolo carried guns?'

'Just hunting shotguns, and Dad swore he never shot anyone.'

'Is that so?'

'He had a mean streak, but I don't see him as a cold-blooded assassin. Anyway, Pierpaolo Guadalupi did kill the two poor bastards with Grandpa's shotgun, which made Grandpa feel even more guilty. He folded the business after that night, stopped talking to Pierpaolo Guadalupi and carried his guilt to the end of his days.'

'Not enough to come forward.'

'What for? The kids wouldn't return from the dead, and he had a young family to take care of. Nothing but a practical man, Dad. Add to that the fact Pierpaolo had the clout to make Dad take most of the fall for the killing of the couple. Whose shotgun had been used? Not Pierpaolo's.'

I saw the point. I didn't necessarily like it, and I needed time to decide whether I agreed with it or not, but I did see the point. 'They say Pierpaolo's death was suspicious.'

Uncle Mario said, 'He shuffled it twenty-odd years later: his boat sunk one night while moored in the harbour. He was sleeping in the under-deck and went down with the boat. An unusual accident, I'll grant you that. As you can imagine, it attracted busybodies like sugar does ants. Some gossip that Dad was behind it.'

'What do you think?'

'Dad stealthily jumping on a boat, putting a man to sleep, then sinking the boat – it's soap opera stuff. Life makes less sense than that: unusual accidents do happen with no rhyme or reason. You'll meet people who have to find an explanation for everything, and any explanation will do, a conspiracy or a monster or the Devil himself, because the darkest of reasons is still better than no reason at all. They want someone to praise or blame, but there's no one, Luca, in the vast majority of cases there's no one and nothing at all. There's no secret plan, no evil schemers and saintly heroes. There's only the wind.'

Ada was uncharacteristically quiet when I met with her at Chocolate Delight. 'How did it go?' she asked, with the swish of a book shutting.

I told her of my uncle's experience with the mirror, and his dismissive attitude, and I stopped there. I wasn't sure if she knew her grandfather was a killer; I wasn't sure if I wanted to be the one to tell her. I wouldn't let old history drive a wedge between us.

'Ferdinando must be rolling in his grave,' was her only comment.

Family history was awkward. I thought that a different topic might jolt her into conversation. 'Do you know anyone who's having a bonfire tonight?' I asked. I wanted her to talk, have a good time with me. It didn't occur to me that she might be silent for her own reasons.

'The Feast of San Lorenzo is for losers. All the boys think they're these great bongo players, there are too many fires to really see the stars, so what's the point?' She went silent again.

I tried a different angle. 'It freaks me out that the righteous man has been AWOL ever since I took the photograph. It feels like the breathing in before an ugly breathing out.'

'Oh, worry not, he's back all right.'

'What? Why didn't you tell me immediately?'

'I didn't want to talk about it just yet, okay?' I heard her stand up. 'Come on, let's go. I did nothing else than sit on my arse today.'

'Where are we going?'

'Ever jumped off the cubes at the pier?'

'Come again?'

'Cool, we're set. Let's go.'

I had to follow her like in the early days: the harbour wasn't a landmark I'd learnt the way to. We waded through a village packed with people. Some didn't move out of my way quickly enough, or at all, and my cane bumped into calves and dogs' paws. I hadn't been around such intense human activity since Turin. A handful of weeks had passed, each of them as rich as a whole year. A handful of weeks since Mum had packed me in the car and driven me from the continent to the Mediterranean, from one civilisation to another, a handful of weeks since I'd had the first hint of the high strangeness troubling the Masseria del Vento.

'It was yesterday afternoon,' Ada said suddenly. 'I was reading in my hammock. *Lady Chatterley's Lover*, another one my old folks would disapprove of. I was *ecstatic* that the works from your place were on pause.'

'Yeah, I get that.'

'I mean, we didn't have one moment of quiet the whole summer. But moving on. The book was less interesting than the back cover promised, if you're not into gamekeepers. The quiet was a welcome change, the wind turned nicely, the hammock lulled me – well, I conked out. And the dream of the blood-red moon returned.' She paused. 'I opened my eyes – in my dream, I opened my eyes – and there I was, on the beach, with that sick moon lording over me. And I heard the same music you heard. Drums and the fiddle.'

I shivered. I shiver now, as I walk through my memories. 'The revellers,' I said.

'The revellers,' Ada repeated. 'That music is terrifying, you were right, but… I don't know. It made me curious.'

For a moment I could have vomited: the revellers made me all but curious. I didn't know whether to admire Ada, or fear her.

'And I set off towards them. The pier,' she announced. 'We're there.'

We briefly walked on sand, then hard cement. On our left was the sea (the wind and the scent left no doubt about that), on our right a wall, breaking airflow and noises.

'It was dream logic,' Ada said. 'One moment I was on the beach, the next I was on the dirt track, headed in the revellers' direction. And then…' She paused again, and I heard the sound of flimsy fabric rolling up. She took one of my hands in hers. 'Touch,' she said, bringing my hand onto her other arm. 'Go easy. It hurts.'

My fingers rested on a bulge on her skin, pulsating with warmth – a bruise.

Ada said, 'And then the righteous man appeared on the track, blocking my way. His presence was… I'm tempted to use the word *indescribable*, if it weren't such a cop-out. He felt *wrong*, not a part of the dream. A loose cannon who'd wandered there on a whim, from some place very far away. He was dressed like in the photograph, exactly like that. He reminded me of… Don't take this the wrong way – he reminded me of Ferdinando, a meaner, nastier version of Ferdinando. What I'm saying is that he could be, I don't know, Ferdinando's brother, or ancestor. He gripped my arms – strongly – and shouted in my face.'

'Saying what?'

'No words, only a sort of bellow. His smell was like a headbutt. I shouted back, and the next thing I know, I'm awake in my hammock, yelling like a madwoman. It's lucky Mum and Dad weren't home, or they'd still be questioning me.'

'The righteous man stopped you from reaching the revellers,' I said.

'Yeah, I thought that too. But did he need to hurt me? And I've got bruises on my back. Did he make those too? Whichever way I turn it in my head, it doesn't make sense. I… I don't know, Luca. I just don't know.'

'What are we wasting time for? Why aren't we out in the fields, searching…'

Ada laughed bitterly. 'You mean, playing.'

She was right. Of course she was right, so I got defensive. 'It's not a game.'

'It's not a game to go searching for clues in your backyard? Messing around in crumbling chapels? You're smarter than that, Luca. You know we were having a laugh. We may as well get a Great Dane and call him Scooby-Doo.'

'The righteous man is not a laugh.'

'No, but we are. Okay, stop here.'

'Ada, we need to talk about this…'

'Luca, *I* need to take my mind off this. I was hurt, and I put on this strong face, what else can I do? But I'm scared stiff. I almost pissed myself in the hammock. I need to get some breathing space. I need not to obsess over bloody monsters for five minutes. I need to jump, okay? I need to jump.'

On our left, where the pier gave on to the sea, scattering the breakwaters, were enormous concrete cubes. From them, you could dive into deep water. I heard knots of kids doing just that, as knots of kids have been doing since the day the cubes were thrown there, and will continue to do until the pier crumbles or humankind dies out, whichever happens first.

'Mauro, don't be a sissy and dive in!' a voice said.

'Chill, Tony, I'm on it,' another answered.

No one approached us and we approached no one. We ventured from the pier to the cubes, which were rough underfoot. There were gaps of different widths between them, from the almost non-existent to the insurmountable. Ada held me while I tested one void with a foot, searching for purchase on the next cube. We got to the last line, which seawater lapped at lovingly.

'Only the big blue sea in front of you,' Ada said. 'On the count of three. One.'

I flexed my legs. *Are you ever going to make a move?*

'Two.'

That wasn't the moment for such thoughts. I thrust my body forward. *For real, I mean.*

'Three.'

Or you can just keep jerking off. It's safer that way. You can't fail that way.

I jumped. I was suspended in a nothingness and a thought came to me, perfectly clear, that when I touched the water, it wouldn't be the sea I knew, but that other sea, in that other place, which was almost a beach, but not quite. The thought took the breath out of me, and I wished I hadn't jumped, I wished I hadn't come, I wished I was safe in Giuseppe Guadalupi's office, with his fingers gently placing mine on the guitar's strings.

Then I hit the water. I sank deep and deeper yet, unable to tell up from down. The pressure of the water on my body showed me the way. I swam, following the line of least resistance, and came back to the world, gulping fresh air, laughing.

Ada was laughing too. 'How cool is that?' she said.

'Unspeakably cool.'

'Another round?'

'First I'm gonna take off my shades. I almost lost them. Which way are the cubes?'

She floated closer and took hold of me. 'Come, I'll give you a hand.'

We jumped maybe thirty times that afternoon. We splashed about with the energy of champions. It was an amazing, exhausting day.

On our way back home, Ada asked me if she could borrow the gun.

I had replaced the shotgun in the secret compartment. With Ferdi on the beach, and Mum and Dad busy chatting about work, it took but a moment to sneak in and take it. Touching the wooden handle made me bigger, stronger. That gun had taken human lives, not so long ago. I brushed the trigger. So much power coiled there.

Ada could not balance both the gun and the bike, and besides, the Guadalupis would be home, so we hid the shotgun in the low-hanging branches of a fig tree beyond the vineyard, close to the spot where we had first met. Ada assured me that the wide lobed leaves concealed our shotgun as well as they had Adam's in the Garden of Eden. 'I'll come and fetch it tonight,' she said.

'Be careful.'

'That is what I need the gun for, to be careful. Thank you, dude.'

She drew closer to kiss me on one cheek, and when her lips brushed me, one moment I flinched, the next I cursed myself.

'Oh, wow,' she said. 'If I have the same effect on monsters, we're sorted. I won't need to fire one round.'

Whatever I thought, I kept it to myself.

When the builders' van arrived, and Piero Quarta, the master mason, climbed out of it, Dad said, 'Mr Quarta, a word in private, please.'

'Yes,' Piero Quarta said, in his thick accent.

My parents, too, were fighting their battles. Once again they forced Ferdi and me to assist. They thought they were putting on a display of strength, after having been humbled by Dr Ranieri before our eyes. They clung to their illusion of being the new power couple in town, and their children were the last audience they had left. It was heartbreakingly ridiculous.

We got to the kitchen, Mum and Dad leading the way, Piero Quarta behind them, and Ferdi and I as the rearguard. Ferdi had spent the night at a bonfire on the beach, and he would still be with his friends hadn't Mum and Dad required his presence. He gave off a demonic vibe of woodsmoke and resentment.

'We couldn't help but notice,' Mum said, 'that you are already behind schedule.'

The master mason lit one of his heavy cigarettes, instantly filling the room with a tear-inducing stench of burning tar. 'Happens.'

'We're not happy with that,' Dad said.

'Happens too.'

'Nothing to offer as an explanation?' Mum asked.

'Your kid slows us down.'

'Please,' Dad said. 'I doubt Ferdi's powerful enough to hold back an entire building crew.'

'Building's hard work. You don't know what could go wrong until it does.'

'And, pray, what is it that is going wrong?'

'The other day, for example.'

'The other day, yes, a perfect example,' Mum said. 'Why didn't you show up for work?'

'You know why.'

'Did you forget who's paying your salary? It's us. Not the council. Not Dr Ranieri. Us.'

Piero Quarta dragged on his cigarette. 'What're we saying here?'

'We are saying that you've been rude since the first day, Mr Quarta. And we aren't happy either with your attitude or with the quality of the work you're doing. We are terminating your contract with immediate effect.'

The master mason took another, longer, drag. 'My boys accepted to work on the week of Ferragosto. Nobody works on the week of Ferragosto.'

'We were going to pay you double for that.'

'You are still paying us. Fair is fair.'

'What part of what my wife said wasn't clear?' Dad's voice rose. It sounded more and more like the keening I had heard the other night. '*We're terminating your contract with immediate effect.* That means today. Now.'

'Yes, and today before we leave you're going to give us what you owe us until the end of August. Double for the week of Ferragosto. Fair is fair.'

'Or what?'

The master mason took another drag, walked to the sink, turned on the tap, and there was a sizzling of a cigarette snubbed under the water. 'You don't have to pay cash,' he said. 'A cheque's all good.'

'That was a cringe-fest,' said Ferdi.

I gave him a non-committal, 'Yeah.'

Ferdi yawned. 'Sorry. Long night.'

An obvious opening. I could have followed with, 'Did you have fun?' or, 'What were you up to?' or a thousand other stock phrases, had I wanted to talk to him, but I didn't. I'd been sitting in the shadow of the carob tree, in the company of *Moby-Dick*. The whale was boring, and boring was better than anything my family had on offer.

Ferdi insisted. 'Mum and Dad won't find other builders until September. I don't think they could afford them anyway, while they're still paying Quarta's boys. I've got the tail end of summer to myself. Small blessings, eh?'

I said, 'Yeah.'

'Scrawny, we haven't properly *talked* in a while.'

'It was great, wasn't it?'

'Are you cross because I told your story to Mum and Dad?'

'Guess.'

'I was worried for you.'

'Thanks to you the only person standing between me and a boxful of meds is Giuseppe Guadalupi.'

'What's wrong with taking medications you need?'

'I don't need them!'

'So you still stand by that story?'

'Why are we talking about this, Ferdi?'

He shuffled on his feet. 'I miss the way things were before.'

'Before you double-crossed me, like Uncle Mario with Mum. Must run in the family.'

'Give me a chance, Scrawny. Tell me, did you have any more… experiences?'

'Why do you ask?' I paused, to allow a thought to form in my head. 'Who put you up to this?'

'Nobody!' he answered, too quickly.

'Was it Dad?'

'Nobody, Scrawny, I…' He couldn't bear to say *I promise*.

'No, not Dad. Bianca Guadalupi? It's her, isn't it?'

He didn't answer immediately. When he did, he said, 'Bianca and Giuseppe both. They insisted. They care for you. We all do.'

I rose to my feet. 'I hate you,' I said, and right then, I meant it.

The phone rang at the time Ada should have been swinging by. Mum picked up and then called my name.

Ada was on the other end. 'Can you talk?' she asked under her breath.

Mum had returned to the kitchen table, where she was filling a pot with coffee. 'Yeah, it's beautiful weather,' I said.

'Just listen, then. I'm not coming this morning. I'm preparing some stuff for later. I'll come and get you tonight. You wanted a bonfire, we'll get a bonfire. Can't give you an exact time, just wait for me on the porch after your family's gone to bed, okay? Can you do that?'

My heart was drumming. 'I don't see why not.'

'Get your towel,' Ada said. 'Your guitar too. It's not a fire without a guitar.'

I am putting order where there was none, organising a story, a fiction of sorts, events that in real life bled into one another with no apparent rhyme or reason. I am sure to be making minor mistakes, misremembering facts, omitting details, perhaps forcing the hand here and there for the sake of clarity, of rhythm (would you be able to repeat beat by beat chats you had twenty and more years ago?). It is small stuff. The crux of the matter is that these events did happen, more or less in the order I recount here, more or less in the world we deem real. That summer our world behaved like a dream, thus showing, I believe, its true nature.

On the night of the bonfire I stole back to the porch after Mum and Dad had retired to their room, as I did most nights, only this time I wore trunks beneath my cargo shorts, and left behind my book to take my guitar and beach towel instead. I eased into the swing, sat the guitar on my lap, and waited. The rocking, the breeze, the call of the hoopoe: everything was mundane and everything was a portent. I was excited, bursting with anticipation. I'd heard, from Ferdi, stories of bonfires on the beach. I'd heard stories of girls.

I prayed the righteous man wouldn't come, wouldn't spoil this for me. When steps rustled the gravel, my heart sank.

'Hey,' Ada whispered. 'It's me.'

I had been expecting the whir of mechanical wings. 'Where's your bike?' I asked.

'I walked. Bikes are noisy.'

I would never hear the whir again. We get to know what our first times are, but seldom our last.

We tiptoed down the drive, and it seemed to me that our feet were impossibly heavy, that the friction of flip-flops on gravel would wake Mum, Dad, everybody within ten miles. As we approached the gate, the beastly roar of cars jumped at us. In the week of Ferragosto, traffic never slept.

'We can't go the usual route,' Ada said.

I'd guessed that much: kids out and about late at night were not an unusual sight in Portodimare, but I was a highly recognisable kid, and people gossiping were not an unusual sight either. We walked on the main road for a short while, then Ada turned right onto another dirt track.

'Where are we going?' I asked.

'Duh, the Little Pinewood. Do you need to ask?'

With a towel balanced over my shoulder, my guitar slung over the same shoulder and my cane in one hand, negotiating a new route required most of my attention, and we spoke little, except when Ada updated me on our progress. Scents of fried fish and stone-baked pizza wafted in the air, and oafish music pumped from gardens. The shore might be quiet tonight, after the excesses of the Feast of San Lorenzo, but nowhere else was.

I recognised the village at once, even though we got to a different part of it than usual. When we entered it, the temperature rose, the noise grew louder.

'Shit,' Ada said.

'What?'

'Freeze.'

I had sensed a wall; I reached out behind my shoulders, and sure enough I touched bricks. I stepped back and stood with my back against the wall, playing possum. Drops of perspiration fell down my forehead and rolled down my neck. We were surrounded by music, happy voices, drunken voices and too many smells to count. I didn't have a clue where danger might come from, or what kind of danger it was.

'It was your brother,' Ada said. 'He almost saw us.'

'But he didn't.'

'No, I don't think so. You know what, better get to the Little Pinewood from the beach. There's going to be everyone and their mum around the village tonight.'

I wouldn't contradict her even if I could. We reached sand, where my cane was hard to work. 'Let's swap,' Ada said. She took my guitar, and gave me her backpack, which was heavy and tingled with glass. She had learnt how to be a faultless guide; I leaned on her elbow with one hand, now free, and it was almost as good as having my own set of eyes, shiny-new.

I'd never be led again with such ease, not by my friends, not by my wife. A certain grace does not belong to adults.

The sand was fresh, the sea barely moved, and as we advanced along the coast the noises from the village sounded less like life and more like memory, until the memory faded too and all was quiet. I recognised the rocks underfoot, and walked to the other side following a trajectory my body had learnt. We kept walking. The scent of damp, burnt wood reached me, a ghost of yesterday's fires.

And we were at the Little Pinewood. I took off the backpack with a sigh of release. The back of my t-shirt was drenched in sweat. 'Heavy, I know,' Ada said. 'You'll be grateful when you open it. I'll go fetch some wood, okay?'

'Do you want me to come with you?'

'No need. You want to make yourself useful, empty the backpack. Be a darling, and set up dinner while I go hunting for the tribe.'

'How can I make dinner if you don't hunt first?'

'Hear, hear, the life of the party is here.'

Her steps drew away. A metallic groan announced that the net to the pinewood was being pulled up. It was a sound I had come to love, but I had grown used to hearing it when the sun was beating on my head. By night, it had a different resonance – louder, deeper. We were far from the village, far from the road, in a spot well beyond civilisation as I knew it.

'Give me a shout should you need anything, okay?' I said.

'Will do,' Ada answered, kind enough not to point out that I couldn't exactly run to the rescue.

She rustled and crackled and crinkled in the woods; she might as well not be herself anymore, no more human, and I might be alone on the beach with an unseen creature prowling among the trees. I unzipped the backpack. I was enjoying myself. I enjoyed the sense of freedom. It was a grown-up thing, to be on a lonesome beach with a girl I was sure was beautiful. Yes, I cared about Ada being beautiful, and if that sounds stupid to you, then you are not listening.

I took out a bottle which, from its shape, I concluded to be wine, and another, squared, which I didn't recognise. This one had a screw-top cap. I opened it, smelt, was assaulted by the chemically sweet odour of strawberry-flavoured vodka. I put the bottles on one side and dove into the backpack again. There were sandwiches, two extra-large creaky packets of crisps, filled-up Tupperware boxes, cutlery, paper cups and plates. For reasons I couldn't fathom, a newspaper. On the bottom, carefully folded so as not to take up too much space, were a beach towel and a plaid blanket. In a side pocket I found a lighter, a pouch which smelt of tobacco, and a strip of cigarette paper. I left them there.

I set everything else on the sand, and waited, my back to the woods, my face pointed at the fresh scent coming from the sea. Some moments are unexpectedly happy, for no exact reason you can point at, and that was one of the happiest in my life. I didn't miss seeing the stars. I didn't miss a thing.

Ada's steps approached. She let something fall on the sand. 'I found lots of dry wood,' she explained. 'It'll take a couple more journeys to bring it all. Wait, I'll be right back.'

When she'd brought all the wood she needed – it was a lot, and it required more than two journeys – she asked, 'Do you know how to build a fire?'

'We didn't have a fireplace in Turin, and this is my first bonfire.'

'A long-winded way to say *no*. Is there anything, anything at all, you're good at?' she asked, in a way which made me feel I was good at *everything*.

'Stubbornness?'

'Better than nothing. Come, I'll show you.'

She taught me how to separate the kindling from the light branches, from the thicker ones, from the big chunks of wood. We dug a large hole, inside which we built a mound of kindling. We ripped pages off the newspaper and crumpled them up. 'Not too tightly,' Ada advised, 'or the fire won't breathe.' We put the crumpled up paper with the rest of the kindling, then piled on light branches, and then thicker ones, always leaving space for the fire to breathe. The proceedings added to the sense of adventure. Ada and I were stranded on a distant shore and were building our fire. We were in the wild, alone, the two of us.

'When you build a fire correctly,' she said, 'you only need to light it once.' A lighter snapped, producing a tiny heat. Suddenly the heat grew into a blaze, then it subsided and remained pleasantly steady.

'We did it!' Ada cheered. 'You did a good job.'

'I followed instructions.'

'That's my definition of a good job.'

'I thought you didn't like bonfires.'

Ada crawled to where I'd left the food and took one of the bottles. 'No, I don't like people.' She tinkered with the cutlery. 'Most of them anyway.' I heard a soft stabbing: Ada was unscrewing a cork. The wine, then.

'Who are the ones you like?' I asked.

'Are you fishing for compliments?'

Embarrassment swept through my body. 'No!' I said. 'I was just asking in general.'

Ada giggled. 'I liked your grandpa.'

'Who else? You must have some friends.'

Ada didn't answer. Had I overstepped? She poured two cups, handed one to me, and finally said, 'So you noticed, then.'

'I noticed what? I wasn't hinting at anything.'

'Cheers,' she said, bumping the back of my fingers with the back of hers, as you do when toasting with paper cups. 'To our fire.'

'To our fire.'

'And long may it burn,' Ada said.

I sipped my wine. It went down strong and thick, almost like syrup, warming me all the way down to my belly.

'I don't have all that many friends,' Ada said. 'Well, I've got one, of late: you. I know people, they know me – small town and all that – but we're not friends, me and them.'

'Why?'

'Most everybody thinks I'm weird.'

'No, you're normal.'

'Slow down with the insults.'

I drank my second sip. It was better than the first. 'Not in the sense that you're banal. You're *good* weird.'

'I sent a kid to hospital once.'

I left that to linger. When it was clear Ada wouldn't say more without a prompt, I asked, 'For real?'

'For very real. Nino, he was called, that annoying little prick. We were in the same school, not same class, but same school. He had this obsession with my skirt. He would come at me from behind and lift it, and chuckle like an idiot. He would do that with basically every girl at school, but he had a special fixation on me.'

'How old were you?'

'I was eight. He was, I think, nine. And I told him to cut it out. I promise, I told him. I told him once. And then twice.'

'And he didn't listen.'

'Isn't that always the problem? People who don't listen. I lost my patience – it'd been a long week, my parents were having a slow-burn, high-intensity fight, you know the drill – and the next time he did his thing, I whipped around and shoved him to the ground. He fell on his wrist, big boy that he was. He snapped it.'

I laughed, helped in this by the wine. 'He had it coming.'

'Yeah, well, I didn't stop there. This white-hot fury washed over me, this sense of violation. Why do people always feel entitled to treat you like garbage? I had with me the book I was reading, *The Neverending Story*. Hardback edition: big tome, heavy spine.'

'No, you didn't.'

'Yes, I did. I hit Nino with the spine. On his head. Repeatedly. It was… it was lucky a teacher came, or I'd have killed that creep. Seriously, I think I'd have killed him, and I'll tell you more, I wouldn't feel a speck of guilt about that. They dragged him to A&E, stitched him, and nothing more came out of it 'cause Nino's old folks were too embarrassed to admit their boy had been trashed by a girl. Now, put Nino in a toy box and he still wouldn't be the sharpest tool there. He was always that way. But kids in town say it was me, that he got simple because of how I beat him on his head. They can't prove it, but they can sure as hell say it, and when enough people say one thing, it becomes sort of true.'

'You should be a legend.'

'If I were a boy, I would be. A brawling girl, though?' She put on a posh accent. 'Surely, darling, that lady is a psycho.'

I drank the last of my wine. My head was already swimming high with the stars. Ada clicked open one of the Tupperwares. 'Aubergine croquettes,' she announced, handing one to me.

I bit into the croquette, and even cold, the tender aubergine's flesh melted into pure flavour in my mouth. 'Oh, wow,' I said.

'I know. Mum's croquettes are…' And she made a kissing sound.

We opened the crisps too. We unwrapped the sandwiches and poured more wine. '*The Neverending Story*,' I said. 'I read that.'

'What did you make of it?'

'I liked the first half.'

'Yeah, it gets too much, I agree. At some point along the way it forgets to tell a story and it starts preaching.'

'Your family is keen on preachers.'

'Mum and Dad, not me. They're Catholic. I'm an atheist.'

'How come?'

'What prick of a god takes a baby from her parents?'

I shut my mouth. Ada's sister, Akela the mad dog, the tragedy the Guadalupis had endured: it had all gone from my mind. Ada's smooth conversation made it easy to forget there was more about her than words. 'But you believe in books,' I said. I was steering the conversation, avoiding a topic I was deeply uncomfortable with. I was, in other words, being selfish.

'You like them too.'

'I thought I was this heavy reader until I met you.'

'When I'm reading a good book it's like I'm in the company of smart folks, folks who have something to say and have raked their mind to find ways to say it. I hope I'll have something to say, one day.'

'You could write about the righteous man.'

She scoffed.

I said, 'No, seriously.'

'If we survive the righteous man.'

'Do you think he's that dangerous?'

'Everything's dangerous.' She drank from her cup. 'Almost midnight,' she said.

'Midnight swim?'

'Yeah.'

The midnight swim was a bonfire tradition I'd heard about, and lusted after. It was known that everything could happen during a midnight swim. I heard Ada's trousers swish down, a sound I had been hearing since the first days of summer, but that night it made something funny happen. I remembered, probably too late, that Ada could see me, and turned my back. My erection pressed painfully against the internal net of my trunks.

Ada must have noticed. She pretended she didn't, and gave me time. She fed the fire, so that it wouldn't die while we were swimming, and then ran to the water, to dive in first. Only when she was in the sea, she called, 'Come!'

I walked to the sea and dived in. The water was warm, soothing. I stretched out my arms and floated on my back, knowing that Ada would rescue me if I were to float far from shore. I kept my head slightly lifted, so that my ears were above water, and I could hear her breathe.

'What are you doing?' I asked.

'Floating, like you.'

'Did you see any shooting stars?'

'Three, so far.'

'And did you make a wish?'

'And can you come up with a cornier question?'

I laughed. 'And would you make a wish for me, on the next one you see?'

'Yes, he could,' she said, in the voice of a football journalist. 'What wish would that be?'

I found I didn't have an answer. Right in that moment, floating with Ada on that perfect water, I had nothing left to wish for. 'Your pick,' I said. 'Just wish something for me.'

For a while there was only our soft breathing and the lullaby of the waves.

'Done,' Ada said.

'What did you wish for?'

'Can't tell, or it won't come true.'

'But it's my wish!'

'Same logic applies.'

We swam and splashed about, and that was the moment – right then! – to draw close and kiss her, during a midnight swim, when everything could happen. I let the moment slip; I didn't find the courage. When our fingers wrinkled, we ran back to the fire. Scented flames licked the water off my skin.

We had some more food, drank more wine. We emptied the bottle. I couldn't take my mind off what Ada might have wished on my account. Was it to do with *us*? I managed to convince myself that surely she had wished for me that I would be manly, for once, and kiss her; an egocentric trip if ever there is one.

I was growing restless. I could just turn and put my lips on hers if I wanted. She was close enough, physically, but I was afraid I would ruin everything – our friendship, our investigation – if that was not what she wanted. I was afraid I would look like an idiot. I couldn't know what the right move was. I couldn't know what the consequences of the wrong move might be.

'Imagine if,' Ada said, her voice slightly slurred by the wine, 'we heard the revellers now.'

It was like plunging in ice-cold water. 'Why did you say that?'

'Just imagine.'

'No, Ada, that is the last thing I want to imagine.'

I didn't notice I had raised my voice until she said, 'Jeez, chill.'

'Sorry,' I said. 'The… the memory of that music. It winds me up.'

'My mistake.'

My heart was beating hard; an echo of the fiddle reached me.

'Should we be heading back home?' I said. 'It's getting late.'

'You didn't play a single tune, yet. You can't have a bonfire without bad music.'

'Who says my music's bad?'

'Show, don't tell.'

While I took the guitar out of the case, Ada opened the vodka. We were officially getting wasted; that might be good for my courage. She handed me a cup. I put away the contents in one shot. The vodka was a synthetically-flavoured grater poking my throat with hot rods and kicking and punching my stomach like an octopus gone berserk. I coughed. 'That's *vile*.'

'It's strawberry. Strawberries are nice.'

'Not one real strawberry was harmed in the making of this vodka.'

'The life of the party *and* the spirits connoisseur. Will wonders ever cease?' She poured a fresh serving of vodka in my cup. 'Have more and it'll taste better.'

Again, I put away the cup in one swallow. She was not wrong. 'What do you want me to play?' I asked.

'Can you do "Champagne Supernova"?'

'Nope.'

'"Lemon Tree"?'

'Let me think…' I desperately pretended. 'Nope.'

'Okay, so, what can you play?'

'"Eleanor Rigby"?'

'Go.'

My fingers flew on the guitar's neck. The plectrum teased the strings. I sang of Father McKenzie and his socks in the best performance I'd ever given. In my imagination, that's how it went. Reality was more dismal. I picked the wrong chords. I had to start again. I played too slow, then too fast, my voice rose and fell at random points.

'Is that the only song you can do?' Ada asked.

I put the guitar aside. 'Yes.'

'I hate to break this to you, but you can't do that either. You're not bad. You're terrible.'

'I won't dispute that.'

'Abysmal.'

'Yes.'

'You suck to the moon and back.'

'Are you going on for long?'

'It'd be my pleasure. Do you even *like* playing?'

'I don't have time to practise.'

'Said the CEO of Microsoft.'

I paused. I wanted to be honest, with myself most of all. 'I never cared about music,' I said, and what a relief to say it aloud. 'It's Dad who wants me to learn an instrument. A blind man who can play – it's poetically fitting.'

'Why doesn't he stick a guitar up his arse if he's so keen on fitting stuff poetically?'

That made me laugh, and Ada Guadalupi laughed too.

I put the guitar back in its case. I never took it out again, not until yesterday. I found fine grains of sand in the case. They must have snuck in that night – sand finds its way everywhere – and remained in place ever since. They carried a memory of strawberry-flavoured vodka, of Ada and our fire. I had to drop the guitar and go for a walk. I am a lucky man, luckier than most, happier than most, and definitely happier than the boy I was, but I will never be that boy again.

'I'm getting the tobacco,' Ada said. 'Ever smoked?'

'No.'

'A night of firsts for you.'

'I didn't know you smoked.'

'A night of firsts for me too.'

I heard noises I couldn't identify. The breeze brought to my lips a fleck of tobacco.

Ada laughed. 'I'm trying to roll a cigarette,' she explained. 'Another first, and it's not as easy as it seems.' Time passed, during which I warmed up to the vodka, and Ada cursed at intervals. Then she said, 'Here we go.' She took a drag. She had a coughing fit.

'Are you all right?' I asked.

She took my index finger and my thumb in one of her hands, and gently put the cigarette between them. She squeezed my fingers to signal me to hold it. 'Try,' she said in a coarse voice, and coughed again.

And I tried. I inhaled freely, not ready for the consequences. The smoke filled my lungs, sending my alarm systems into overdrive. I choked, I coughed, I burnt, I felt close, too close, to being sick.

'I would say it takes some getting used to,' Ada proclaimed, taking back the cigarette. 'Wash it down with vodka. It helps.'

Once again, she was not wrong.

I did not kiss her that night. Why? There is of course no shortage of sensible answers (I was afraid to make a mistake, I was awkward, it was all part of my learning curve, I had so much on my plate) but the one which is truthful is, *because*. There are moments you seize and moments you don't, and you must live with both, and you will regret some of either. I did not entirely forgive that boy for what he didn't do. I am not convinced he should be forgiven.

Yet, it was a magnificent night. Ada and I exchanged cigarettes and drinks. We got drunk and then drunker. We talked, we laughed, we fell asleep by the fire.

A voice yelled in my face. Hands grabbed me. Ada cried out. I screamed and flailed with my hands. One landed on my aggressor's nose with a satisfying *thwack*, and a crack, and my aggressor let go.

'Ada!' I called.

The answer came in my mother's angry voice. 'Stop it, Luca! It's us.'

'You're in trouble, kid,' Dad said, talking as if through a tea towel. It was his nose I had whacked.

Where was I? What time was it? Thinking hurt; magma flew through the vessels in my brain and a storm raged in my stomach. I turned my head and vomited. The sun beat on the nape of my neck. It was hot, but not unbearable. A ten-ish sun.

Then the night came back to me: the alcohol, the cigarettes, the midnight swim. The not kissing Ada. I'd believed I had all the time in the world, before running out of it. I wiped my mouth with the back of my hand.

'Was it only alcohol?' Giuseppe Guadalupi's measured voice asked.

I knew better than to admit to having drunk.

'Luca, it's important,' he repeated. 'Was it only alcohol you had?'

Ada said, 'Cigarettes too.'

'Nothing else? No drugs?'

'No.'

'Are you sure?' Giuseppe Guadalupi insisted.

'I'd remember, Dad. What do you think?'

'You are in no position to be clever,' Mum said. 'Neither of you.'

Dad's voice was returning to normal. 'Luca, do you have any idea how worried you had us?'

'Dad—'

'We had to call the police. The hospital! In case you were in A&E.'

'Dad—'

He shouted, 'We've been looking for you everywhere!'

'And who fuckin' asked you?' I shouted back.

After a beat, Giuseppe Guadalupi said, 'I'm disappointed.'

That hurt, coming from him. I felt I had to defend myself, defend Ada. 'Nothing happened,' I said, the unfortunate truth.

'Please, Luca, don't start. This pathetic little scene is the least of it.'

I didn't understand what he meant until later in the day.

Giuseppe Guadalupi shipped Ada back home while Mum and Dad took me to the Masseria del Vento. They gave me barely enough time to get a shower and a hold of myself before marshalling me to the kitchen, where I faced a firing squad thinly disguised as a jury.

'Good morning, Luca,' Bianca said.

Ferdi said, 'I'm here too.'

'Where's Ada?' I asked.

Bianca said, 'Don't worry about her. She is fine, considering.'

I was feeling better, and I was able to think more clearly (I look back with jealousy at the amount of punishment my body could take back then, when I didn't know what to do with it). I had learnt from witnessing similar scenes play out with Ferdi that nothing I could say would improve my situation, and everything I might say would worsen it, so I said nothing at all, until Dad asked, 'Well?'

'What?'

'How do you justify yourself?'

'I don't have to. We were having a good time, and it's none of your business.'

'How dare you…'

'Nobody got hurt, Dad. We got carried away, that's all.'

'You were drunk!'

'Weren't you ever?'

'Not at thirteen.'

'I'm a quicker study.'

Mum said, 'Your brother set a bad example.'

'How is this my fault?' Ferdi protested.

'Luca must have learnt to act this way from someone, and it's not me or Dad.'

'So where did *I* learn?'

Bianca cleared her throat, and everybody shut up. 'The gun,' she said, and with those two words it dawned on me that yes, I was in trouble, deeply in trouble.

'What gun?' I tried.

Bianca pretended I hadn't spoken. 'When Ada didn't show for breakfast, I checked on her. She was not in her room, not anywhere in the house. She did not answer when I called her name in the garden. Giuseppe made a phone call to your family, waking them up, and no, you were not home either.'

Dad said, 'We searched your room and Ada's.'

'You had no right,' I said.

'That is broadly correct,' Bianca conceded. 'But we were concerned, Luca. We were looking for any clue as to what might have happened to you two. And do you know what we found buried deep in the back of Ada's wardrobe?'

I didn't say a word.

'A shotgun,' Bianca said. 'A *loaded* shotgun. That, I will admit, made us mad with worry. We searched the fields, the village. We were grasping at straws. It is lucky that your brother is such a clever young man: he noticed your guitar was missing, and your towel and trunks too. It was his idea that you might have gone to the beach. I stayed home in case a phone call arrived, and Ferdi stayed here for the same reason, while Giuseppe and your parents scouted the coastline.'

Dad, who couldn't stay silent for a minute, said, 'We smelled you before we saw you. Booze and cigarettes: I thought I'd raised you better.'

Mum asked, 'What was Dad's shotgun doing in Ada's room?'

I thought I had an answer ready – I usually did. Not this time. I might say I didn't know, and if they believed me, I would be betraying Ada, leaving her to fend for herself. I might tell the truth instead, and before I knew it I'd be swallowing pills, and Ada wouldn't be any better off. I could make up some bollocks on the spot, but I didn't know what Ada would say, how much her bollocks would differ from mine. I was confident she wouldn't sell me out, but apart for that? No idea. I was trapped, walls closing in on me from every side.

I didn't say a word.

'Talk,' Dad ordered.

Ferdi said, 'Dad, give him some space.'

I didn't say a word.

'I hope you realise how grave this is,' Bianca said. 'Guns kill, Luca. They don't only hurt, they *kill*.'

I didn't say a word.

'Is there any connection between last night and your recent episodes? If there is, I'm begging you, tell me now. We love

Ada and we love you. We are angry at you both at the moment, indeed we are, and I am not going to deny that, but we do love you with all our heart. We are trying to understand, and we need your help.'

I didn't say a word.

'Did you know that Ada has a history of mental illness?'

A history of mental illness.

The blow had landed, and Bianca kept pummelling. 'Rage outbursts, unchecked emotional reactions. Self-harm. I'm telling you this in confidence, Luca, because Giuseppe is very fond of you, and so am I. Nobody in town knows, for reasons you're more than capable of understanding. Ada's issues have become manageable, with a lot of hard work on her part, but they could easily resurface. Does she know of your episodes, Luca? Did she share them with you?'

Most everybody thinks I'm weird.

'Did she *inspire* your episodes?'

I didn't say a word.

Bianca Guadalupi sighed. 'You are going to take this as a punishment, but I hope you will find it in yourself to entertain the idea that it might be the opposite of that. It is common for people who have experienced comparable problems to be attracted to each other. Common, yes, but not healthy; I am afraid you and Ada are feeding into each other's problems. We made a decision, your family and ours, for the good of you both.'

'You will not hang out anymore until we have those problems worked out,' Dad said.

My world crashed down all around me, walls and ceilings and everything, and I was left alone in the void, to face spooks without a shield, a sword, a friend. The righteous man was coming, and I had no one in my corner. Ada had no one in hers. I hated my querulous voice when I said, 'Bianca, don't do this.'

'It's for the best,' she said.

It was an echo of the fight my parents and Ferdi had when I started showing symptoms, only their roles were reversed, and this time my presence was required.

'The main thing you need to remember is we love you, Luca,' Dad started. I knew fresh trouble was on my way.

He had gathered the whole family in the kitchen after a frosty dinner. He felt safer within the walls of the house he and Mum had half-destroyed.

'I know,' I said.

'If we didn't love you we wouldn't worry for you, isn't that obvious?' he went on, in the reasonable tone he still uses when he wants to convince himself that he is on the right track.

'Yes,' I said.

'Giuseppe and Bianca are good people, but they don't love you as much as we do. Nobody loves you as much as we do. They take care of their daughter, as is only right, and we take care of you.'

'Cut to the chase,' Ferdi said.

'See?' Dad snapped. 'Your attitude, exactly your attitude, Ferdi, is what brought us here. You were an awful influence over your brother, awful.'

Ferdi didn't answer; in hindsight, I think he believed that too.

Dad's voice brimmed with satisfaction for the point he had scored. 'This isn't about you. It's about Luca, who needs us, more than ever. He needs *his family*. I'm not angry at you,' he said, without saying my name, and it took me a second to understand he had shifted his focus back to me. 'You made a mistake, but we do share the responsibility. I've been saying since day one, since you came out with that troubling story of yours, that we had to intervene, without dithering, and I was right, wasn't I? I was so right. Giuseppe insisted we wait, your Mum took his side, and I said, fine, let's go along with that, for now. But I knew it wasn't a good idea. I don't think we can wait anymore.'

'Dad,' I pleaded. 'Please, don't put me on meds.'

'Bianca agreed it might not be necessary,' Mum said, in a tone which was less than half-certain.

'You're all being like children,' was Dad's answer.

'She's a doctor…?'

'Doctors make mistakes too.'

'Luca didn't mention any more visions,' Ferdi said.

'Come again?'

'Luca, your beloved son, the one whose side you are on, didn't show any more worrying signs.'

'He might not be telling.'

'So you're going to medicate him for something you just think he might be doing?'

'I don't *just think* that he did what he did last night!' Dad shouted.

'Christ,' Ferdi shouted back, 'he was messing about with a girl! He screwed up, fine, ground him, put him in a bloody building crew if that's what gets you hard, but it's not material for a *psychiatric intervention.*'

'He stole a gun.'

255

'You guys took us all the way down here and nobody's sectioning you for that.'

'We're not sectioning anyone,' Mum said.

'Dad,' I implored. 'Please.'

I didn't go to Ferdi immediately. It took me two days, during which I swung violently from boredom to anxiety and back, always, always, missing Ada with the same intensity I had missed sight on the first days after curtain fall. Giuseppe too – I had been exiled from the Guadalupis' warm bosom. Dad kept me under a tight watch, jonesing for an excuse to medicate me, to prove to himself that he was still in control, still powerful. He had failed his one job in Turin, making sure that Ferdi would sit his exams; he wouldn't fail with me, whatever the cost. I was hanging by a frayed thread, and I would plunge at the first wrong move, the first wrong word. I would plunge, that was for sure. The only question was what I would manage to do in the run-up to that.

I dragged myself around an eerily silent space. I had been using the building works as an aural anchor which, with the builders gone, had now been cut. But the silence, of course, was no silence at all – with the humdrum chaos of the works gone, the countryside was no less vibrant than the city. More so, in fact. It was alive with birds chirping and hooting, a buzzing of wasps, the deep howl of the wind, rising and falling, the hum of pylons. Days stretched on for ever, and the righteous man didn't show, which made me wonder what he was planning for Ada and me. Ada: I hadn't made a move with her on the night of the bonfire, and who knew when I'd get another chance.

I went back and forth on the idea of talking to Ferdi. In the end, I had to. By inaction, I had missed something precious at the bonfire, and I flat-out refused to make the same mistake twice. I've made a point to avoid that particular mistake ever since, which has gained me a reputation in town.

Ferdi was in *Da Klub*, smoking one of his sweet-scented cigarettes. When I stepped in, I heard him jump from the couch and put out the cigarette. 'Scrawny?' he said.

I couldn't stand his voice. I couldn't stand his stench, his presence; no one had ever let me down as massively as him.

Also, he had protected me from Mum and Dad.

I went straight to the point. 'I didn't tell our old folks where I got the shotgun from.'

'Scrawny, can we talk?'

'No, Ferdi. I talk, you listen. I could've thrown you under the bus and I didn't.'

'I know.'

'Unlike what you did with me.'

'It's different.'

'Oh, yeah? What were you doing with the gun in *Da Klub*, Ferdi?'

'I took it here last summer. It was just lying around. Mum and Dad had forgotten about it! I shot at things to let off steam. Grandpa used to do the same.'

'I don't know, Ferdi, that sounds unstable and violent to me. I'm worried for you.'

'Scrawny, why are you being like that?'

'Because I'm desperate,' I admitted. 'And I want you to listen very carefully to what I'm going to say.'

'I always do.'

'Spare me the crap and hear this: What I'm saying here, it stays here. If you get all worked up for me and run to Mum and Dad, I'll tell them where I got the shotgun, okay?'

'Blackmail, Scrawny? We're at that?'

'Yes. Yes, we're at that. I'll tell you what – say that we have a deal, or I turn and go vent my worries to Mum and Dad *right now*. And by the way, I don't know what you're smoking, but it's not tobacco. I'm going to mention that too, just in case I should be more worried for you than I already am.'

Ferdi sighed. He lit his cigarette again. "Kay,' he said. 'Go on.'

'Ada is in danger. Physical, immediate danger. The story I told you? Yes, I stand by it, one hundred per cent. Something wanders our fields, something which does not belong to this world, or not entirely, and I did end up on an impossible beach. This is a fact, and it sucks that you don't believe me, but it doesn't change reality.'

I stopped, to give him space to comment. He didn't.

'Ada had odd experiences too,' I went on. 'She saw the same beach I ended up on in her dreams, and she heard the same blood-curdling music. She got it worse than me though. She came out hurt.'

'Hurt?'

'Hurt, yes. She was too afraid of her family's reaction to mention that, and she was right as it turns out. She made me promise I wouldn't talk to a living soul. I am breaking that promise now, which makes me a snitch, no better than you, but I don't know what else to do. She met in her dreams the same thing I met in the fields, and the thing left traces on her *in the real world*. That's what Ada took the gun for: protection. She wasn't playing. She was terrified. We've been investigating the wanderer, the two of us, and I think we pissed him off. He comes and goes as he wants, Ferdi.'

'You say *he*.'

'He smells like a beast and looks like a man. Last time I met him, in our vineyard, I took a photo. Before you say it, I know that a photograph only proves there was a trespasser, but it is something, right? A starting point. Will you do me a favour and look at it? Will you look at the light in his eyes?'

Ferdi said, 'Do you have the photo here?'

I took the photograph out of my cargo pants and held it out. Ferdi's fingers took it from mine.

'Oh, Scrawny,' he said. 'Please, don't hate me.'

'If you're selling me out again, you—'

'There is no man in this pic,' he interrupted me. 'There's a barn owl. That's it: a barn owl, flying from the vines.'

'Do me a favour.'

'Why would I lie?' he said, with real compassion in his voice.

And why would Ada lie?

A history of mental illness.

But I'd touched her cuts!

Self-harm.

As I relive the last conversation I had with Ferdi in *Da Klub*, I relive the turmoil I went through at the time – anger and sadness and that unyielding loneliness which strangles you until you beg or die.

A barn owl.

I was like a glass sculpture shattering under one neat hammer blow. When I'd made a leap of trust and confided my experiences to Ada, my Ada, the girl I'd wanted so badly to kiss and hold, she had taken me for a ride. Pranking the blind kid, what a laugh.

'She's unwell,' Ferdi said. 'Don't hate her either.'

I groped my way through a wine-scented jungle, between tall, luscious vines which had taken over every crevice and free space. Almost ripe for the harvest, the fat grapes marked the progression of summer more precisely than calendars. I walked to the far side of the vineyard and continued until I met the almond tree. I read the initials I'd carved on the trunk with my fingers. I moved on.

From the almond tree to the rock, I minded the length of each step and any potential deviation. It would be inconceivably cruel of Ferdi to be lying. It would be inconceivably cruel of Ada. Perhaps the photo looked differently to different people. Perhaps it was magic.

From the rock to the bush, I kept walking. I took into account mistakes I might have made the previous time, when Ada and I had failed to locate the hollow tree. I wished I would fail again. That would go to show that Ada had told the truth, that she hadn't seen the tree, rather than just pretended not to. How'd that be for cruelty?

My cane touched a jutting root. My hand rested on a trunk gnarled and twisted like a giant fossil of a rope. I felt for the hollow, and there it was: a large mouth of wood.

That was no supernatural wonder, just another old tree. Ada couldn't have missed the sight of it. She had played me for a fool. She had been lying smoothly, adapting her story to mine in real time, making fun of me, as all the while I toyed with pathetic fantasies of kisses and smooth moves.

God, I was stupid. I leaned with my back against the trunk. The occult investigators, two against the world – sweet, fanciful bollocks. Of course Ada could make light of the revellers; she didn't know what she was talking about.

I sniffed a trace of the feral smell.

I imagined calling out to the wanderer. *Where are you?* I'd say. *Get out!* Coming to blows with it, with something, anything – I wanted that. Or to scream, if that was all that was left. I didn't do it, only because screaming to an empty field was too much like my father.

It was a glaring scent once you picked up on it, not getting any stronger or weaker, but lingering like an aftertaste. A reality no less indisputable for being subtle.

Why don't you come out, you coward? I would yell.

I'd been surprised when Ada had said the wanderer seemed human, for it didn't walk the way humans do. But it did walk, unlike owls. It had pushed me, and how could an owl do that? It was all very confusing.

The echoes of the voice in my mind died out. I wriggled inside the tree, found a spot between the creepers and the mouldy growths, and sat enveloped by a cool shade, protected by hard wood. It was safe in there.

I had to talk to Ada.

I think back with some awe (and pride too) to the boy who, lonely, haunted, betrayed, and with Damocles' sword of unknown medicines hanging over his head, found it in himself to embark on a quest to confront a girl. I doubt I'd have the guts to do the same today.

After another of the tense dinners which were the hallmark of that summer, dinners in which not one word was uttered that reflected what the speaker was actually thinking, Ferdi made off for the village, Mum and Dad retired to bed, and when their snores filled the space outside their room I grabbed my cane and headed out.

My parents and the Guadalupis had exchanged house keys. I had never felt the Guadalupis' ones and couldn't recognise them, so I went to the rough ceramic bowl where my parents kept the keys and emptied the whole contents into my cargo pants' right pocket.

It was the night before Ferragosto's eve and the echoes of distant parties made it to our secluded dirt track. I knew the way to the Guadalupis' well enough to walk it without a cane, almost. Their gate was not locked, like Grandpa's had never been. I pushed it open, waited until I was satisfied that the creaking hadn't rippled to the house, then waited a little longer. No sound made its way back to me. I went on.

I was confident no one was in the garden: that was the size of my certainties. I could not be sure that Bianca and Giuseppe would be in bed. I could not know if lights were lit. Likewise, I could not locate Ada's window.

I could get to her room, though, opposite Giuseppe's office, a place I'd visited many times. I had thought at first I could steal inside her room, but I wasn't a perv, and also, I didn't want to risk giving her a scare and making her yell. Less ambitiously, I would slip a note under her door and get out. On five sheets of printer paper I had written in stamp letters: *Hollow tree. Noon. I will be there every day*. Five copies of the same message, so that Ada would be able to reconstruct it in case my writing was too hard to read. If her folks let her hang in the fields, she'd know where and when to find me. The mention of the hollow tree was to tell her I was wise to her deception. Yes, I had given the matter a lot of thought.

I made it to the front door. The keys in my pocket tingled when I dug my hand to get one at random. With the fingers of the other hand I felt for the lock, then I left the fingers on the lock and used them as a guide to try the key. It took me many attempts before I managed to make the key touch the lock in a way that assured me that the key was wrong and not me. I dropped it into the left pocket, took another. I tried again. I moved slowly, steadily. It is amazing how quiet humans can be, and how much they can do, if they do not rush. When we think we are blundering idiots, we are only fretting.

One key fit, and turned, and the handle went down, and the door slid open. My heartbeat was neither slow nor quiet. From this moment on, everything could go wrong. Everything was already going wrong: I was trespassing, and if I were to get caught a quick retreat was not on the cards for me. Once in, I was in at the deep end. I wondered whether Giuseppe had a gun. I wondered whether he was easier to scare than he seemed.

I confusedly felt that I had come to an important juncture in my life. I could step in and make myself into a burglar, a snoop who abused other people's trust. Or I could turn back, and remain what I was, a nice boy. The price would be to accept that I could not fend for myself, that I was indeed no more than Luca the blind one, the sweet handicapped guy whose job in life is to make you feel good about yourself when you help him cross the street. I would make myself into *that*.

Fuck that.

I stepped in.

I had to be careful with the cane, for the sweeping sound it made but I knew that living room as well as I knew my own. I inched forward until I reached the staircase. I held on to the banister and climbed the first step. I thought I heard something. I climbed the second. Yes, there was a voice. I froze.

It was the kind of call a human throat might let out when it is too hoarse, or hurt, for proper words. Another sound, a whacking one which I could not identify, boomed at intervals. Doors and distance made the sounds dreamy: I would have missed them in a city home. A voice meant people being awake, it meant I had to leave immediately.

I didn't want to be the kind of man who shrugs off a voice in pain.

Whatever was happening, it seemed to be happening roughly where the kitchen was, if my mental map was correct. It was not a part of the house I had often been to. Venturing there would be dangerous. What is that Ada said? *Everything's dangerous.*

I went back and passed through a doorway, to find myself in a room smelling of garlic and basil. The chances of getting lost were sky-high: my mental map didn't stretch to here. I might have left after all if I hadn't noticed beneath the usual odours a whiff too incongruous to be ignored. Frankincense – the substance priests burn in church. The inchoate voice and the whacking sound came from my left-hand side.

I followed them up to where sturdy wood – a closed door – stopped me. With my ear flush to the wood, I listened to what came from beyond. The sounds were far and full of echoes, as sounds become when they have to climb up from a cellar to reach you.

The voice was Ada's, gurgling and coughing, in pain. There was a second voice, much lower in tone, Giuseppe's, who, with his charming lilt, chanted Latin words, '*Averte mala inimicis meis et in veritate tua disperde illos.*' The whacking sound, which came at intervals, was harder to recognise. I was not at all familiar with it. *Thwack.* I imagined it as an onomatopoeia in a comic book, and I figured which kind of scene it would be attached to. Something violent. *Thwack.* Something unpleasant. *Thwack.* For all their flaws, my parents had never hit me.

It was the whack of a hand that slaps a body.

I drew back. I made my way out without hurry. I locked the door behind me, pulled the gate and headed back home, with all the calm in the world, and only when I was inside the Masseria del Vento, inside my room, did I give myself permission to shake. I lay on the bed, on one side, hugging my knees. In time, I drifted off.

That was the first night since we had moved that I slept soundly, with no interruptions or nightmares. I gorged myself on sleep until I was full to the brim and couldn't take it anymore. I woke up late, I woke up refreshed and I woke up angry.

It beggared belief that this was the beach. An aerosol of sweat, ashes and deep-fried foodstuff landed on my tongue every time I parted my lips; a thousand songs gave me no quarter, and children screaming, and adults fighting and flirting, and mouths chewing. A draught threw offensive stenches (unwashed bodies, burnt oil) at us, the next one offered mouthwatering scents (grilled fish, ripe peaches). Every time my senses zoned in on a feeling the feeling changed, except for the sand underfoot, which was steadily sticky. It was out of the question that I could move on my own: the beach was too packed to use the cane. Every inch was taken up by bodies, bowls, dogs, radios, tables, bottles, bonfires, chairs, cans, tents, footballs, umbrellas and a plethora of things I was far from able to identify. A still-burning cigarette stub burnt my toe, making me jump and yelp.

'All good?' Dad asked.

'Yeah.'

I leaned on his arm to wade through the crowd. He was doing his best, I had to admit, but he was no Ada.

That chaos robbed me of the self-reliance I had claimed over the course of summer. In the barrage of garish stimuli I could not locate myself in space. I couldn't tell where the sea was and where the road, I couldn't tell what was in front of me and what behind, and if a wrecking ball had come at me, I wouldn't have noticed until steel smashed my face. Tomorrow townsfolk would celebrate the day in which the Virgin Mary had been bodily taken up into heaven. Tonight, they partied.

Aunt Betta's shrill voice rose, saying, 'This way!' She and Uncle Giorgio had invited friends to join them for a night-time picnic on the beach, as people did all along Puglia's endless coastline. We reached her, and she kissed us on the cheek. 'I'm so happy you came in the end! Mario's already here.'

'I see him,' Mum said, every word a blade of permafrost.

There had been a long debate over whether to attend or not. Mum and Dad dreaded meeting Uncle Mario, but if they didn't come that would mean that, after ripping them off, he was hounding them out of their social circles. So they were, in their minds, holding their ground.

'Luca, I'm sorry your girlfriend can't be with us,' Aunt Betta said.

'I don't have a girlfriend.'

'Sure,' she said, in the mysterious voice of one who's part of a secret.

The Guadalupis wouldn't come. Bianca said it was better for Ada not to be around large crowds for the time being and had produced a run-of-the-mill excuse about a cold. *It is better for Ada to be kept in a cellar.* What was going on in that house?

'How's my little sister?' Uncle Mario's voice came.

Mum said, 'Not too bad, thank you.'

'I've been trying to get a hold of you for days.'

Dad said, 'We've been busy.'

'I heard! You've got to tell me absolutely everything. Glass of wine?'

Apart for the Guadalupis, no one knew what Uncle Mario had done to us. He was the local, Mum and Dad the unknown quantity: they had to be careful or they would come out as backbiters. That one thing at least they got right.

Aunt Gemma hugged me tight – her geranium scent and her soft body did little to ease my confusion. 'I don't see Ferdi,' she said.

'He's at a party with friends.'

'My daughter too. I promise, sweetheart, we'll endeavour not to be dull.'

'You couldn't be dull if you tried.'

She offered me her arm, and I trailed behind her. She met and kissed and chatted to an endless queue of people.

I'd planned a heart-to-heart with Uncle Mario, but I had not factored in the sensory overload, which made it impossible to tell where he was at any time. I got a hold of his voice when Aunt Gemma took me to fill my plate with crudo of prawns, then I lost it, and found it again after a long while, telling a joke to a small, amused crowd. More time went by. The adults got drunker. I remained in trail of Aunt Gemma, who was the kind of person who considers a prickly pear too much of a commitment, and was giving signs of being tired of the novelty I had been. I overheard a snatch of a conversation between Uncle Mario and some lady, and told Aunt Gemma to go on without me. She was relieved to get her freedom back.

I hovered around Uncle Mario's words until the lady left, at which point I called, 'Uncle.'

'Hey, Luca. Having a good time?'

'We need to talk.'

'About what?'

'Do you have five minutes?'

'Swing by next week?'

'Now. Please.'

Laughter exploded somewhere on my right. When it died out, Uncle Mario said, 'Come.'

He led me to the shore with his heavy step. I let fresh water lap my feet.

'You're trying a charm offensive with Mum,' I said.

'Let bygones be bygones, I say. Is this what you wanted to talk about?'

'No. It's the Guadalupis.'

'Again? I gave you all I had.'

'Grandpa had it in for Pierpaolo but was friends with Ada.'

'It'd been self-defeating for Dad to believe that the sins of the fathers should be visited upon the sons.'

'What did he have against Giuseppe, then?'

'It was personal. He considered Giuseppe a leaf from his father's book, a bloody thug with a glossy coat of paint.'

'He was right.'

Uncle Mario sounded surprised: 'I thought you were best pals with Giuseppe Guadalupi.'

'He beats Ada,' I said.

'Do you know that for a fact?'

'Yes.' I did not mention the Latin chanting and the incense. I did not want to spoil my one chance to be trusted.

And my uncle, to his credit, did trust me. 'Forget it. It's none of your business.'

'How can you say that?'

'Because it's none of your business.'

'Bianca must be in it too, or at least know about it.'

'None of your business, Luca. Record these words and play them on a loop in your mind, 'cause they're the most useful words you'll ever come across and they'll serve you well for the rest of your life: *None of your business*. Dad knew that Giuseppe beat Ada.'

'And he did nothing?'

'He gave her shelter when needed. Iced tea and cake too.'

'That all?'

'What else? If Dad had to play knight on a white horse for every girl being beaten round here, he would've done nothing else in his life.'

'Ada's situation is bad, Uncle, real bad.'

'Are you deaf as well as blind? *None of your business*. You're too early in life to let women drag you down. Don't get in

Giuseppe's way; he's not an easy man to handle, nothing like your father. No offence. The goings-on are ugly? One more reason to stay away.'

'I hear you've got some handy contacts.'

After a moment, Uncle Mario laughed. 'Aren't you something,' he said. 'Yes, yes I've got my contacts, and there's no way in hell I'm going to bother them with this.'

'Uncle…'

'Take a word of advice, tough guy: When you ask for favours, you're putting yourself in somebody's debt. I'm not going to do that for your girlfriend, and neither should you. There's plenty of fish in the sea, have you heard that one?'

'That's callous.'

'That's life. Don't waste your time, Luca. Praise God, never the wind.'

I was angry, I was disappointed, afraid and tired. I had my shields down. They let a wild thought pass through, a thought that took hold of my mind.

We drove back home at dawn, with the first sunshine gradually heating up the car's rooftop. Mum and Dad were chatty, borderline drunk. They made a huge deal of the impression they must have left on the people at the party. They didn't remember the last time they had such a good time. The moment we arrived at the masseria, they staggered up to their bedroom.

I was not sleepy.

I felt an anger intense enough to part the sea: half of it was teenage angst, and half, frankly, justified disillusion. It was a fact that everyone I cared for, friends and family, dead or alive, had let me down. Grandpa had let horrors continue in Ada's household, offering nothing more than iced tea and cake, Uncle Mario was a smug bastard, Ferdi, my parents – let's not go there. The girl who stole my nights had reduced my awe-inducing experience to a Three Investigators farce; her father, my hero, was an abuser, and his wife too. Bianca, she was the worst. She'd set a trap that would snap were I to breathe the wrong way – I had lost my sight to bad luck, but she had taken my speech from me on purpose. I was alone, in a corner. I was, in other words, dangerous.

Praise God, never the wind.

What is forbidden has been done before. *Praise God.* Scores of downtrodden folk in history have turned to prayer: when you've been stripped of your clothes and robbed of your food and bound and gagged, when this world has failed you, appealing to others is nothing but sensible. *Never the wind.* To whom were they praying, though?

This is the question I meditated on while I rocked on the swing on our porch in the early hours of Ferragosto. Ferdi hadn't returned (he might stay on the beach until late afternoon), and except for my parents' snores slithering out of their open window, I couldn't discern any other human sound. Fracas would explode again later in the day, in one last blaze of glory; for now, the human soundscape had abated, and a better one flourished.

Ada's house loomed large over the edge of my consciousness. Nothing came from that direction, but that house had thick walls. I rocked the swing. A zephyr touched my face. *Praise God, never the wind.*

They all praised God. Ada's parents said grace, Grandpa read the Bible, Uncle Mario was keen on being seen at Mass. All good people, all good Christians, the whole lot of them. I was not good, not like them. Their God? Giuseppe Guadalupi's God, Grandpa's God, the God whose wrath I was supposed to fear, were I to worship false idols? I'd experienced that wrath, and I was still standing. I was not afraid of him and I was not in awe of him. He had nothing on me. He had nothing for me either.

The zephyr did not ask me to stand up and go; I will not shift responsibility by pretending otherwise. It hummed, it invited. It did not ask. I grabbed my cane, entertaining some ridiculous thoughts, but I had no fucks left for *ridiculous*. Those thoughts of mine, they were old thoughts.

I marched into the vineyard.

The breeze was picking up. The grape leaves were thin, coarse hands. Each of their five lobes was a finger tickling and prickling my arms, my neck, the whole of my face. The deeper I went into the vineyard, the stronger the breeze grew, the more restless the grape hands got, the more their fingers tickled and prickled. The vineyard stretched on and on, deeper than it had any right to be. The wind built up. Grape hands swayed all over me. A feral smell rose. It made me all the more furious. I wouldn't be chased away anymore.

I stumbled out into the fields beyond, and all sounds but the wind died out. The wind kept coming gust after gust.

From the vineyard to the almond tree, I walked in perfect silence, except for the gusts. *Praise God, never the wind.* The feral smell surrounded me, but I heard no *tap, tap*. I kept all focus on my steps, my rhythm and my landmarks. I held on to my cane while the gusts raged, sliding on me, pushing and pulling. There was a rhythm in the wind, a language I didn't speak. I reached the hollow tree.

Praise God, never the wind.

I didn't know how to pray. It was one of the skills my parents hadn't taught me. It is a neglected skill among Christians too; the church-goers I know ask for favours and give thanks, all very politely, but prayer, the prayer I have learnt, is no teatime chitchat. It is a blasting open of doors and a shout in darkness, and when you call, you are never quite sure what will be awakened. *Praise God, never the wind* – for the wind may answer.

I thought about kneeling, discarded the idea. If the wind was another overbearing bully who wanted me on my knees, it wouldn't have me at all. It kept getting stronger, gust after gust. I wished Ada were with me; she was good with words.

'I praise you,' I started, my voice instantly stolen by a gust, which snatched my words and stuffed them back down my throat. 'I praise you!' I repeated, shouting now, expelling the words out of my throat with all the power stored in my young lungs. 'I praise you, oh wind.' I opened my arms to take it on all my body. 'You were here before we came,' I shouted. 'You were here before the small God of priests came. You will be here after we leave. You will be here after God leaves.'

The wind didn't talk. It roared, it invited.

I unbuttoned my shirt, and the wind tore it out of my hand. I took off my shoes, all my clothes, and stood naked, the gale smashing on me with the weight of avalanches, stealing my breath, making it nearly impossible to stand. I laughed.

I wouldn't be anywhere else than there, exposed, and free. I howled. 'And this is my praise to you,' I shouted.

The wind rose.

It came at me in full force, on every inch of my body, inside my open mouth, in my ears and my nostrils. It undid me. It took away my tongue and my skin, then my heart, my brain, all my organs, it sprayed my blood all over the fields, and blew on my bones until they were dust, and then nothing at all.

I was the wind.

I was every gust, every flurry. I was the one who rustled the leaves and shook the trees, I was the one who made the waves by blowing over the sea, I was the one gathering clouds and wishing them away. I was the wind, and I knew what the wind knows.

I knew that Grandpa had been young. I was drying his tears when he wept over Grandma refusing his proposal, and I was a draught when he danced and laughed after she came back with a change of mind. I breathed cold on his face on a Candlemas day, when he planted a carob seed in the garden for Grandma, whose favourite treats were carobs. I brought his curses to his God when Grandma died before he did. Grandpa was not a talker. I had never imagined he had been so profoundly in love, but the wind knew.

I knew, because the wind knew, that Pierpaolo Guadalupi and Grandpa had a great time for years. I was blowing on embers on the beach when they roasted two-day-old bread, and a bass they had just fished. I carried to the stars the scent of the red wine they drank, and I sang bawdy songs with them, and listened to the stories they shared, almost true, made taller in the telling. I knew that Grandpa never forgave Pierpaolo for being the man Pierpaolo was, and never forgave himself for befriending such a man.

I knew that Ferdi had a fling two summers ago, a local girl, and again last summer: I kissed them both as they kissed each other. I knew this year he was preoccupied with me and had no time for her. I knew he was devoured by guilt: he could have spotted my illness earlier, and he could have done more for me after curtain fall. I knew he missed me and hated himself, and he thought our parents were right to treat him as a good-for-nothing. I thundered when he shot cans in the fields, I curled the smoke from his cigarettes in my fingers, I dried the tears he cried when I was the only one there with him, the way I dried Grandpa's. I knew Ferdi was lost. He had been smoking alone, unsure of how to get our friendship back, and afraid that I might be breaking down, or that he might be.

I was a zephyr when Ada died. I ruffled the fur of Akela, the gentle giant, in whose head a wire went wrong, just because. I breathed with him when he shut his muzzle on the girl's little body, I breathed with Giuseppe who cried in horror, I breathed with Bianca who rushed to get a knife, and I breathed with Ada, until she didn't.

The wind knew that Uncle Mario was right, that bad things happen, with no rhyme or reason.

I knew that Uncle Mario had looked after Mum when she was young, a sweet, starry-eyed girl, easy to like, easy to forget. Uncle Mario was there when some boy broke Mum's heart the first time, and he was there when she decided she would dump Dad, six months before the marriage. I was Sirocco that day, and I put nasty thoughts in people's minds; I had turned into Tramontana, fresh and young, when Mum and Dad brought their first baby to the Masseria del Vento. The wind knew that Uncle Mario might have turned into a different man by making one different choice at one juncture in life. The wind did not judge the man he had become.

The wind did not judge the ancestor who started squandering the family wealth, with madcap investments intended to show to his father – at last! – that he could take care of business. And the wind did not judge his descendants, who drank and gambled away what was left. The wind didn't care and neither did I. All stories are human to the wind, all stories equally small and endless.

I knew there was one who wandered in the wind, who was not human and never had been. Neither was it anything I could put into a jar and label. It was older even than the wind, much older. When time started running in our fresh, green universe, the wanderer was there; it was not haunting our grounds, as much as we were haunting its. It did not walk between worlds, as much as it knew where all worlds are one. The wind knew its name, and so did I. It had not been spoken for uncounted millennia.

I was the wind. I was breathing on the grapes and on the dirt track, and on Ferdi, walking home. I was breathing on that other place which masqueraded as a beach (not on the revelry; nothing breathed there). I breathed on drystone walls and makeshift boundaries, I made the Guadalupis' gate groan, the gravel on their driveway roll, the pine needles sway smoothly, and I rocked a hammock with a girl in it.

'Ada?' I said.

'Luca! How did you get here?'

'Can you see me?'

She coughed. 'Shouldn't I?'

I reached out to her, with a hand, not a gust. Where I was expecting flesh, I prodded something sturdy.

'A cast,' she explained. 'I fell down the stairs and broke my arm. Stupid, eh?'

'What are they doing to you?'

'Who's doing what to whom? You're strange today. Me, I feel fabulous.' Her breath was ragged. 'I *am* fabulous. Your loss for not being able to see me. How did you get here anyway? That's the second time I asked.'

'Ada, I heard the chanting.' I paused. 'The slapping.'

'Oh,' she said. 'That.'

'That.'

She asked, 'Did you sneak into my house?'

'Not your room.'

She laughed, which made her cough again. 'Never less than chivalrous.'

'Your folks,' I insisted, 'what are they doing to you?'

'Don't just stand there. Come and sit in the hammock.' She repressed a cry of pain as she changed position. I sat next to her, my feet on the ground. Her body radiated heat, not a healthy heat. She asked, 'Why did you sneak into my house?'

'I wanted to talk to you.'

'Cute.'

'And I heard your voice, in pain, from the cellar. What was going on in there?'

'They're putting me right.'

'You're right just as you are.'

'You say that, Luca. If you knew…' Her voice trailed off.

'I know you lied.'

'Oh.' After a while, she asked, 'Ferdi?'

'Yep. I showed him the photograph.'

'You must hate me.'

'A little. Did you make everything up? Dreams and all?'

'From first to last word, commas included.'

'Why?'

'Because I'm awful.'

'Be more specific.'

She laughed and coughed again. 'Do we agree your story is a hard sell?'

'I'm not stupid.'

'It's also awesome. I didn't buy it, but I didn't disbelieve it either – I loved it for what it was. It caught my eye. I think I saw a chance to speak up through it.'

'About what? What does it mean that Giuseppe and Bianca are *putting you right*?' The air was still; I was the wind, and I was not moving. 'Help me understand.'

'They never got over Ada's death,' she said. 'The good Ada, the better Ada. The *real* Ada. I was the substitute, I was yogurt to her gelato, chicken to her steak. There wasn't one day in my life – one day – in which they didn't remind me of that. The real Ada never cried. The real Ada had spoken her first word at ten months and could read by the age of three. The real Ada *never* gave them a headache or a sleepless night. The real Ada *never* cried. She was adorable around strangers, but cautious too. She was cute as a button and smart as fuck.'

'She died at four.'

'It's easy to be perfect when you're dead. Me? I was alive, so flawed. Mum and Dad made it their life's mission to put that right.'

'By doing what, killing you?'

'Did you notice the incense?'

'Yes. What was that?'

'Exorcism.'

'Ada, please.'

'Exorcism, for real. Mum, or Dad, I don't even know who started it, but they put in their mind this idea that I had a shot at being a good girl, every bit as good as the one they'd lost, in fact. Shame I had the Devil in me. The actual Devil, the unclean spirit who possessed Akela when he tore my little sister to pieces. That Devil jumped into my Mum's belly when Akela died. Into me.'

'It's… crazy.'

'It's the reality I grew up with. Mum and Dad's life mission became using all possible means to scare the Devil into letting me go. Then I'd be as perfect as the other sister. They have this notion that the Devil is afraid of prayer, because he's the Devil, and of a good thrashing, because everybody's afraid of a good thrashing. All my life, when I did something wrong it wasn't me, it was the Devil, and they would tie me up, sing prayers, burn incense. And thrash the Devil.'

'And the cuts?'

'For many years they couldn't stand the idea of slapping or punching me; it was too much like hitting their daughter, when instead they were fighting the Adversary. They hate hurting me. I think they do. I've seen them cry while they were bleeding me senseless. They used to be scrupulously careful to minimise the traces they left, hide them, but they've got clumsier of late. And they've lost all qualms about hitting me. The war over my soul is almost lost, they say.'

I felt – and I am ashamed every time I think of it – a touch of resentment against Ada. Knowing those horrors had been happening next door year after year, while my family had alfresco dinners and leisurely chats, made me feel sick. It ruined some of my happiest memories. I thought, *Why is she doing this to me?* before getting a grip and taking in that it wasn't about me. I grew a little older in a heartbeat. 'I'm sorry,' I said.

'I wished I could be like other kids,' Ada said. 'Like, not possessed. I tend to act out around them. I told you about Nino. I made it look like it was a one-off, but, breaking news, it wasn't. Every time I acted like that, it proved I wasn't like them, it proved I had something dark inside.'

'Ada, you don't.'

'No need to tell me that,' she said. 'Not anymore, although once upon a time it might've helped. I used to take for granted what I'd been told. Mum and Dad are always right when you're little, aren't they? Seriously, put yourself in my shoes. The beatings, the chants, this presence within me – it was my normal, all I'd ever known. Imagine you've been told all your life that you can't walk – what do you think is going to happen? You won't try to walk and you'll feel self-conscious when you find yourself staggering and stumbling, and the fact that you can't walk will become sort of real. But I've been reading books, articles from Mum's library. I've been thinking, chatting with Ferdinando, and you. I got the refreshing point of view of folks who don't think I'm evil incarnate. And I started thinking. *I don't care* whether Mum and Dad are right or not. That's not the main thing. The main thing is, if they're actually doing God's will then I'd rather play for the other team. I said it in that many words after they busted us on the beach.'

'It didn't go down well.'

'They're going to kill me.'

The wind stirred and I stirred. 'No,' I said.

'It's going to happen. Tonight. Tomorrow. Soon, anyway.' She took my hand and put it on her cast. 'This is a first. The things they've been doing… Mum has this whip, an original piece, an antique, which she never used, only teased. She took it out two nights ago. They say they won't let me, well, *the Devil in me*, ruin you too. They think the world of you, Luca, honestly they do.'

I said, 'Let's go. Now.'

'Where? Yours won't believe me, the Carabinieri – Mum is their *consultant*. Thanks to her, I have a detailed clinical history of self-harm, paranoid tendencies. Whatever I say or do, it will only prove her point. Same for you. She's clever.'

'You're cleverer.'

'Thank you.'

'Tell me the plan, Ada. You always have a plan.'

'The plan's not changed. No one's going to rescue me, and I've got to rescue myself.' She paused. 'Guns a' blazing.'

'Okay, I'll go get Grandpa's shotgun for you.'

Ada giggled, then chuckled, then laughed. A fit of coughing interrupted her. It lasted longer than the ones before, and when it was over her breath was more laboured. She spat. 'Oh, Luca, my chivalrous Luca. If only.'

'I'll handle that, I swear.'

'You're not really here.'

'What?'

'You're naked, barefoot. I can't see your cane. What the hell? I got a detailed masterwork of a dusting last night, first-class stuff. I've been feeling foggy ever since. My brain's making up a fairy tale to distract me from how majestically fucked up reality is in my last hours. You're a coping strategy, Luca Saracino. It's a handy brain, it knows the good stuff. I wish you were real.' Cracked lips skimmed my forehead. 'I wish we'd had time.'

My forehead was breeze and air in motion, my body was a whirlwind of gusts. I was the wind, and I had to move on. I blew between the pines and the driveway. I blew above a drystone wall, and I blew into the hollow of a tree, and there I rested for a while. The gusts settled. They condensed and made bones and organs, blood and flesh, until I was in the tree, a human boy again. I lay there for a little longer. It was very nice.

After, I crawled out of the hollow and went fishing for my clothes. It took me a long time to find most of them. I had enough and decided to make my way back with my shirt and left shoe still missing. I was expecting to find my family asleep.

But I didn't.

Giuseppe Guadalupi's voice spread through the air with the smoothness of oil rubbed on skin. It made me want to run the other way, go back to the tree and hide in its hollow until the next morning. Then what? Then Ada would die.

The scent of pipe smoke and coffee got deeper as the voices got more defined. They were ready for battle on the porch – my parents, and Giuseppe.

'Here you are,' he said, relieved.

Giuseppe Guadalupi, my own white whale. I hadn't fully grasped the notion of hatred until that moment; I understood Ahab at last. *Breathe in, breathe out*, I told myself. *Slow and steady*.

Dad's voice was harsher than his. 'Luca, what happened to your clothes?'

'You're covered in dirt,' Mum said.

Giuseppe said, 'The important thing is that you're here. Ten minutes more and we'd have set up a search party.'

His concern for me was nothing but genuine, as was his concern for Ada. Bianca and Giuseppe truly wanted the best for us. They were the good guys in their story, and people will cheerfully kill and maim and ruin lives when they are the good guys.

'No need,' I said.

Someone touched my shoulder, making me jump. Dad said, 'We know what you did.'

'Okay.'

'You're admitting it, then,' Mum said.

'I don't know what you're talking about, but okay. You've made up your mind.'

'We told you that you shouldn't see Ada, for the good of both you.'

They waited for an answer. I kept my mouth shut.

Giuseppe said, 'You came to our place, earlier today.'

'Did you see me?'

'I heard your voice, from the hammock. You left before I managed to get there. I ran here immediately, and you weren't home.'

'Fucking klutz you are, that a blind man moves faster than you.' In the course of summer I had outgrown my early desire to keep using hand gestures, but that time, I flipped Giuseppe Guadalupi a middle finger.

Dad told me off with a resounding, 'Luca!'

'Were you there?' Mum said.

An idea was forming in my mind.

'If I told you I wasn't, would you believe me?'

'I'd ask you again what happened to your clothes, and why you look as if you dug your way out of a hole in the ground.'

Because I was the wind. 'I've got something to say. I have to give it a go, for my peace of mind.'

Giuseppe said, 'Please, do.'

'Okay, here we go. Giuseppe, you and your wife are scumbags. I will take you down. Maybe not now, maybe in ten years, or thirty, but I will take you down. It's not a threat, it's a fact. I'll take you down for what you did.'

I was expecting an explosion which didn't arrive. Dad was going to talk, but Mum cut him off. 'What did they do?' she asked. She was listening.

They lied to me, I thought. I had nothing to lose, so I went on in a steady voice. 'Giuseppe and Bianca have been beating Ada on a regular basis since she was a little child. I talked to her. I touched her cast. They broke her arm the other day. She is in a bad way, and she is afraid they're going to kill her this time.'

'No,' Mum said, in a low voice. 'Oh, please, not this too.'

'I am sorry,' Giuseppe said. 'I am so, so sorry: I take full responsibility. Bianca had foreseen that a situation exactly like this would happen. I was the one who insisted on a light-handed approach, but I was wrong. I'm sorry, this is my fault. We should have listened to her.'

'No one's listening to *me*,' I said.

'Sure we are,' Dad said. 'Sure we are.'

Giuseppe said, 'Listen, Luca: Did Ada tell you that we have been casting out devils from her? That we believe she is possessed, and that we want to make her as good as...' His voice trailed off. 'Our other daughter?' he concluded.

'Mum, Dad, this is what is going on next door.'

Giuseppe said, 'It is not a secret that Ada is hurt. We took her to a hospital when she broke her arm! She did that to herself, by throwing herself against a wall.'

This was a waste of time. Mum's voice had given me a stir of hope, but no, my judgement had been passed long before I arrived. 'Okay,' I said.

'Ada's story is a fabrication, although it contains more than a grain of truth. Her issues originate at least partially in old mistakes of mine: I've failed her as a father I don't know how many times. When our…' He was on the verge of tears. 'When our other daughter died, it broke me; Bianca barely managed to put me back together. She agreed to name our baby after the girl we'd lost. She tried to convince me it was appallingly unhealthy, but unfortunately for Ada, my wife loves me more than I deserve. I'm *ashamed* when I think of what we did, what I did. Ada grew up in the shadow of her sister, obsessed, I would say, with the sister she'd never met. She created this whole fantasy world in which our dog had been possessed by a spirit when he'd…' He paused again. 'And in which the same spirit now possessed *her*. She self-harms to cast out the Devil. She is highly manipulative, as a part of her clinical presentation. We should've shielded you better from her, Luca. We failed our duty of care.'

'I told you we had to act,' Dad said to nobody in particular.

'All I can say in our defence is this: So far, Ada never mentioned her fabrication to anyone but Bianca and me. It is not an excuse. We will do everything in our power to set things right.'

I said, 'Can you even *hear* this man?'

Giuseppe asked, 'Tell me, Luca: Would this be the first time Ada lied to you?'

'No,' I admitted.

'And yet you believe her?'

'Completely.'

'Why?'

I was grateful to him for asking that question, so that I could find an answer for myself. I didn't know what I was going to say until I said it. 'Because she's my friend.'

'Is that all?'

'You said I was mental. Now she is too. Are you guys the only sane people in town?'

'Not mental!' Giuseppe said. 'Unwell, troubled, in pain. Bianca could explain it better than me. It is sadly common for teenagers to feed each other's fantasies. It might be UFOs, or fairies, or devils, or abuses, or a mix of everything.'

'Mum, Dad, do you guys buy this crap?'

Mum was crying. 'Luca, you wanted us to believe you visited another world.'

'I told you,' Dad repeated.

That was it: certainties are comfy beds on which to doze, and my parents would never forgive me for threatening to shake them awake. It was like Ada said; no one was going to rescue me. I had to rescue myself. I sighed. 'Okay. What's it going to be?'

'We're not your enemies,' Mum said.

I swallowed a *Fuck you, Mum* and repeated, 'What's it going to be?'

Giuseppe said, 'My family are leaving tomorrow. It is obviously unhealthy for you and Ada to live in such close proximity.'

Dad said, 'I appreciate your forfeiting the end of your summer for us.'

'Nonsense. You have nowhere else to go. We do. Luca, we are going to run a battery of tests, with your parents' permission. I promise, we'll get to the bottom of this.'

I had one night.

They realised that too. They would not go as far as locking me in my room – I might need the loo, and they were going to great lengths to convince me, against all the evidence, that I was not a prisoner – but they made it very clear they would lock the front door and move the keys from the bowl, in case I got ideas in my head. Giuseppe Guadalupi took back his house keys. He made embarrassed noises and gave ample reassurance that it was nothing to do with trust or lack thereof, only with the peculiar situation that had developed, and Mum and Dad *of-course*d all the way. Dad's manners were those of a stung man; another piece of his pretence of being a local had been taken from him. A cunning, well-liked entrepreneur in his head, a dupe that his neighbours couldn't trust with house keys in everybody else's.

I was not allowed to spend time on the swing after dinner. Ferdi proposed to stay with me and keep watch, and for the briefest moment I almost believed he might be some help. It would be cool, and simple, and not how life goes. 'No, I'll go to bed,' I said.

'Scrawny…'

'I've got a name, it's *Luca*.'

Mum and Dad recovered to their room. Ferdi, who was of that age when you are able to sustain yourself on sunshine and friends, found the energy to go out again, to say goodbye to one of his summer party who would leave the next day. I was left alone in my room, fully aware that crickets and hoopoes and thick walls hid cries.

I knew a name.

I had to get out of the house, and the wind wouldn't help, for the wind did not owe me anything. Back in the fields I had received a gift of extraordinary grace, and I understood, though I had no words to explain, that grace cannot survive gluttony, and miracles disappear when you want them on tap. I knew a name, that was my gift, and I could not ask for more.

Ada had said, *If they're actually doing God's will, then I'd rather play for the other team.* Well, the wanderer was, without any question, the other team. Not the Devil, not in the way Giuseppe and Bianca understood him – the wanderer was older than that, and stranger. The idea that the primal sounds forming its name could vibrate with my strings, march out of my throat and bend my tongue to come into the world again for the first time in millennia gave me a sense of violation. It made me curious too.

I reached out for my cane.

Where would Mum and Dad hide the shotgun? I ruled out their room, because Dad would not sleep with a gun in his room, especially not Grandpa's. Then, where? Not in the kitchen, the busiest room in the house. Not in Ferdi's room either. It must be in a cupboard or a wardrobe or something like that. The masseria was littered with worm-holed furniture.

I can only scan what I touch, which makes searching hard labour. The upside is that the sighted believe that I cannot search at all, and when they hide things from me, they are sloppy. I went room by room, most of which had been abandoned for decades. I opened doors. I passed my hands over layers of dust and crusty insect husks. I broke age-old cobwebs with my face, sliding through the night like a clumsy ghost. I had to resist the impulse to speed up. I proceeded slowly, methodically, piece by piece. That way I found the gun.

I had climbed on the seat of a chair (a perfectly terrifying thing to do) to search the top of a mouldy wardrobe in a room where the glass in the window was completely gone, leaving a gaping hole in the wall, which let in a breeze and a barking. I touched steel first, then the soft fur that covered the cartridge belt. There were not many cartridges left. It was immaterial: Ada wouldn't get a chance to fire more than once or twice. I set the belt around my waist and I slung the shotgun over a shoulder. Now I had to find a way out.

I didn't know how much time had passed since I'd started searching for the shotgun; a couple of hours was a realistic estimate. I could not waste any more time searching for the keys, and there was a fair chance those would be in Mum and Dad's bedroom. I thought of leaving through a window. I tested the shutters of one, then another: they were closed. They were old things, noisy, which would wake the whole house if rolled up. An overwhelming helplessness washed over me, the same I felt immediately after curtain fall and on the first days in the Masseria del Vento. It was a feeling I thought I'd left behind. It was also a luxury I couldn't afford; while I wept over my bad luck, Ada was suffering.

I headed to the little loo on the ground floor, a minuscule room with only a WC, a bidet, and a sink. There was a tiny window there, with a tiny shutter. I slowly closed the door behind me and brought a hand to the shutter. It was already halfway up. They must have judged the window too small for anyone to pass through. I grabbed the string and pulled. The shutter produced what to my ears felt like a nuclear explosion, but it was objectively nothing more than a scratching. I pulled again, again the shutter scratched. I left my cane against the wall and used my hands to test the opening. The window was small, but so was I. My bones were young, they could turn in ways that would be impossible in ten years' time. I put my head through. I was about to test a theory I'd read somewhere, that if your head passes through a space, then the rest of your body must be able to pass through too.

I brought my cane down on the other side of the window and set it against the external wall. Next, with all the care of a tightrope walker, I brought down the shotgun. I dropped the cartridge belt with almost no noise at all. Then it was my turn.

I wormed my way through masonry head first, but I had to accept after a few attempts that I did not have enough space to turn and let myself fall on the other side legs first. So I went back, and this time I climbed on the windowsill with a knee, held on to the edge of the window frame, and squirmed outside with both legs. Now came the scariest part of any task, the letting go. I knew the ground had to be ridiculously close, but to me it was like jumping into a bottomless abyss.

I let go.

I fell for a long time, enough to get to the other side of the planet, and further still, although in the real world I was crashing down onto the pavement outside probably only a fraction of a moment later.

I did not stop to consider the enormity of what I was about to do, but I did stop to load the shotgun with a *clack*. I didn't know yet how to get inside the Guadalupis'. One thing at a time.

I stopped again before turning onto the dirt track, stretching my ears for Ferdi's steps. I was under no illusion about what he would do were he to see me in the street, intent on playing a miniature Rambo. I heard nothing, and ventured out. I felt exposed, a kid with a gun and a white cane sweeping his way towards the house of good, God-fearing people. I hoped it was not a full moon; Uncle Mario's comment stayed with me.

If I heard anyone, I decided, I would fire. In the air, just to scare them off.

But no one saw me and no one called; only the crickets kept me company. I turned into the Guadalupis' driveway, and after checking that no sound came from the house, I headed to the door. As I walked I scouted for ideas on how to get inside, finding none. Ada would have come up with three plan As and two plan Bs by now. I was not stupid, but she was brilliant. If any devil did try and mess with her, he would be in for a ride. I made it to the door, tested the handle.

The door opened.

I stood there on the threshold, afraid to move another step. In a comic book this would be a trap. I knew miracles were another fact of life, but I doubted they were ever this straightforward. Giuseppe and Bianca would not leave the door unlocked, tonight of all nights, nor would the wind bother to open it for my sake.

Ada, I thought.

Ada was brilliant.

The house stood silent, not empty. I listened with ferocious attention, being rewarded with the singsong melody of people sleeping the sleep of the just. Nothing came from the kitchen, and what whiff of incense there was, lingered as a leftover.

I took the stairs. It was obscene that it had not changed, that these were still the same steps I climbed and still the same banister I held on to when I came here to hang on Giuseppe Guadalupi's every word.

I stopped before Ada's door. Absurdly, I thought I should knock. I was halfway there when I caught myself. I opened it. Nothing that came to me from the other side was in the neighbourhood of *right*. The space smelt of illness and blood. Ada's breath was laboured. It came to a halt. She wheezed, 'Earlier, on the hammock – you vanished.'

'I was the wind.'

'You were really there.'

'Yes.'

'I left the door open for you.'

'You were great, as always.'

She coughed for a long time. When she caught her breath she said, 'I wasn't lying either. Not this time.'

'I know.'

'You know why I wanted the gun so badly?'

'I think I do.'

'I'm not going to kill both of them,' she said. 'Only one. I'll be safe, in jail.'

'If that's what you want, Ada.'

'I have a right to *live*!'

'Of course you do.'

'You think I'm a bad person?'

'You're the most amazing person I ever met.'

'You know what scares me? That it might be the Devil in me in the driver's seat. That this... this thing I want to do, this bad thing, it doesn't come from me, it comes from him.'

'You don't have any devil in you.'

'And isn't that scary too?'

'A little,' I said.

'Are you afraid of me, Luca?'

'A little,' I repeated.

'Damn, I flunked. I was aiming for utterly terrified.'

'You've got stiff competition.'

She coughed and coughed, which was all she could do in the way of laughing.

I asked, 'May I say something?'

'As long as it's short.'

'There is a terrible smell, and your breath and your voice sound awful.'

'Charmer.'

'This has gone well beyond anything your old folks might get away with, even factoring in all the psycho-babble they can muster up. Cuts, yes, bruises, even a broken arm, but this? This is lunacy. We can call the Carabinieri. They will have to make an enquiry. Let's go home.'

'You trusted Ferdi, and see how it turned out.'

'I gave *you* a second chance.'

'It's not a risk I can take.' She paused to gulp some air, and something within her whistled like a broken door. 'I'm drowning,' she said. 'My lungs are filling up. I'm drowning on dry land.'

'Hospital first, Carabinieri later.'

'Thirteen years, Luca. It's all my life. They've taken all my life.'

'You've got plenty more to go.'

'If they did that to you – would you let them walk?'

'No,' I said, after a moment's reflection.

'Leave. I'll say I stole the shotgun. I won't get you in trouble.'

'I won't let you do this alone.'

'But you'll ruin your life.'

'We'll see about that.'

I would have done it myself, had I been sighted; I might as well take the fall with my friend. That summer I came to think that the place of some people is six feet under, and I never changed my mind.

Ada coughed, and moved, and stifled a cry. 'Appreciate.' She hauled herself up and limped towards me, her wheezing rising and falling with every step. She took the shotgun I was holding out to her; she wrapped her plastered arm around my shoulder. 'A little help?'

We left the room, Ada leaning on me while guiding me to her parents' room. I stopped when she stopped. She brought her lips very close to my ear, and whispered, 'The door.'

I reached out and found a handle. I wondered what kind of man Grandpa would think I was if he could see me. *Better than you*, I said to his ghost in my mind, *better than you, who didn't offer this girl more than tea.*

I slung the door open, and Bianca's sleepy voice jumped, 'What…?'

'Boo,' Ada said. 'The Devil is here.'

I heard her move the shotgun; I supposed she was pointing it.

'Ada?' Giuseppe said. 'Luca!'

Bianca was calm when she said, 'What are you doing?'

'I'm getting free,' Ada said.

'Don't be silly.'

Ada's voice faltered. 'I'm not silly…?'

I'd never heard her like this: a word from her mother, and the Ada I knew shattered, to be replaced by a trembling doe. If I didn't hate the Guadalupis before, I hated them from then on.

'Pull that trigger,' Bianca said, 'and you'll be a prisoner for evermore. All you are going to do is give the Devil free rein over you.'

'Bullshit.'

'You know I am telling the truth. Don't give up, Ada, my love. Don't let the Devil win the war over your soul. Be strong. Make us proud.'

Ada let out a whimper. Her body next to mine was going limp. 'I can't, Luca,' she said. 'I just can't.'

I heard Giuseppe walk towards us.

I shouted, 'Ada, go!' and threw myself on him.

It didn't even rank as a scuffle. I confusedly heard Ada run, Bianca following behind her, while I swung with my cane, but white canes are made to be light, harmless. It is possible I did connect with Giuseppe Guadalupi and it did not make a lick of difference. He got to me, took hold of my wrists and squeezed, and I lost my grip. 'Calm down,' he said. 'Calm down, son.'

He spun me until I didn't have a sense of where I was, and stepped back, leaving me staggering, nauseous. 'It is only you and me,' he said, in a warm, compassionate tone that almost made me love him again.

'I know,' I said.

'Let's talk. There is a chair in the corner behind you.'

Ada and Bianca made no noise; they must have left the building. I sat down.

Giuseppe stood not far from me. 'You probably won't understand, Luca, but you must know how sorry I am.'

'Sorry enough to let me go home?'

I was not afraid of him. I don't think it was bravery, there was more than a touch of folly to it. I was well aware that Giuseppe Guadalupi would do as he pleased with me if Ada didn't return soon with help, but I was too disappointed in him to be afraid.

'Sorry enough not to let the Devil go,' he said.

'The Devil, your devil – that's not a thing.'

There was the swooping of a drawer being opened, the rasping of a match being struck, and pipe smoke filled the room. 'How can you say that, after you met him?'

'So you did believe me.'

'When Bianca and I heard of your trial, we understood two things. First, we were doing too little with Ada. Second, we had a responsibility towards you too. The Devil roams these fields. Your family knew, my family knew, every old family knew in the olden days. But they forgot. They thought it was enough to look the other way, to ignore the problem, and the problem would go away. Fools! Our Lord is the Lord of Armies, and we, we are the armies. If you look the other way from the enemy, all you're doing is showing him your shoulders. And the enemy will jump on the opportunity and attack, I can assure you. The Devil will, and he will take what you hold dear. He will maim and slay and eat your little girl.'

'The wanderer is not the Devil, Giuseppe. It's older than that.'

'Did he tell you as much? Beware, my poor boy. The Devil is Belial, the Lord of Lies.'

'That's not his name.'

A crack of enthusiasm broke Giuseppe's self-collected facade. 'Did he give you another one? Names have power. We might be able to harness it against him!'

'You're pathetic,' I said. 'You talk and talk, but you don't know the first thing.'

Giuseppe came nearer, set his arms either side of my body on the chair's arms. He neared his mouth to my face. 'What's his name?' he asked, in a whisper.

Suit yourself, I thought, and spoke the name.

I had been afraid I wouldn't be able to pronounce it correctly. The sounds I was meant to produce were nothing like anything my larynx had been trained for, and I had thought that pronouncing them would be hard. I was wrong.

When I breathed in the air I would shape into those sounds, my body purred in anticipation the way it did on Christmas Eve when I was little, or on the last day of school before summer. Those were the most natural vibrations that would ever pass through my lips. Older than the sloppy sounds writers wrestled with, older than the approximate words of human languages, they came from a time when reality spoke in its own voice. My body remembered them perfectly, for they were as natural to it as its other rhythms, the drumming of a heartbeat, the surge of strong blood, the electrical fizzling of neurones. Those vibrations were as natural as death, sex and beauty.

As I spoke the word, I understood (or remembered) that it was not exactly the wanderer's name. Rather, the word was the wanderer, not a label imposed on a thing, like other words, but the thing itself. You can talk and run and cook and read and you are still the same person, under different guises but fundamentally the same, and similarly, the wanderer was that word no less than it was its gait and feral smell.

It was a short word. When my lips joined again, Giuseppe was recoiling, as if sucker-punched. 'The language of Hell,' he said, with a heavy breath.

I pitied him. He groped for a ledge he could not reach.

He took a panicked smoke from his pipe. 'The Devil got such a strong hold on you,' he said. 'He takes the best and brightest of us, the ones we hold the dearest. We were too soft on him, and for that I will never finish making amends until I die. Oh, but it ends tonight. I promise, Luca, we'll deliver you both from evil tonight, once and for all.'

'You won't lay a finger on Ada.'

'I'd never harm my daughter.' He paused. 'It's the Devil we're after.'

A feral smell was rising. I listened. Was it a strange gait I heard?

'You've been harming Ada plenty,' I said. 'For her whole life.'

'If one's leg has gangrene, a doctor amputates it. The doctor is not harming the patient, the doctor is *saving* the patient. Ada's bodily pain is nothing, absolutely nothing, less than nothing. You must think in terms of eternity, Luca. Not a million years, not a billion years, but all the time that will ever be. *That* is what we are fighting to preserve for you and her. Bianca and I are doctors of the soul. A temporary discomfort of the body? It's the prick of the needle of a lifesaving jab.'

Tap, tap.

The feral smell was stronger.

I could have laughed. 'You have no clue,' I said.

'I have all the clues that the Lord saw fit to give me.'

'The wanderer is older than your God too. Much, much older.'

'See? This is the Devil, talking through you. He grabs your vocal cords and twists them into horrible blasphemies. I am so, so sorry, Luca,' he said, and there was nothing but sincerity in his voice. 'It ends tonight, I promise, whatever the price for Bianca and me.'

'You guys want to kill us.'

'No! We'll deliver you to a new life, before your souls are damned for ever. We were going to deliver Ada, and try other routes with you, but you have gone too far now.'

Tap, tap.

The feral smell was intense enough to cover the pipe.

'This smell,' Giuseppe said. 'This walk. Is this the Devil?'

'The wanderer,' I said.

'Good,' he said. 'I'm ready.'

I heard him fumble with something. I asked, 'What are you doing?'

'Arming myself.'

I imagined him holding a cross and a rosary against the wanderer, like a child aiming a water pistol at a tiger, and this time I couldn't contain the laughter.

Giuseppe said something, something I didn't hear, for an explosion from outside covered his voice.

We stood in silence as the echo faded, and when it faded the *tap, tap* was closer.

Giuseppe started mumbling in Latin. The words he spoke were manufactured: small, toy words. They sounded childish against the stark reality of the feral smell which was everywhere, in the steps, in the walls, exuding from our bodies. I had been right to be afraid of it. I was still afraid. I was also in awe.

Tap, tap.

Another step approached, advancing across the ground floor and up the staircase, a dragging step, faltering, all too human, and it came in tune with the wanderer's.

Ada's scent of coconut, vanilla and gunpowder burst from the doorway.

'Dad,' she said, in tears. 'Please, Dad, please, let us go.'

'Where's Mum?'

'I had to…' She stopped. She sniffed. 'Please, Dad, I'm begging you, I'm begging you, let us go, don't make me…'

'Sure,' Giuseppe said. 'Sure, I'll let you go, my love.'

Tap, tap.

Giuseppe moved towards Ada's voice. And before I could yell to Ada not to trust him, before I could yell at her to either run or fire, another explosion boomed, ricocheting from wall to wall, getting stronger and meaner with every bounce, and when it was ready, it assaulted me brutally. I brought my hands to my ears and screamed.

I couldn't hear my voice.

I stretched my hearing for my heartbeat without finding any; I stretched for the wanderer's gait and couldn't find it either; and when I clapped my hands, nothing was there. I panicked. I stood up. I felt the full weight of my heavy breath but not its broken rhythm in my ears. It is not an exaggeration to say that being deaf used to be my worst nightmare, before I met my wife and my bad dreams started revolving around other kinds of loss. Deafness would make me virtually a prisoner in my body.

Meanwhile things were happening around me, a carnival of air in motion and shifting feelings underfoot, but in my state I was no more able to read them than I was able to read printed words. I received no images, no sounds, nothing I could work with. Shifting feelings and nothing more.

Gradually I became aware of a brackish whiff and a fine spray of water on my face. I sensed the clean taste of sea salt on my tongue, and hard, flat rocks beneath my soles. The feral smell was gone. My ears whistled.

A hand touched my shoulder.

I jumped. I turned.

'It's me,' someone said, from another planet. 'Ada.'

The whistle was subsiding. 'We're on the beach,' I said. '*That* beach.'

Ada's voice became more defined. 'It's not a beach.'

'Your father…'

She asked, 'How do you feel?'

'My ears are still ringing, but I think I'm all right. You?'

'I'm better.'

Her breath was almost normal, her voice firmer. Yes, she was better. 'Your father…' I repeated.

'He was my father,' she said. 'I knew when he was lying.'

'Did you…'

'Don't ask. Not yet. I'll tell you everything, but first I need some time to process, let my thoughts settle. Will you give me time?'

'Of course.'

'You know I only ran because I thought I'd find help faster, right?'

'Didn't doubt that for a moment.'

'I'm sorry I couldn't pull the trigger at first. I almost got you killed.'

'You couldn't shoot your parents in cold blood, that doesn't make you a wimp.'

'My blood's never cold.'

'And I love you for that,' I said before I knew what I was saying.

She laughed, without coughing. 'Strong words.'

'Let's go home,' I quickly said. 'We're going to have to answer a million questions.'

'I wouldn't mind staying a little longer.'

'As long as you like.'

'Just a little longer,' she said. 'Come, sit with me.'

I sat next to her, and she put her head on my shoulder. One last time, she was close enough that I could kiss her. She reached to my hand, took it in hers and brought it in her lap, and I was happy to stay with the breaking ashore of those strange waves and the calls of the beings that peopled that land.

After a while an immense tiredness weighed me down. I let my head fall onto Ada's; I drifted off with the scent of her hair in my mouth.

When I woke up, my ears didn't whistle anymore. My senses, all four of them, had returned pristine. Ada said, 'I think we should go.'

She handed me the cane. I folded it, and, leaning on one another, we walked on the rocks, away from the sea. I said, 'I know it's not a beach.'

'It looks like one. Almost.'

That was all I needed.

We reached the dirt track; there we heard from afar the bleak music of a fiddler and other revellers. 'Mum and Dad are with them,' Ada said, barely slowing her step.

Then we went home.

Ada Guadalupi left me at her driveway, where I said goodbye, expecting to see her again in a matter of hours. I turned into the

Masseria del Vento's. I felt a presence on the porch, someone who was fitting a key in the door. It stopped. 'Scrawny?' Ferdi said, surprised.

'Before you ask,' I said, 'this is how it's going to work. Whatever happens tomorrow, you won't say to a living soul that you saw me now. Not a living soul, Ferdi. You will never, ever mention that we met, not even to me, and you won't ask questions, not now, not tomorrow, not ever. I don't care how much you're going to worry. I don't care how curious you'll get, you will have to live with it, because I was never here, tonight. I was in my room, sleeping like a drunk baby. Say yes, Ferdi, please, and keep your word. Give me a chance to be your friend.'

After a while, he said, 'Okay.'

'I'm sorry about your exams. It sucks that you couldn't sit them, and it sucks that I was a pillock about it.'

'Yeah. A little.'

I yawned. 'Gotta go to sleep. Good night, brother.'

I took a shower before jumping into bed; I had salt on my skin.

The following days and weeks did not play out as I'd thought they would. I had put in my mind that Ada and I would be fine from then on. The enemies vanquished, the danger removed, we were going to ride into the sunset bathed in glory, and I would make my move before summer's end. I didn't understand that summer was over.

It was late morning when the commotion started. We heard cars, an ambulance. Mum and Dad were still debating whether to check on the Guadalupis, at the risk of appearing nosy, or wait for them to call, at the risk of appearing uncaring. The Carabinieri put them out of their misery coming to the masseria.

They were two highly unpleasant men, arrogant, demanding, as enforcers of all stripes often are. They ignored Mum except to ask her for a cup of coffee, and talked only to Dad, the man of the house. When they addressed me they talked slowly, as if to an idiot. Projection, psychologists call it. I filed their names in my memory for future reference. Apparently, there had been a call from the house next door; apparently our neighbours had vanished overnight, leaving behind both their cars (one an expensive make!) and also, by the way, their daughter. Did we know anything? Unfortunately, none of us did. Not even Ferdi.

That evening Aunt Betta paid us a visit for an aperitif and a spot of gossip. Ada was in hospital, and we were not to mention a word of this to anyone, but she had accused her parents of abuse. She had seized the chance to call the Carabinieri when she had woken up and her Mum and Dad were not home. The Guadalupis, such nice people – who would have thought it? Aunt Betta was entirely sure that Ada was telling the truth, shocking as it was, for one cannot simply hurt oneself the way she was hurt. (Aunt Betta's cousin had married a chiropractor who worked at the hospital, and had first-hand information.) 'She will be marked *for ever,*' she said, in a saddened tone, and she meant the scars on Ada's back, which as far as she was concerned were immensely more serious than any scar that was left in Ada's mind.

After she left, Mum and Dad grilled me. They asked if I knew more than I said, if I was hiding something, as if my being right was a fault I had to justify. In the course of the conversation a shift happened. They convinced themselves they had suspected all along the Guadalupis were off. Bianca was so eager to feed me pills – how come? And with all the blabbing Giuseppe did about music and guitars, I hadn't progressed all that much. They *knew* it.

More details came to light by the next morning. The Carabinieri had found Bianca Guadalupi's body in the fields behind the house, against a drystone wall. What was left of the body, that is. Bianca had been mangled by dogs with a ferocity which apparently made not one but two Carabinieri throw up.

Giuseppe was nowhere to be found, and an official theory took traction that he might have killed his wife. Considering the state of her body, it was difficult to say any last word on the cause of death, but she had been shot from close range with a hunting shotgun. If that gave my parents pause for thought, they never showed it. For a week or so they tut-tutted at the widespread circulation of guns in this corner of Italy, then they forgot about it.

I got the last reality check of that summer, and a harsh one, when I found that Aunt Betta was once again an unlikely exception to the rule. My weird gothic fantasy all but forgotten, now the Guadalupis were the talk of town, and the folks who believed Ada's story were as few and far between as those who had believed mine. The girl was temperamental, she had kicked this boy's nuts and pulled that girl's hair, she was not demure, and she didn't dress properly. Her parents, though? They were exquisite hosts, and they were doctors. The wild brat was fibbing, truth would out. She couldn't be the killer, for she was a girl after all, but she was lying about the abuse, that was for sure.

The Carabinieri returned for a half-arsed attempt at interrogating me. They were resentfully putting checks on boxes. A blind boy couldn't be a reliable witness, and I didn't disabuse them of that belief. I didn't say that I had known what was going on next door, and neither did Mum and Dad. What for? I could do without the hassle of being called as a witness. I'd step up if need be, but only if need be.

Grandpa's shotgun never came up. It was never found, nor were cartridges, holes in the masonry or birdshot. Seven or eight years later, Mum and Dad realised they had lost the gun, and they convinced themselves the builders must have stolen it, although they had kicked out the builders before they hid the gun. In their memories things had worked the other way round, and if that was good enough for them, it was good enough for me.

One morning Uncle Mario dropped by the masseria for a quick coffee. He was patiently at work on the ice wall between him and Mum, which he would manage to thaw in time for Christmas. My parents would rather forget they'd been duped. They came to tell the story as if they, the world-weary city people, had taken slight advantage of that country bumpkin relative of theirs – only slight, because family is more important than money. I hope I don't have their same power for self-delusion.

On a moment in which we were alone, Uncle Mario said, 'Have you heard?'

'What?'

'Giuseppe Guadalupi's body. They found it: it was washed up on the beach. The Carabinieri will make the news public later today, I think. The fish had...' He stopped. 'The body was in no better condition than Bianca's.'

'What a tragedy,' I said.

'Do you reckon we will ever get to the bottom of this story?'

'I wouldn't expect that, no.'

'Mmm,' he said.

Ever since then, Uncle Mario was never less than friendly with my family.

The truth did out, and the truth was Ada's. The marks on her body left little space for doubt, her DNA had been sprayed all over the cellar's walls, and the Carabinieri found an antique whip drenched in her blood like a biscuit fattened with milk. Even so, a sizeable amount of people stubbornly kept disbelieving her about the abuse, and to this day you might hear at the café disparaging comments about 'that lying girl'. Some people lack the humility to admit they're wrong, and some lack the brains.

The great puzzle remained – what had happened to Bianca and Giuseppe Guadalupi? The theory of homicide-suicide gained traction. It did not explain much, but it sounded sensible, and in time it solidified into a well-known fact.

As Aunt Betta put it, whatever had happened, Ada Guadalupi, the poor little angel, was free. She was also thirteen, and could not live on her own.

She called me in September, some days before school began. I had fallen into the habit of saying goodbye to her every night, aloud, and imagining she was there with me. I missed her in a way that still makes me wistful when I think of it.

I took the call in the kitchen; Ferdi shepherded Mum out. He clicked the door closed.

'Ada!' I said.

'Hey.'

'How have you been?'

'I've not been tortured of late.'

She made me laugh. 'All shares are on the up.'

'I never said thank you.'

'You did most of the work.'

'You helped.'

'One last day at the Little Pinewood before school?'

'I'm leaving tomorrow.'

And still I didn't get it. 'Where for?' I asked.

'Rome.'

'When are you back?'

'Not for a while.'

I heard the words but it was beyond me to put them together. 'School starts next week.'

'I'm going to school there.'

'What? Why?'

'I'll be staying with a cousin of Mum's.'

I'd heard about this cousin: the word on the street was she had volunteered to take care of Ada, temporarily. I hadn't thought she might not live in Puglia. How could she possibly not live in Puglia? A lump blocked my throat. 'Rome is far away.'

'I'll call.'

'We could hang tonight.'

'I don't know if I can do that.'

I hated her, and I understood her. 'Will you come for Christmas?'

'Probably,' she lied. 'Next summer for sure. And I'll call.'

'It's expensive to call from Rome.'

'So don't be a cheap bastard and call me some time.'

309

'I'll need the number.'

'I'll give it to you when I have it.'

'Okay,' I said.

'Okay,' she said.

I didn't hear her voice again until last week.

That was another bad winter. I kept waiting for Ada to call, and meanwhile I started school with boys and girls younger than me. I was tainted by my silly spooky story, my association with Ada Guadalupi and my troubles in joining social activities such as riding bikes, playing football, roller skating. I was a magnet for a certain type of girl, the type perpetually on the lookout for a harmless charity case to patronise, and for a certain type of boy so low on the food chain that even bullies do not bother with them. They did not bother with me either. They didn't know, of course, what had become of the last two people who had tried, but they sensed it, the way carnivores sense dangerous waters.

My one meaningful interaction that winter was with the boy who everybody agreed was the local weirdo, Arturo Musiello, called Art. A little older than me, he was the one who had played a prank on the town of Casalfranco two years earlier, pretending that he had disappeared for seven days when he'd only been hiding. He came to the masseria one afternoon, on a bike which did not sound at all like Ada's. I barely knew him: I could not imagine what he might possibly want from me.

He wanted to know about the wanderer. He wanted to know about the beach, about the rumours he'd heard. There was an intensity about him which reminded me of Ada's. He asked questions for no other reason than to hear my answer. I started out tight-lipped, but when it became obvious that his curiosity was sincere, I told him all that I had told my brother. And I stopped there, before the last act, which was for Ada and me only.

Art asked, 'That's the last time you met the wanderer?'

'Yes.'

'Where did Giuseppe Guadalupi die?'

'What do you mean?'

'You know.'

'I don't.'

He didn't debase himself by pretending to take my word, but he didn't push the point. He politely took his leave, and we never talked again. He left Casalfranco after school, to return some years ago, as most people who leave end up doing. I don't know his whereabouts, although I could find him easily. I should do that, now that I think of it. I suspect there is more than a prank to his seven-day flight.

A new summer came, and I didn't hear from Ada. I expected someone – her, her new family – to occupy the house next door by the end of June, but no one came. The house stood empty that summer, and the next, and for all summers to come. Its wooden doors rotted, trees and shrubs reclaimed the porch. It went the way houses go when humans leave their belly. Houses are hungry for company; when left alone, they wither, like dogs, and become feral.

My life took the opposite trajectory. I managed to cram the study of two years into one. I made friends, and I learnt, by trial and error, how to be almost popular. I have, if I can say so myself, a good head for practical problems.

It served me well. My parents kept working on the grange, and kept bleeding money until they were dry. Dad found a job as an accountant, and Mum gave private lessons to the thickest of the local kids. They didn't become the power couple they'd fancied themselves to be, and were happier for it. They were never cut for power.

I hated Ada, truly hated her, for a while. I hated her for disappearing. It took me years to understand that a girl who had been so thoroughly abused, a girl who got to a point at which she did to her parents what we did to them, could not just shrug it off and get on with her life. I had occasional news of her through people in town, social media. I heard she went through therapy, lots and lots of it, received help and made no secret of it. I heard she was faring well, far from here, far from me.

I took on the Masseria del Vento.

With my parents focused at last on realistic concerns, and Ferdi back in Turin, there was no one left to take care of the masseria. We lived in a small part of it, the way Grandpa had in his last years, and there was more than enough space for the three of us. It was a pity, though, to let such a proud old building decay.

I gradually stepped in. I was acquainted with the masseria on a level at which no one had been for generations: the time I was the wind, I had puffed into every nook and cranny, I had sung with the trees and kissed the bushes. I was seventeen when I realised I was in love with the land, with its odours subtly changing every week, with the holy intensity of its flavours, with its summer heat, the spacey sea that let you float for ever, and with the astounding power of the wind when it roars and howls and comes at full force.

I studied Economics at the closest university, in Lecce. There I started raising funds to put the works back on track. I had to learn how to write a business plan, how to sweet-talk potential investors, until, after many failures (one of which, in particular, was truly embarrassing), I managed to convince two successful art gallerists to bankroll me.

Their daughter went to university with me. I had been marginally aware of her as someone quick-witted and scholarly and one afternoon, after a meeting with her parents, the two of us walked together back to campus, and ended up talking of Robert Frost. Although he was falling out of fashion, considered too sentimental by the anaesthetised literary cliques in which we moved, we both remained proud fans, and she could recite 'Stopping by Woods on a Snowy Evening' by heart. It's a short step from poetry to sex, and I had learnt the hard way how important it is to make a move when the time is right. It was meant to be only one night; we ended up married, and I have blessed my good luck ever since. She is the only woman, or man (I have been around), I ever loved as much as the land. And she loved my project – she made it hers.

With a lot of work, an inordinate amount of good luck, and going through more setbacks than a human being can contemplate, we made the masseria into a centre for ecotourism, exhibitions, cultural events. We don't do weddings. Ada would never forgive me if I did. My in-laws had a good return on their investment, which is invariably the first thing about me my father-in-law mentions.

My wife and I married in church, for it was the wise thing to do for Southern business people. Yet, she knows that my allegiances lie elsewhere.

After our first daughter was born, when we went back home from the hospital my wife and I brought her into the fields beyond the vineyard, where the hollow tree stands. The wind came to greet my firstborn, and I showed my firstborn to the wind. I told the wind her name, and asked the wind to be a good friend to her, if it pleased, as it was with me. The wind roared and boomed.

I presented our second baby to the wind too, and the third. I have been teaching them to stand naked in the fields and take the wind fully on their body. My wife understands. I told her my story, all of it, up to the last time I heard the revellers, with Ada, and she accepted all of it without as much as a *but...*, because it is my story. I confessed to her my hope that I will get to be the wind again, once, before I die. She said that the wind might be what we become after we die. See why I love her so much?

I have taught my children to notice the wanderer. It is not difficult once you know it might be there, although it never again manifested as strongly as it did to me in the summer of '96. My children, and my wife too, are convinced they have spotted it at this time or that, as a flicker at the corner of the eye, an unusual gait heard in the fields. I imagine that it had gone unrecognised for such a long time before me because first people believed that it was evil, and then they stopped believing altogether. Reality is a polite fiction and they clung to theirs. Every now and then a guest complains of an unexplainable smell in their room, and I tell them it is nature, it is how real life smells. Every now and then they spot a strange shape in the fields and I remind them I am blind and I wouldn't know what to say.

I idly ask myself whether, by acknowledging its presence, I made the wanderer stronger. And if that is the case, how come its presence has been so much subtler after the events of '96. I wonder how much stronger we are making it now. What is it planning?

I never spoke its name again. I don't know what might happen. Maybe nothing, or maybe – I don't know. I keep the name, and I will pass it down to my children when the time comes, and I hope a new family tradition might come out of that. Yes, I am aware that I will have to speak the name in order to pass it down. It will be what it will be.

My eldest daughter swears she saw the wanderer one night among the fires of Saint Giovanni, at midsummer, and it looks like an enormous bull with large twisted horns, but I don't know.

We had a good run. I don't want you to think my life is perfect, for it is dotted with sorrow and trouble like all lives are: Mum died too early, Ferdi had a blood cancer scare six years ago and a messy divorce last year, my wife and I went through a rough financial patch recently. Dad is still Dad, and Mum's death didn't make him any easier to deal with, or to take care of. But we had a good run. The tide is going to turn sooner or later, for every summer must end. Meanwhile I praise the wind for every day our good luck holds.

Ada Guadalupi called last week.

'You didn't change the number,' she said. Her voice had the bittersweet sound of an old mixtape.

'I take my time with decisions,' I answered, as if it were normal talking to her, as if we were still spending every waking hour together, the way we did for a short period of time twenty-five years ago.

'No, you're lazy.'

She was going to fix her old house, and I expressed my enthusiasm at the news that I would get rid of the haunted ruins next door. She said, 'Why, the Masseria del Vento isn't haunted anymore?' and I said, 'More than ever.'

She asked to get coffee, and I said we could do that at the grange, she would love what we had done with it, my wife and I.

I was tense while I got ready. The masseria wound back in time; it was once again a draughty wreck full of mysteries. My wife shaved my head and my face, and gave me the shirt she says suits me best, white, clean and crisp. I put on my favourite cologne, a new brand which is not dissimilar from the one Uncle Mario wears, and whose entire stock he says he bought. 'How do I look?' I asked. 'And how do I smell?'

My wife asked, 'Should I be jealous?'

'Always.'

She laughed and gave me a kiss, and said I looked and smelt yummy.

I said, 'Why don't you stay? You should meet Ada.'

'Another time.'

She took the children with her, to spend the afternoon with Maddalena's family, and they left me alone in the Masseria del Vento, to wait for Ada Guadalupi, decades after the summer of '96. The echoes of that season are with me always.

And now I sit on a swing on the porch, in the company of those echoes, waiting. I know Ada won't come with a whirl of mechanical wings, and yet it is so hard to believe.

TOASTS

The story is over; it is time to go home. But before you gather your things and head to wherever life and reading habits will take you next, please, indulge me while I toast to some friends who were with us along the way, making magic from behind the curtain.

Starting with the folks who went through sight loss and were kind enough to answer my silly questions. I raise a glass to Ian Morris, a gentleman if there is one, who helped me get rid of misconceptions and gave me tons of insights into the day-to-day life of a blind person. Thanks, Ian!

Then, a glass to Hussein Pattwa. We got in touch through the Royal Society for the Blind, and without our conversation, I wouldn't know a thing about the options a blind boy had in the nineties.

Through the Royal Society for the Blind, I also got in touch with Shelley Rogers, to whom I raise the next glass. You talked to me about reading Braille, and that made its way into the story.

I did a lot of research to try and get an understanding of Luca's lived experience. I was light on medical details: I was more interested in his new life than in how he got there. Even so, my cousin, George Turner, saved me from some ludicrous scientific errors. The ones which are left are entirely my own. Thank you, George, and a glass to you!

I will raise the next three glasses to people I never met and yet helped me immensely. The first is John M. Hull, a blind theologian whose memoir, which I read in the edition titled *Notes on Blindness*, became my well-thumbed guide. Of all the books on blindness I devoured, none stayed with me like Hull's: his voice gave me food for thought about life and spirituality. The documentary and the virtual reality experience based on his memoir are as strong an invitation to empathy as I've ever felt.

Then there is Tommy Edison, whose YouTube channel is a treasure trove of facts and trivia on a blind person's routines. When I rage against social media for dividing us into fractious petty tribes, I try to remember the work of folks like Edison, who are using them to create wonderful new bridges.

I did not have yet the pleasure to meet Professor Jeffrey J. Kripal in person, although we did exchange emails. Jeffrey, your book *The Flip* was a huge influence on my thinking about the so-called supernatural. The idea that the world sometimes behaves like a dream comes from there. Cheers!

And now let's move closer to home, with Piers Blofeld, my long-suffering agent: Piers, thank you for the hard work, the friendship, the creative sparring, and, more than anything, the trust. Not many would bother to help me navigate the strange writing paths I'm drawn to. May the Norfolk–Puglia axis prosper. Here's to you!

Then I will raise a glass to George Sandison, my wonderful editor and fellow Hooklander, who not only knows books, but also knows Puglia. George, every editor worth their salt can discuss semicolons, but the topography of vineyards and Mediterranean shrub? That's unique. I bow to that.

Let's now raise a glass to Ella Chappell. Ella, thank you for being a top-notch beta reader and even better friend. Yes, there are black snakes in our fields, and yes, they're good chaps, I promise.

And a glass also to Fabrizio Cocco. Fabrizio, without your knowledge about guitars, I would have embarrassed myself in multiple ways. Thank you for sharing with me.

Two last rounds and I'm done, I promise. A toast to Fortuna, the Roman goddess of luck. I was finishing this book when a tiny bastard of a virus sent our world grinding to a halt: death surrounded us from all sides, and the only sounds coming from the streets were ambulance sirens. Whatever will happen from today on, when the world ended, I was writing in a nice house with a fireplace and a full pantry. My family was spared the worst. If I didn't say this is undeserved good luck, I would be a moron.

And then my last toast, to Paola. You are patient, you are kind, you are forceful, you are bright. I toast to you at the end of the night, because I wish this toast to last after the night is over, and for all the days and nights to come.

ABOUT THE AUTHOR

Francesco Dimitri is a prize-winning writer of fiction and nonfiction, a comic book writer and a screenwriter. He published eight books in Italian before switching to English. His first Italian novel was made into a film, and his last was defined by *Il Corriere della Sera* as the sort of book from which a genre 'starts again'. His first English novel, *The Book of Hidden Things*, a critical and commercial success, has been optioned for cinema and TV.